Zero Friction

Kestrel Class Saga Book Five

by

Toby Neighbors

Zero Friction - Kestrel Class Saga Book 5
© 2020, Toby Neighbors

Published by Mythic Adventure Publishing, LLC
Idaho, USA

ISBN: 978-1-952260-03-2

Books By Toby Neighbors

Avondale

Draggah

Balestone

Arcanius

Avondale V

Wizard Rising

Magic Awakening

Hidden Fire

Fierce Loyalty

Crying Havoc

Evil Tide

Wizard Falling

Chaos Descending

Into Chaos

Chaos Reigning

Chaos Raging

Controlling Chaos

Killing Chaos

Elder Wizard

Lorik

Lorik the Defender

Lorik the Protector

Spartan Company

Spartan Valor

Spartan Guile

The Vault Of Mysteries

Lords Of Ascension

The Elusive Executioner

Regulators Revealed

We Are The Wolf

Welcome To The Wolfpack

Embracing Oblivion

Joined In Battle

The Abyss Of Savagery
Dragon Team Seven
Uncommon Loyalty
Total Allegiance
Kestrel Class
Jump Point
Gravity Flux
Modulus Echo
Charter
Jack & Roxie
Third Prince
Royal Destiny
The Other Side
The New World
Zompocalypse Omnibus
My Lady Sorceress
The Man With No Hands
ARC Angel
Battle ARC
Broken Crucible
Lost Kingdom

Toby Neighbors Online

www.TobyNeighbors.com

GOODREADS

www.GoodReads.com/TobyNeighbors

FACEBOOK

www.Facebook.com/TobyNeighborsAuthor

INSTAGRAM

Instagram @TobyNeighborsAuthor

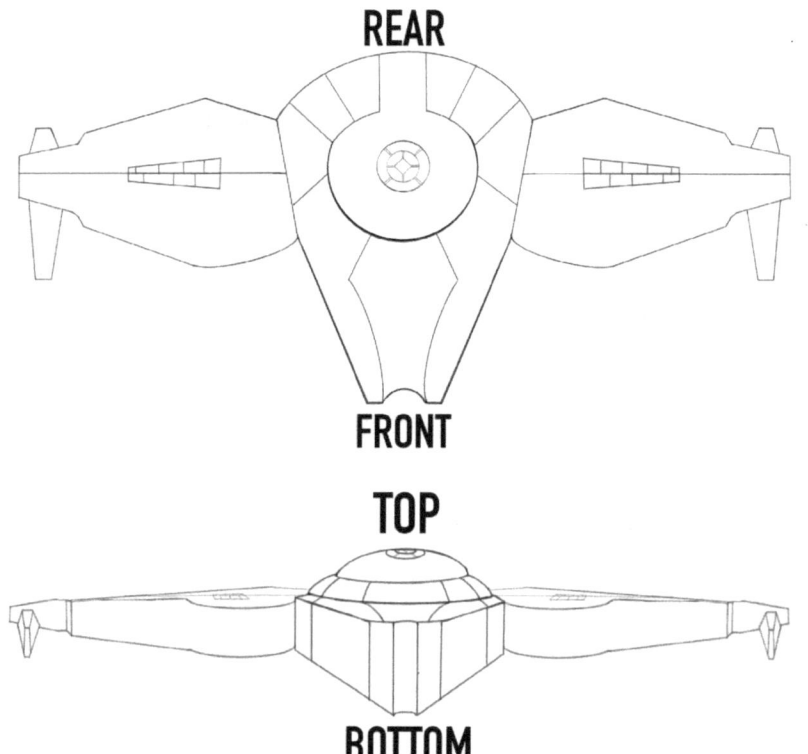

UPPER LEVEL

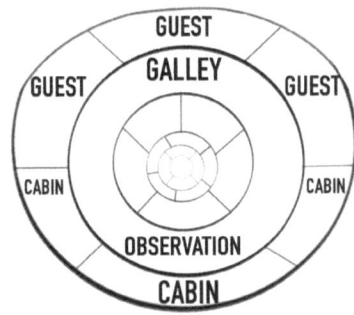

GUEST

GALLEY

GUEST

GUEST

CABIN

CABIN

OBSERVATION

CABIN

MID LEVEL

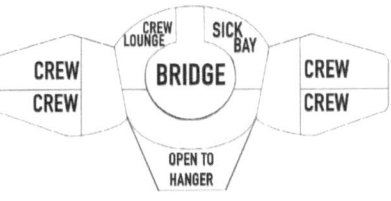

CREW
LOUNGE

SICK
BAY

CREW

CREW

BRIDGE

CREW

CREW

OPEN TO
HANGER

THE MODULUS
ECHO

LOWER LEVEL

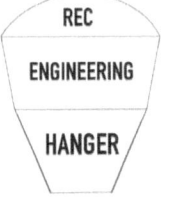

REC

ENGINEERING

HANGER

Prologue

"Coming up on another one," Kim said.

"Alpha team," General Pershing said into the ship's comms. "Prepare for EVA."

"Roger that," Staff Sergeant Visher replied.

"How many is that?" Ben asked.

"We've picked up three escape pods," Nance said. "This is the last pod. The rest are in space suits."

The plan had worked. Using the Confederate ships as stealth bombs had destroyed the armada of alien ships. Ben had hoped his idea of rigging the hydrogen tanks in the Confederate vessels would have disabled the alien vessels, but most had been completely blown apart in the explosions. Ship debris was everywhere, forcing Kim to weave around chunks of metal and melted components. Occasionally they even saw the bodies of the aliens who had crewed the strange-looking spaceships. None had worn protective gear, and they didn't survive.

The Special Forces commandos on board the *Modulus Echo* had worked diligently, capturing the escape pods and wrangling them onto the Kestrel class ship. Holt was taking the Confederates under his wing, making sure they were okay after abandoning their ships. Ben could only imagine how unhappy the displaced crews were. Everything he owned was on the *Echo*, and he knew most of the Confederates lived on their ships. The promise of a new spacecraft for each of the displaced crews was generous, but Ben guessed it did little to reassure the Confederates. He could only hope Duke Simeon followed through on his promise and got them all quality interstellar vessels.

"Will they be able to come to us?" Kim asked, referring to the Confederates in space suits.

"I doubt it," Ben said. "Unless they had time to get their gear together before they abandoned ship, they'll be drifting."

"We need to rescue them as soon as possible," Pershing said. "We can't afford to lose even one."

Ben agreed, but he was certain it was for a different reason than the general's. She needed pilots and soldiers to carry out her war, while Ben just hated to see anyone hurt because of his plan. It had been his idea to scuttle their ships. The aliens had adapted to the weapons from the Confederate ships much more quickly than Ben had expected. Their own tactics remained the same. The aliens chased down their prey and used their grappling arms to capture any unfortunate vessel in their path. They would use those same grappling arms to hold the captured ships, or even fragments of ships, to their own hull while they continued the fight, or hunt, depending on one's point of view.

"I'll go down and let Holt know," Ben said. "Magnum and I can even help in the rescue efforts."

"Very good," Pershing said.

Ben got up from his console and headed for the stairs that led down into the cargo hold. Magnum met him at the landing.

"Want me to get our gear?" the big man asked.

They were already in space suits as a safety precaution during the fight with the aliens. But, just like the Confederate personnel they were going to rescue, Ben and Magnum had no way to maneuver in space without additional gear. They needed thruster packs and rescue kits that included ropes, magnetic hooks, and emergency O2 tanks.

"That would be great," Ben said.

They hurried downstairs, with Ben heading across the cargo bay and Magnum turning into the engineering section. Holt was waiting by the plastic barrier that sealed off the airtight interior of the *Modulus Echo* and allowed them to open her wide rear hatch. Ben could see through the clear plastic to the dark void of outer space. The Special Forces team was carefully moving the escape pod, which was roughly the size of a ground transport, into the ship. The artificial gravity had been dialed back so that it covered the bridge and most of the cargo bay but still allowed the escape pods to drift in and settle on the deck with very little effort.

There were nearly a dozen people standing around, looking bedraggled. Most were staring in disbelief at the pallets of food and supplies in the cargo hold of the *Echo*. Ben had to admit, the sight of so much abundance was awe inspiring. It was more than he had ever owned, and although it was in his ship, he knew it was still the property of the Royal Imperium.

"Looks like they're almost in," Ben said as he approached Holt. "We'll be going after the refugees next."

"They aren't refugees," Holt said. He was obviously in a sour mood. "They're patriots who have sacrificed more than you can imagine."

Ben let the insult slide. He was used to as much from Holt. The gruff old Confederate didn't like him, and the feeling was mutual.

"At least we haven't had to use the medical supplies," Ben said.

"Not yet," Holt said. "I imagine things will be different for the survivors in space suits."

Ben wasn't sure what to say. He knew there was a possibility that some of the Confederates had been injured. Some might have simply run out of oxygen as they drifted through space, but it couldn't be helped. If they hadn't abandoned their ships, they would have been captured or killed. That was the one irrefutable fact that Ben clung to as his guilt nagged at him. He couldn't help but wonder what he'd have done if the general had ordered him to scuttle the *Echo*. That thought made him shudder, and he pushed it away.

"Magnum and I are going to help," Ben said.

"That's the least you can do," Holt grumbled.

"What's your problem?"

"My problem is that you dragged us into this mess, cost my people their ships, and you've barely lifted a finger to help the cause."

"You're out of your mind," Ben said.

"Am I? When are you turning over the research you've stolen from Professor Jones?"

"I haven't stolen anything," Ben said. "Your people put us together, and all I did was apply it to our ship."

"That tech could have changed the tide in the war," Holt argued.

"The war is over," Ben said. "We have a new enemy now."

"Spoken like an Imperium stooge if ever I heard one."

"That's not true, and you know it. I shared the shield technology with the engineers from the Brimex Corporation with the condition that they sell it equally to both sides."

"The Imperium doesn't deserve it," Holt snapped.

"I don't think you have the right to say what anyone deserves. And you can climb down your high horse. You brought an explosive device onto this ship once upon a time. So don't talk to me about not knowing what your people have sacrificed.

"You just love that, don't you?" Holt said. "I took precautions with you, and somehow that makes you superior to me?"

"That's the difference between us," Ben said. "I don't think anyone is superior to another."

"Tell that to your Imperium puppet masters."

"I'm telling you, Holt. Get your act together before we kick your sorry butt out the air lock with the rest of the garbage."

"Better watch yourself, Ben," Holt threatened. "We outnumber you now. That mouth of yours might cost you your ship after all."

"They'd be a fool to follow you, Holt. And you're a fool if you haven't realized the danger we're in. Not just the Confederacy, but the planets you claim to care so much about. There are innocent lives at stake here."

"The way I see it, that isn't my problem," Holt declared. "The general didn't hesitate to order the destruction of our ships. We're just pawns to her and that's no surprise. I'll be letting my people know exactly what happened here."

"That we stopped an attack by the aliens?" Ben asked.

"That your precious general sacrificed the good people who came to her aid. I wouldn't count on any more help from the Confederacy, Ben. We're through listening to a traitor like you."

Ben was furious and wanted to keep up the argument. In fact, he wanted to punch Holt right in the face, but he kept his emotions in check as Magnum returned with their gear.

"Everything okay?" Magnum asked.

"Yes," Ben said, ignoring the cold fear whispering tales of doom in his ear. "Let's get ready. We have work to do."

Chapter 1

"Lord Racca," Grubat said with a bow. "I have come to report to the council."

Racca was an imposing figure, standing head and shoulders taller than Grubat on magnificently manufactured legs. His torso was still flesh and blood, at least Grubat supposed it was. Both of the warlord's arms were made of gleaming metal, and his headdress included a throat shield that surrounded his neck. Both of his gleaming eyes were enhanced, and the warlord's sensory tendrils hung past his waist.

"Enter, Chieftain," Racca said, his voice mechanically modified to a deep, rumbling timbre. "We have been awaiting your arrival."

Grubat knew he was delivering bad news. It was a dangerous prospect. The warlords could slay him for his failures, or worse, strip him of his caste. A disgraced warrior was shunned by all. His son would try to protect him, but Grubat would never allow his own failures to disgrace his followers. Whatever the council of lords decided, Grubat would take full responsibility. If they stripped him of his caste, then Grubat would do the only honorable thing he could and let the cold darkness of space take him. It had been a long time since fear had poisoned Grubat, but he felt it attempting to steal his strength as he stood before his masters.

"Where are your ships?" Tusgar asked. He was a hideous figure with only one eye. His skull was misshapen, and the left side of his face was a mass of scar tissue. What he lacked in physical appearance, he made up for in wealth and strength.

"Lost," Grubat admitted. "The inhabitants of this galaxy are more formidable than I anticipated."

"Your offspring reported that the species of this place are cowards," Racca said. "Did he lie?"

"No," Grubat said. "They are weak, frail creatures who fight with projectiles."

"We have fought scum such as these before," Warlord Oligar said.

"And we are always victorious," Prass said with disdain.

It was an accusation, but not an unexpected one. Grubat endured it without offense. He had lost focus, allowed his Yarls to mutiny, and lost his Thralldom. All that remained in his control were the *En'Galla,* and the *Trom'Mal,* which technically belonged to its shipmaster, Yarl Kraglo. The ship which had been his home for decades as he led his followers on raids through their old galaxy was grounded on the nearby planet, never to rise again. The Worker caste was probably stripping it of components to build the first Krah settlement at that very moment.

"We enhanced our defenses," Grubat said. "We've added grappling arms to the ships, but the humans, that is what this species calls itself, allowed their ships to be captured."

"They didn't flee?" Racca asked.

"No, my lord. The crews abandoned their ships and set explosive charges."

There were growls from the assembled warlords. The long tendrils of their headdresses began to wave with agitation. Grubat understood their response. For hundreds of years, the Krah had ruled their own galaxy without a home world. They were nomads who mercilessly stole or salvaged every piece of usable space technology they could find to expand their ships and build their space stations. To willingly destroy a ship was unthinkable to the Krah.

"Which they used to destroy your ships," Oligar said.

"Yes," Grubat admitted. "Nine vessels were lost."

"Nine?" Prass said in disbelief.

The warlords were masters of large Thralldoms, but Prass was the youngest and consequently poorest of the warlords. Grubat guessed Prass had twelve or thirteen vessels in his Thralldom. The thought of losing nine at once was unthinkable to the brash warlord.

"All but one," Grubat said. "The *En'Galla* returned to report the defeat."

"Reports of thirteen ships passed through the portal under your command," Tusgar said.

"Where are the others?" Racca demanded to know.

"*Nog'Deit* is on the planet. As you have heard, it is a pristine world."

"We will get to that," Tusgar said.

"That's twelve," Prass said. "What about thirteen?"

"It was sent in pursuit of the humans," Grubat said. "Before we captured the prisoners and gained access to their navigation technology. I expected it to return with news of more human settlements."

"But you don't any longer," Oligar said. "Why is that?"

Grubat was beginning to sweat. His tendrils were growing stiff with fear. The emotion was getting the better of him. Perhaps it was due to the way the warlords questioned him, or maybe he was just out of practice controlling it.

"The ship it pursued," Grubat admitted, "returned. We watched the vessel. Unlike the others we have encountered here, it has a powerful shield that we failed to penetrate. It made a pass through the system, then left again."

"But your thirteenth ship has not returned," Racca said. "You believe it was destroyed."

"Disabled, certainly," Grubat said.

"But it's more likely been destroyed like the rest of your Thralldom," Prass said with satisfaction.

"There is wealth here," Racca said. "Perhaps more than one can fathom."

"How so?" Prass asked.

"Only a species so fabulously rich in technology would sacrifice their own ships," Hochum said, speaking for the first time since Grubat had been granted access to the council.

"But also danger," Oligar said. "The time for raiding will come, but first we must secure the system."

"We have over two hundred vessels," Prass said. "That's more than enough—"

"Stop," Oligar snarled. "Did you hear nothing Chieftain Grubat said?"

"Careful," Prass said. "You do not command me, old one. And to challenge me is death. I have ascended on the corpses of those who dared to question my strength."

"We cannot afford to underestimate our enemy," Grubat said, trying to turn the hostility back where it belonged. "Their star map reveals that they have proliferated throughout the galaxy. They have exceeded our own technological advances in terraforming. Two hundred ships are more than enough to subdue a species in our galaxy, but it will not be enough to stop the humans."

"Grubat speaks wisely," Tusgar said. "We should not rush to the spoils and lose what is most important."

"Nor can we afford to cower here and allow the natives to converge against us in this system," Racca said. "We must work together."

"To secure and hold this system," Oligar insisted.

"Tell us about the world you have found," Tusgar said to Grubat.

"It is the fourth planet in the system," Grubat said with a touch of pride. "The air is breathable and clean. I have never seen a world so pure."

"The humans haven't infested it?" Racca asked.

"Only a single settlement," Grubat said. "My prisoner revealed it was home to the ruler of their kind."

"An entire world?" Prass asked.

"Indeed, the humans are rich beyond our comprehension," Tusgar said.

"They have a settlement, which we will easily overrun," Grubat said. "I have landed the *Nog'Deit* on the planet, and my workers have begun building. If it pleases you, my lords, I will send my son to bring more workers and priests to consecrate the world as our new home."

"You would settle for a single planet?" Prass said with contempt.

"Breathable air," Racca said. "What else?"

"Clean, abundant water," Grubat said. "Liquid water. It flows through the landmasses in rivers."

The warlords looked at him with disbelief. Grubat, anticipating their skepticism, powered on a small, portable hologram projector. An image appeared before Grubat in vivid color and detail. He had recorded the footage in the brightest part of the day, filming the river, the trees, and part of the clearing.

"Is this real?" Tusgar asked.

"This is New Krah," Grubat said as the image continued to pan and the spaceship came into view. "That is the *Nog'Deit*. There are seemingly boundless wildlife and flora of many kinds. We could spend centuries exploring all that the planet has to offer."

"What is the temperature?" Racca asked.

"Stable in the acceptable range," Grubat said.

"Wouldn't we be better off taking a world that is rich with technology?" Prass asked. "There is nothing on that planet but dirt."

"Yes," Racca said. "Which is precisely why it is so valuable."

"If you say so," Prass replied.

"Hold your tongue," Oligar snapped. "We already know you're a fool. There's no need to prove it."

With a roar, Prass launched himself at Oligar. Prass was built like a war machine; his mechanical legs were optimized for strength and speed. His left arm was enhanced with a thick blade snapping out of the outer portion just below the wrist. He brought his weapon over his head, his tendrils standing straight out behind him. Oligar never moved. Prass would have split his skull, but Grubat threw his shoulder into the young warlord, knocking him off course.

"Stop this," snarled Racca as Prass crashed to the deck.

"I challenge him!" Prass screamed. "I'll have his heart!"

"Not on my ship," Racca said, his voice a deadly hiss. "This is a council of war, and we accomplish nothing with your vain conceit."

"I will go down and see this planet for myself," Oligar said.

"As will I," Tusgar added.

"Hochum will stay and command our ships," Racca said. Hochum nodded but didn't say anything.

"The priests made me a warlord," Prass said. "I will not be excluded."

"No one is trying to exclude you," Racca said. "But none of us got here because we're weak. You'll be wise to remember that."

"I'll be glad to show you our new home world," Grubat said, his chest still heaving from the anticipation of the fight.

"No," Racca said. "Return to Algonny Outpost with your son."

"What?" Grubat asked. The shock on his face was plain to see. His headdress tendrils writhed like snakes, unable to cope with his emotional state.

"Your time here has been put to good use," Racca explained. "But we cannot overlook the loss of ten ships."

"Perhaps in time you can overcome the disgrace you've brought on your Thralldom," Tusgar said.

"But the planet was my discovery," Grubat said. "My ship established my claim."

"Your Yarls and workers will not be abandoned," Racca said. "I will see that they are redistributed myself."

Grubat's consternation was quickly replaced by rage. The warlords were using the defeat in the Yelsin system as an excuse to cut him out of his rightful claim to the planet. He was losing not only his flagship but also most of the Krah under his command.

"If you disagree, you can challenge him," Prass said. "That is law."

Racca didn't even bother to turn to face Grubat, yet the chieftain knew that fighting the warlord would only result in a long, exhaustive battle. Even if Grubat won, he would surely be gravely injured in the process. There wasn't time to spend a month in recovery while the human threat was so dire. And while a victory would by rights give him control of Racca's Thralldom, Grubat would never be able to hold his place. There were at least two dozen chieftains serving the warlord, and Grubat knew that each and every one of them had ambitions to overthrow Racca. Prass had only suggested the challenge because he hoped to steal away some of the shipmasters pledged to Racca and thereby bolster his own forces.

"Unlike you, Chieftain Grubat is not a fool," Oligar said calmly.

"Return with the priests and meet us on the surface," Racca ordered. "We must consecrate this world and begin planning our next conquest."

"Yes," Grubat said, acknowledging the order.

He turned and left the council chamber. Racca's flagship was a massive vessel, and it took Grubat several minutes to make his way back to the hangar where his small landing craft was waiting. He did his best to settle in his mind the fact that he would have to be content with his life. The warlords could have demanded it from him for Yarl Hassik's foolish and wasteful loss to the humans. Grubat's one consolation was the knowledge that he alone had come to know their enemy. The warlords would need him soon, or they would suffer the same fate as Yarl Hassik. In some cases, he mused, that might not be so bad.

The Krah Empire had gone unchallenged for so long that their ranks had become bloated, and few had managed to rise above the station they had held for decades. Grubat had been so close, yet one mistake had cost him everything. He was determined to change his fortune, and if the humans continued to prove themselves to be dangerous adversaries, he might not have to wait long to do it.

Chapter 2

In space, life was precarious at best. Hard vacuum offered no air to breathe, and it was so cold that without protective gear one would freeze to death instantly. Yet as Ben glided through space toward the drifting Confederate he was attempting to rescue, he couldn't help but contemplate the beauty of it. On board the *Echo,* outer space seemed almost distant. They viewed it using cameras mounted on the hull, or through the transparent steel of the observation deck, but nothing compared to being in space with nothing between your eyes and the vast cosmos but a thin layer of plastic.

"Coming up behind you," Ben said.

There was no response from the person in the space suit drifting in a slow spin through space ahead of him. Not that Ben expected there to be one. Most of the Confederates who had abandoned their ships to the Krah had only short-range com-links. Without knowing their exact frequency, Ben couldn't communicate with them. He spoke more to himself than to anyone else.

"Almost there," Ben said.

He waited until he was close, then reached out and snagged a loop on the unsuspecting Confederate's shoulder. The momentum of the Confederate's spin caused Ben to start drifting off course slowly. He turned the person he had caught around and saw a pleasant face. It was a woman, her blonde hair floating around her face inside the helmet. She was smiling, but Ben also saw water floating around her face and more was beaded on the visor of her helmet. Ben couldn't blame her for crying. She mouthed the words *thank you* and held onto Ben with a fierce grip.

He nodded at her.

"Don't worry," he said, even though she couldn't hear him. "You're safe now."

With one hand, he held onto the woman whose name tag on the space suit said Nomstrog. His other hand worked the simple controls of the jetpack he wore. A few thrusts later, they had turned back toward the *Echo* and were moving slowly toward the air lock. Corporal Dial was tethered to the ship, helping his squadmates pull in more refugees from the battle near Yelsin Prime. Ben could see the planet, and the system's blue star sent light glittering on the debris from the battle. There were plenty of large chunks of metal, but some of the explosions had turned the ships, or at least sections of them, into space dust. Fortunately, as the hours of their rescue mission passed, the more dangerous pieces of debris had spread wide enough that the *Modulus Echo* and the rescue operations weren't in danger.

"You got one," Corporal Johnathan Dial said.

"We've got each other," Ben replied. Nomstrog was still holding onto him desperately.

"At least she's alive," Dial said.

Several of the refugees had died from lack of oxygen. It chilled Ben's blood to think that something as simple as forgetting to fill a space suit's oxygen tanks could cost someone their life, but that was exactly what had happened to six of the Confederates they had rescued.

The air lock opened, and Ben helped his refugee inside. They waited while the outer door closed and the chamber filled with air. When the inner door opened, the woman removed her helmet. She had blue eyes and her hair was nearly white.

"Thank you," she said.

"No problem," Ben said as she stepped through the air lock and into the cargo bay.

"The soldiers have the last of the refugees," Professor Jones said to Ben.

The professor was administering first aid to the refugees who needed medical help. Most were fine, just a little frightened. Others were like Holt, their anger simmering just beneath the surface. Ben did his best to stay positive. What else could he do? But it was impossible not to feel like any number of the Confederates would happily slit his throat and steal the *Echo*.

Ben removed his helmet and went immediately to the engineering bay. He pulled off the bulky space suit, and with the lesson they had learned from the Confederates still fresh in his mind, connected the O2 hose to his suit to refill its air supply. Once he had seen to the space suit, he checked the ship's systems on his workbench console. All the ship's systems were in the green. There was plenty of Zexum, and the ship's auxiliary batteries had nearly completed their recharge. With so many people on board, Ben switched the hydrogenerator off so that the fusion reactor, which burned Zexum gas and released pure oxygen, could keep the atmosphere in the ship balanced.

Ben was just coming out of his work area when he ran into the woman with blue eyes and a strange name. She smiled at him again and Ben felt a tingling buzz through him.

"I wanted to thank you," she said.

"You did that already," Ben replied.

"I guess so," she said, looking down. "I don't know, it just doesn't seem like enough."

"You made the sacrifice," Ben said. "Losing your ship."

"The *Denmark Eight*," she said. "It wasn't much of a ship. No real loss."

"Tell that to the aliens," Ben said.

She smiled and the tingling shot through Ben again.

"I'm Van," she said.

"Ben," he replied.

"Is this your ship?"

"Yeah," he said proudly. "The *Modulus Echo*."

"Are the rumors true?"

"I don't know," Ben said. "I haven't heard them."

"That you flew her through a black hole?" Van asked.

"Well, I was on board," Ben replied, feeling a pang of guilt. "But the credit goes to Kim, our pilot."

"I can't wait to meet her," Van said.

"Why wait?" Ben said. "Come on, I'll introduce you."

He hurried up the stairs and Van followed. Ben felt strange. It wasn't like he'd done anything wrong, yet for some reason he felt as if he had. They came up to the main deck and found more refugees loitering in the atrium between crew quarters and the bridge. Ben made his way through the refugees and stepped up onto the bridge near his console. He turned and helped Van up beside him.

Kim was focused on her instruments and didn't see them. Ben felt a small wave of relief. He didn't want to have to explain to Kim what he was doing chatting with another woman on the bridge.

Magnum was still helping with the rescue efforts, and Nance had gone to the upper deck to help make protein drinks for the refugees, but General Pershing was at her console monitoring the comms of her Special Forces team.

"It may not look like much, but this is it," Ben said.

"It's a palace next to the *Denmark Eight*," Van said.

"This is my console. We have communications, computer systems, fire control, and that's General Pershing at the navigation station."

"You run with a full crew?"

"No, we started with four and picked up the professor a while back."

"He's the medic?"

"Yes," Ben said, leading Van down toward the pilot's seat. "And this is Kim, our pilot."

Kim looked up with a frown that deepened when she saw Van.

"It's a pleasure to meet you," Van said, extending a slender hand.

"What's this?" Kim asked.

"Kim, this is Van. She was the pilot of the *Denmark Eight*," Ben said.

"Wonderful," Kim replied.

"She was asking about our trip through the black hole," Ben went on. "I told her we only made it because of you."

"I'd love to hear the story," Van said.

"There'll be plenty of time for that," Kim said. "Sorry I can't get up. There's still space debris I have to keep an eye on."

Ben knew they were in the clear, but he understood the need for Kim to remain at her station. The real fear was that more alien ships could show up at any time. And almost as if Ben had willed his fear into reality, a beeping sound began to chime from behind them.

"Proximity alert," Kim said. "A ship just popped out of hyperspace."

Ben ran over to his station and hit a few buttons to bring up the ship on the main display. He was afraid it would be one of the bulbous alien vessels, but instead it was a sleek, dark-colored craft.

"That's an Imperium ship," Van said.

"Yes," General Pershing said. "The R.I.F. *Siren.*"

She pushed a button to activate the ship's communications system, and a voice boomed over the bridge's speakers.

Modulus Echo, this is the Siren actual. Is General Pershing still on board your vessel? Over.

"Yes, I'm here," Pershing said.

General, we were hit by a fleet of alien ships, the voice from the other vessel explained. *We didn't have the firepower to stop them. Once our defenses failed, we all ran. I'm not sure what happened to the other ships, but I'm guessing from the looks of things it wasn't good. Over.*

"Your guess is correct, *Siren,*" Pershing said. "We got back with a flight of Confederate ships and were forced to fight. We're mopping up the survivors now."

Do you need help? Over.

"Not here," Pershing said. "Make a sweep of the planet. There are some escape pods that missed orbit."

Roger that, General. Moving to pick up survivors near Yelsin Prime. Siren, out.

"At least it wasn't the bad guys," Ben said.

"Indeed," Pershing said without looking up from her console.

"Come on," Ben said to Van. "Let me show you the upper deck. You can get a bite to eat and catch some rest on the observation deck until we decide what to do next."

"Sure," Van said.

She stepped off the elevated platform of the bridge, and Ben cast one last look back at Kim. She, too, was studying her instruments, but he could tell by the tension in her shoulders that she wasn't happy. How did he get himself into trouble without even trying, he wondered. He had to force himself not to shake his head as he led Van across the crowded atrium toward the stairs to the upper deck. He promised himself he would leave her there and come right back down, but still he doubted that it would be enough. Kim would want answers, and he had none to give her. Nothing had happened, and yet he knew he had inadvertently crossed an invisible line. Trouble was brewing over the horizon, and Ben had no illusions of escaping the fury of the storm to come.

Chapter 3

Pershing felt anger welling up inside her. Nothing was working in her favor, and while she didn't expect war to be a simple matter, she felt as if she couldn't get her head above water. Worst of all, there was no place to escape the scrutiny of the people on the *Echo*. Ben and his crew of misfits were bad enough, but the Confederates were openly hostile and the royals had an air of superiority that chafed Pershing's own ego.

Once the rescue operations were over, Pershing allowed herself the luxury of getting something to eat. She was used to self-denial, and her willpower over her appetite was a point of pride for her. But the stress of their situation weighed on her even as she ate. The aliens were expanding into the galaxy, and Pershing still didn't know how they had found the Yelsin system.

"There she is," Holt grumbled as he stomped up the metal stairs to the upper deck.

Pershing forced herself not to look his way. Her hold on the leadership of the Confederates was tenuous at best. She couldn't afford to let Holt think of her as an equal. He made his way to the table where Pershing was eating, followed by several of the Confederate crew members who had lost their ships in the battle.

"Well?" Holt demanded.

"Are you addressing me?" Pershing asked. "This is a military operation, and I am a brigadier general. If you want my attention, I suggest you approach with a little more respect."

"Excuse the hell out of me," Holt said. "But since my people just saved your precious planet and this ship, I think some respect is due to the Confederates. When are we getting those new ships you promised?"

"I didn't make you any promises," Pershing said. "That was Duke Simeon. And while I'm sure he's a man of his word, I would not try to speak for him."

"Nice," Holt said, turning to the other Confederates. "I told you she'd stall and try to get out of it."

"We are on our way to Yelsin Prime to ensure that the survivors are all rescued. Once that is done, I will see about transferring your people to the *Siren* where they can be taken to the nearest shipyard. In the meantime," Pershing said, picking up her empty tray and standing to her feet, "I would appreciate it if you wouldn't stir up trouble. I'm not your enemy."

Pershing was headed for the stairs and nearly ran into Staff Sergeant Visher as he came up. He gave her a quick salute, but he looked exhausted and Pershing didn't make him stand at attention.

"As you were, Staff Sergeant," Pershing said. "Where's the queen?"

"Still in her quarters, I think," Visher said. "We've been busy, but I haven't seen her since she slipped inside during the battle."

"Very well," Pershing said. "Get something to eat, Staff Sergeant. Your people can catch some rest once we reach orbit."

"Are we going back down to Yelsin Prime?"

"That depends on the queen," Pershing said. "She may want to keep you around as her guard."

The look on the staff sergeant's face wasn't pleasant and told the general exactly how Visher felt about the idea of staying on as the queen's protective detail. Her people were highly skilled warriors, but they weren't trained to protect the royal family. Still, until they had transported the queen safely to the Mersa system, someone would need to fill the role.

General Pershing stood aside as the commando squad lumbered up the stairs to get something to eat. Once the way was clear, she returned down to the bridge. Kim was flying the *Echo* back toward the planet.

"Any news?" Pershing asked.

"There's a steady stream from the planet," Kim said. "They're busy ferrying the survivors back to the base."

"What about the escape pods that didn't make it to the planet?"

"I've got a few on the plot, but the *Siren* is en route. They'll reach the survivors before we will."

"What's our plan?" Ben asked.

He and Kim were the only crew members on the bridge, although there were more than a dozen Confederates loitering on the atrium nearby. Pershing had no doubt they were listening to every word. She wished there were some sort of partition between the bridge and the rest of the ship. It was not up to military standards, especially with passengers on board.

"We'll make orbit," Pershing said. "And ensure that everything on Yelsin Prime is secure. Once the Confederates have been ferried to the *Siren*, we'll make our way to the Celeste system."

A look came over Ben's face, but he didn't say anything. Kim, on the other hand, didn't know the meaning of discretion.

"Why go back?" Kim asked. "We don't have the means to fight the aliens."

Warfare is a three-pronged stool. It only works when each of the legs is secure."

"What's that supposed to mean?"

"It means we need intel. One of the prongs of any battle is knowing what the enemy is doing. Without good intel, you're at a disadvantage right from the start."

"What are the other two prongs?" Ben asked.

"Strategy and force deployment," Pershing said. "It does no good to send too few people into battle, or too many. Just as it would be wasteful to send troops in without the equipment or support they would need to get the job done."

"Makes sense," Kim said, which Pershing supposed was a compliment.

Not that General Alicia Pershing needed acceptance or approval from the crew of the *Modulus Echo*. She was a career soldier, a woman who had devoted her life to military service, while they were just an expedient way to accomplish her current goals. Without their ship's prototype shield, she would have arrested them and impounded the *Echo*. She was already yearning to return to a proper military vessel, but until she had the ships needed to ensure that she could continue to fight the aliens, the *Echo* would have to do.

The ship's comms system beeped, and Ben announced that they had an incoming message from the *Siren*.

"Put it on the speakers," Pershing said.

General Pershing, this is the R.I.F. Siren. We have collected the escape pods and are ferrying survivors down to the Spec Ops base on Yelsin Prime. What are your orders? Over.

"*Siren*, this is General Pershing. Once you've delivered the survivors back to the surface, have your shuttles dock with the *Echo*. We have allies in need of transport."

Roger that, General. We'll drop off our passengers and head your way.

"Kim, bring us into orbit as close to the *Siren* as we can safely get," Pershing ordered. "Ben, find Holt and decide where to send his people. They're no good to us without ships. And I want to know what his people are going to do."

"You mean the Confederates?" Ben asked.

"That's right. They should have gotten our message by now. We need to know if they're willing to help. Once we know what we're up against, I'll have to know what resources we have to fight the aliens."

"Okay, I'll see what I can find out," Ben said.

Pershing sat back in her seat. It was more comfortable than a military-issue console chair despite the fact that it was almost certainly older than she was. She couldn't help but be aggravated by how much she was coming to like the Kestrel class ship. It was old and patched together with refurbished components, yet it had character. She was used to military vessels and their spartan designs. The *Echo* wasn't merely comfortable, it was capable. And as a woman who valued results, she couldn't deny that the little ship was effective.

She looked at the displays built into her console, but her mind wandered. The need to know about the aliens was almost overwhelming. All she knew was how their ships operated, but who the aliens were, what they wanted, or how they thought, was still a mystery. She didn't have to know them or understand them to fight them, but it would help. If she knew what they sought, she could pinpoint their weaknesses and drive them out of her galaxy forever. But to do that, she needed help. She needed more ships, more soldiers, and more time. Unfortunately, she had none of those things, and unless that changed soon, they might never gain the upper hand on the aliens. The problem clouded her mind, frustrating her need to find answers, but she knew they would come. They had to. The only alternative was defeat and death, both of which were unacceptable to Alicia Pershing. She was in the habit of winning, and she didn't see that trend changing if she could help it.

Chapter 4

"The Kruggare Yards is closest," Holt said. "But if they're willing to replace the ships we lost, it would be better to do it in the Androsis system. They have five times the inventory, and their reputation is better."

"Okay," Ben said. "That shouldn't be an issue."

"Shouldn't be," Holt grumbled. He was pontificating in front of a group of Confederates. "You think this is all just a temporary inconvenience, don't you?"

"No," Ben said.

"You do realize that even with new ships, we'll have to spend weeks making modifications, and that doesn't include finding weapons to mount up and sync with a ship's systems that are brand new to us."

"I get that," Ben said. "But if you're fighting with the Royal Imperium, it stands to reason that they would supply the weapons you need."

"And that right there is your problem," Holt declared. "You trust these tyrants. There's nothing reasonable about the Royal Imperium. They enslave entire worlds, cripple everyone with unreasonable taxes, and poison their own citizens, or have you forgotten what you discovered in the Mersa system?"

"I haven't forgotten anything," Ben said. "And none of this is my idea."

"You sure seem comfortable with your new alliance," Holt said. "I'm still waiting to hear how that happened exactly."

He was being overly sarcastic, but Ben understood why. In Holt's eyes, they had partnered with the enemy, and nothing else mattered. Ben sat down at the table where the Confederates were gathered. Nance brought him a mug of ale, and Ben leaned in, speaking low so that he wouldn't be overheard.

"What do you know?" Ben asked.

"I know we set you up with the professor," Holt said. "And you apparently took him straight to the Imperium. What'd you do, trade his research for immunity from the military?"

"No," Ben said. "We did some work together, just the way you planned it. He used our data from the black hole, remember?"

Ben let the challenge hang in the air between them. The Confederates, including Van, hung on Ben's every word, while Holt tried his best to look disinterested.

"Then we went to Torrent Four," Ben continued. "We needed parts to build the experimental rocket the professor had designed. The Imperium caught up to us there. They were planning to make an example of us."

"Instead, they turned you," Holt said.

"Instead, we all found out just how well the new shield I designed works," Ben said.

"We've heard the rumors," Van said, her blue eyes shining with excitement. "Did you really take on an entire armada of Imperium ships?"

"We didn't have a choice," Ben said. "They pushed us off the world and into orbit where their fleet was waiting. We never fired a shot, but their own weapons rebounded from our shields and destroyed their own vessels. Then panic set in. Most of the damage came from their ships crashing into one another."

"Likely story," Holt said.

"Talk to the general," Ben challenged the older man. "She has footage of the entire incident. She was on board a stealth ship with orders to record their victory. Instead, she saw the collapse of their armada firsthand."

"She'd say anything to back you up," Holt said.

"You're getting desperate," Ben said. "You can spin this however you want, but you know we did what we had to do."

"Rumor has it, you were in the Celeste system when the wormhole opened and destroyed the Royal Imperium Fleet," Van said.

"We were," Ben said. "But not by choice."

"What's that supposed to mean?" Holt asked.

"It means the Imperium, under the command of the late admiral general, threatened to bombard ten planets if we didn't surrender to him in the Celeste system."

The group began to grumble. It was exactly the type of tyrannical behavior that drove people to the rebellion. Holt's eyes narrowed as he considered what Ben had said. It was clear that he didn't want to believe Ben, but the one thing he hated more than the young engineer was the Royal Imperium.

"What planets?" Holt asked.

"Ten of your planets," Ben said. "The ones with the biggest support for the rebellion."

"And these are the people you've allied yourself with?" Holt declared. "Worse yet, you've pulled us into your deal with the devil."

"We went to the Celeste system," Ben went on, ignoring Holt's accusation. "We were there when the wormhole opened. We saw the destruction it caused."

41

"The entire Royal Imperium Fleet," Van said with pride.

"Most of it," Ben corrected her. "Some of their battle cruisers escaped."

"They ran like the cowards they are," said another Confederate, a burly man with a thick mustache.

"The Royal Imperium Fleet was decimated," Ben said. "Their entire HQ space station that housed the administrative wing of their military was destroyed. When things settled, the general took her spy ship through the wormhole and we followed."

"Why?" Holt asked.

"The professor urged us to," Ben said. "We were all curious."

"Where did it go?" Van asked.

"We weren't there long enough to find out," Ben said. "The aliens had already attacked and captured the general's ship when we arrived. We picked up her escape pod and came home."

"That still doesn't explain why you joined the Imperium," Holt said. "You should have let her die in space or, at the very least, shoved her out an air lock once you knew who you had found."

"Maybe, but let's be honest," Ben said. "The Confederacy wasn't in a hurry to come to our aid. We were out of Zexum, down to the dregs in our galley, and with no means to get anymore."

"There's always a way," Holt said. "You didn't have to deal with the enemy."

"Where could we have gone that we wouldn't have been captured or killed?" Ben said. "The general offered us the same deal she gave you. Amnesty in exchange for our help against the aliens."

"And you jumped at the chance to betray your friends," Holt said.

"I jumped at the chance to save my friends," Ben corrected him. "My priority is the crew of this ship. I was never a member of your rebellion."

"You were more than happy to take the Zexum we gave you."

"You never gave us anything," Ben said. "We earned everything we got by putting our neck on the line. We even let you record us destroying the space station in the Bannyan system. You used us, then sent us into exile."

"The cause is bigger than any one of us," Holt said.

"Which is why we're helping you," Ben said, his attention turning from the obstinate Holt to the rest of the group sitting at the table or leaning in from all around. "I can't guarantee you freedom, or that the Imperium won't go back on their promise, but we do have a common enemy. It's your chance to earn the right to be heard. It's a chance to give your people the option of returning to the families they were forced to leave behind."

"That's just Imperium propaganda," Holt said.

"It's common sense," Ben said. "The aliens are the enemy now. We fight them together, or we fall to them one system at a time."

"There's no difference between fighting the Imperium and fighting your so-called aliens," Holt said. "That's what we do, and we're damn good at it."

"If that's truly how you feel, then nothing I can say will change your mind. But you all saw the aliens. You fought them.

They're bigger and faster than we are. Our weapons didn't make a difference to them. We need the Royal Imperium's resources to fight them."

"They need our help," Holt argued.

"They need fighters," Ben said, "because most of their fleet was destroyed when the wormhole opened. But we need them too. We need their weapons and their facilities. Look at what they're offering."

Ben waved his hand toward the galley, where the smells of cooking food were strong. There were crates of fruit, real vegetables, and packages of sealed foods that would have cost a fortune in most worlds. There were kegs of ale and drink dispensers with flavored beverages, including coffee, tea, and drinks with electrolytes.

"You're a sellout," Holt said.

"No, I'm a survivor," Ben said. "The Confederacy isn't going to save the galaxy without help."

"Neither is the Imperium," Van said.

"Which is why we need to work together," Ben said. "It's the only chance we've got."

Chapter 5

Grubat stood on the bridge of the *En'Galla* as the ship moved slowly through space toward the ring of fire. The system was crowded with ships. Over two hundred had been brought over with warlords, and Grubat knew there would be more amassing at the nearest space station. It made navigating from orbit over New Krah, known to the humans as Gershwin, difficult. Yarl Quissi was at the ship's controls, moving the Explorer class ship toward the portal that led back to the galaxy the Krah had first conquered.

The chieftain felt the bitter taste of disappointment souring his headdress tendrils. They hung limp around his shoulders, and there was a hollow sensation in his mind from the lack of information they normally supplied. He was vulnerable, partly because he couldn't sense what was happening around him, and partly because his will to fight was so low.

How had he gotten himself into such a mess, he wondered. Never in all the decades he had spent scouring through space had he dropped his guard the way he had on the planet he was leaving behind. Perhaps it was the place. It was possible that something about the pristine planet had seduced him into a sense of vulnerability. All his life, Grubat had hated excuses, yet he could not stop himself from searching for something to explain his failure with Yarl Hassik.

"We're approaching the portal," Grubat's son, Yarl Cherbak, said.

Grubat did not respond. He could see the fiery ring through the *En'Galla*'s transparent bulkhead. Yet it wasn't the report that bothered Grubat, but the fact that his own son saw him as a failure. And being on the ship his son had commanded for so long only added to Grubat's disgrace. He was an interloper, trapped in a tiny ship that seemed to be almost suffocating the life from him after having marveled at the wide-open spaces of the planet he had been forced to leave behind.

"I have a report."

The voice was not of the Warrior caste. It came from a builder, high pitched and too rapid to be a warrior. Grubat turned and found the *En'Galla*'s a highest-ranking builder, equivalent to a Yarl.

"Chieftain Grubat," Yarl Cherbak said. "This is Connar. He is in charge of acquisitions."

"Give your report," Grubat said.

Connar was thin, with his ring of enhancements standing out from his narrow waist where they were folded up like spider legs. On his face were bulky eye enhancements, which only made him look more insectile.

"Yarl Cherbak tasked me with exploring the damage to our grappling arms from the small alien ship," Connar said.

"Humans," Grubat said. "That is what the aliens call themselves."

"Humans," Connar said, memorizing the word. "As you know, mighty Chieftain, our attempts to capture the human ships were only thwarted one time."

"By one ship," Yarl Quissi said.

"I know this vessel," Grubat said. "We first encountered it on our side of the portal."

"That is correct," Connar said. "While we encountered it here, and in the Yelsin system."

46

"And you have discovered its secret?" Grubat asked.

"I have analyzed the damage we sustained," Connar said. "It appears they are using gravity waves to shield their ship."

"Gravity waves?" Grubat said.

"It's the only explanation," Connar continued. "The grappling arms that encountered the vessel were either torn off and flung away, as if by magic, or crushed. The only known force with such power is gravity."

"Gravity is not that powerful," Grubat said.

"Artificial gravity is not," Connar said. "Nor is planetary gravity. But the gravity of an anomaly, say, a black hole, is powerful enough."

"That makes no sense," Grubat said. "If they used gravity, what keeps it from destroying their ship? You must return to your research, builder. Find truth, not mere conjecture."

"The evidence we have supports our theory," Connar insisted. "Were you not drawn to the portal by energy spikes similar to those caused by black holes, my lord?"

Grubat looked at his son. His tendrils were beginning to move, sliding around his shoulders and neck as his mind went back over the data first captured by the *Nog'Deit* in their own galaxy. They had left the Algonny Outpost and were preparing to begin a hunt of the Visanti system when his own ship had picked up strange energy readings. They had gone to investigate the anomaly and discovered the ring of fire, as well as a human vessel. After capturing the strange ship, another vessel had appeared from the portal, the same ship that had damaged the *Nog'Deit* with a strange kind of shielding.

"He is correct, Chieftain," Yarl Quissi said.

"We should not be surprised that the humans have advanced technologies unlike anything we have possessed," Connar said. "I have inspected their vessels. They are different in many ways."

"There is no need to point out the obvious," Grubat said. "Can you replicate this gravity shield?"

"Not yet," Connar said. "None of the ships we have captured thus far have the advanced shielding technology."

"If they did, they would use it to flee from us," Yarl Cherbak said.

"What else do they possess that could be put to use?" Grubat said.

"Their weapons are being studied, although the systems on the ships we have captured are woefully inadequate," Connar said. "The ships that fired upon us in the Yelsin system were more advanced, but those vessels were lost."

"Yes," Grubat said with a growl. "Don't remind me."

"At the moment, that is all we know," Connar said.

Grubat turned away from the workman and watched as the *En'Galla* passed the ring of fire. The view from the ship's bridge changed to a swirling vortex of strange light. Yarl Cherbak dismissed Connar, and Grubat knew what he needed to do to regain his standing with the warlords in command of the Celeste system. Once he returned to the human galaxy, he would need to capture the ship that had eluded him or one with the same shielding technology. With such a treasure in hand, the council of warlords could not dismiss him so easily. Other ships would rally to him, and once he had enough strength, Grubat could petition the priests to convey upon him the rank of warlord.

Grubat felt his headdress tendrils moving with more life. He could sense the tension on the bridge. Everyone felt the shame of Yarl Hassik's betrayal. Guilt would keep his people loyal for a while, but Grubat needed a solid victory to keep his subordinates from abandoning him. And he needed their strength to regain his standing before he could return to New Krah. He would reclaim what was rightfully his, even if he had to challenge the other warlords one by one.

The very idea of redeeming his good reputation fired his ambition. The blood quickened in his veins and he felt strength returning. It all started with the mind. He was down, but not out of the fight. Not yet... Not if he had anything to say about it.

Chapter 6

"That's it," Kim declared. "We have a stable orbit."

"Very good," Pershing said. "Don't go far."

"You're kidding, right?" Kim said.

She was exhausted. Her body ached from sitting in her pilot's seat for hours on end—first, during the battle with the alien ships and then dodging the debris as they rescued the Confederates who had abandoned their ships.

"We're leaving the system as soon as we transfer the Confederate crews to the *Siren*," Pershing said.

"Where to?" Nance asked as Kim rolled her eyes.

What she wanted was sleep, and maybe to give the general a piece of her mind, but she kept her mouth shut. She knew complaining wouldn't change Pershing's mind, and she didn't have time to waste.

Ben was just coming down from the upper deck, and she grabbed him by the arm and pulled him toward her quarters.

"Hey," he said. "What's going on?"

"Zip it, mister," Kim snapped over her shoulder as she opened the door to her quarters.

She stepped over the threshold and tugged Ben into her room. Once he was inside, she hit the controls to close the door and pushed him against the wall. His eyes were open wide with surprise. She leaned against him, pinning him to the bulkhead, a finger pointed to his face.

"What were you doing parading that tramp around the bridge right in front of me?" she demanded.

"I...uh..."

Before he could answer, she kissed him hard. Her lips pressed against his. Her fingers dug into his shoulders. There was no resistance from Ben, and Kim held the kiss just long enough to feel Ben's surprise turn to passion, then she pushed herself away. They had been through a lot together. It had been difficult to settle her feelings about Ben and to actually trust that he wouldn't trample her emotions. She didn't really think he was being unfaithful, but she liked reminding him who held his heart.

"Don't do that again," she said, turning her back on him. "I get jealous."

"So I see," Ben said.

His hands gently took hold of her shoulders and he turned her around. Kim couldn't keep the grin from her face. They both laughed, then he bent low and kissed her softly.

"You're the only girl for me," Ben said. "I promise."

"Good, that's the way I like it."

"You look tired," he said. "It's been a long day."

"And only getting longer," Kim replied. "Pershing wants to leave the system as soon as the Confederates are offloaded to another ship."

"She does?"

"Yes, we're going back to the Celeste system, which means there's no rest for the weary. But I should have time to get a shower."

"I'll fix you something to eat."

"Make sure you get me a caffeinated drink," Kim said. "Something strong. I don't care what it is. I can't be falling asleep at the controls."

"That wouldn't be good for any of us," Ben replied.

She kissed him again, then he left while she got cleaned up. The shower helped, but she needed sleep. Unfortunately, the trip through hyperspace to the Celeste system was short, and Kim guessed that General Pershing would want to break it up into microjumps that would keep her in the pilot's chair the entire time.

After her shower, she towel-dried her short hair, put on a clean flight suit, and let Ben back into her room. He had a tray with a plate of hot food.

"What is this?" Kim asked.

"It's called pasta," Ben said. "And those little things are actual shrimp."

"Shrimp?"

"It's good," Ben said. "Trust me."

She couldn't deny the rich meal smelled wonderful. She dropped into her colorful armchair with its thick cushions and took a bite. The food was warm, creamy, and delicious. The delight showed on her face.

"I told you," Ben said.

"This deal with the Imperium isn't so bad," Kim said after she swallowed. "I could get used to this."

"We have to enjoy it while we can," Ben said. "There's no telling what the future holds. By the way, the *Siren*'s passenger ship is on its way. The Confederates will be gone soon."

"That's good," Kim said. "I prefer our ship less crowded."

"Me too," Ben agreed. "What else can I do to help you?"

"Nothing," Kim said. "I need about ten hours of rack time, but there's no chance of that anytime soon. Any idea what the general wants to do back in the Celeste system?"

"No," Ben said.

"We could be there a long time," Kim replied. "I understand the need, but it seems like someone else could do it. I mean, we've done enough, haven't we? We're not even a warship."

"I know," Ben said. "I'm afraid our luck is going to run out."

"Don't say that," Kim replied. "Let's not tempt fate."

After her meal, Ben walked Kim back to the bridge. They were last of the crew to arrive, it seemed. Magnum was at his station, along with Nance, who hardly ever left her beloved computers. The general was there, but that was no surprise either. Kim couldn't say much about Alicia Pershing as an individual, but as a general, she was a machine. It seemed the woman never got tired.

Even the professor was back at his station, and Duke Simeon was standing near the general. Kim went past the others whose stations formed a semicircle around her large, rotating pilot's seat and controls.

"The *Siren*'s passenger transport is locked on," Nance said. "I'm cycling the air lock now."

"Very good," Pershing said. "Once the queen is on board and comfortable, I'll give the okay for the Confederates to disembark."

"And then we're going to the Celeste system?" Kim asked.

"That's correct," Pershing replied.

"Nance, do you have the jump point set?" Kim said.

"The navigation computer is plotting a course now," Nance replied.

"I'll go down and make sure the air lock is secure," Ben said.

"And do a visual inspection of all ship systems," Pershing said. "Once we're underway, there will be no turning back. I want to ensure we have everything we need at optimal performance."

"You've got it," Ben said.

Kim watched him go. She felt a small pang of regret. There was no doubt that Ben's place was in the engineering bay, but still, she liked it when he was on the bridge with her. And it didn't help matters that the duke slid into Ben's chair and gave her a charming smile.

Kim rotated her pilot's seat so that she was facing the front of the ship. The big bridge displays showed Yelsin Prime glowing in the light from the system star. Beyond it was dark space, sprinkled with stars. Kim wanted to get lost out there, far from the fighting. If they went far enough, she guessed that the crew of the *Echo* could live long, happy lives before the invading aliens reached them. Perhaps they never would. Kim knew it was certainly possible that General Pershing could fight the invaders without their help.

Ben might have felt guilty for opening the wormhole to another galaxy and destroying most of the Imperium Fleet in the process, but Kim didn't. The Imperium got what it deserved, and in her mind, the galaxy was better off struggling against aliens than fighting the overwhelming forces of the Royal Imperium.

She ran a quick system check. The main drive was online, and there was plenty of Zexum in the fusion reactor. Her wing engines were synced, and the only issue at that moment was the air lock, which she could see was still open.

Modulus Echo, we have the queen, said a voice that came over the bridge speakers.

"Roger that, *Siren*," Pershing replied. "Sending the Confederates to you now."

Are these orders correct, General? a woman said. *We're to take them to the Androsis system after ferrying the queen to Mersa Prime?*

"That's correct," Pershing said. "Duke Simeon has already sent word and issued a line of credit to replace their ships. Drop them at the shipyard and return here. Until further notice, the Yelsin system is our operational headquarters."

Copy that, came the woman's reply. Kim couldn't be sure, but she thought she detected a note of resentment in the woman's voice. Not that it was hard to understand. The Royal Imperium had just lost thousands of ships and the duke was replacing Confederate vessels. Old prejudices wouldn't be easily swept aside.

The com-link crackled to life. Kim heard Ben's voice over the loudspeaker and also from the tiny speaker on the collar of her flight suit.

"The Confederates have all moved over," Ben said. "I'm closing the air lock now."

Modulus Echo, this is R.I.F. Siren, the male voice from the Imperium ship said, his deep voice carrying through the bridge on a signal much stronger than the crew's personal com-links. *We are disengaging. Stand by for space bridge release.*

Kim didn't hear the airtight seal break. There was no alert on her monitor screens, but Nance changed the external camera feed on the big wall display. Kim could see the accordion device that had tethered the two ships together being retracted into the *Siren*.

"We'll wait until they move away," Pershing said.

"Jump point is set," Nance announced. "Our departure has been accepted by Ground Control."

"Very well," General Pershing replied.

"Are we going straight to the Celeste system?" Kim asked.

"Negative, we'll be making a series of jumps," Pershing explained. "Standard military protocol for wartime maneuvering will be observed."

"Great," Kim said, even though she had no idea what the standard military protocol was.

Over the com-link, Ben replied again, "Air lock is secure, General. All systems are green."

"Outstanding," Pershing said without the slightest trace of enthusiasm. "Pilot, take us out of system."

"Great, I don't have a name, just a title now," Kim said quietly as she pushed the throttle forward and guided the ship out of orbit.

"No one is going to forget your name, Kim," Duke Simeon said. "We're making history here. You can count on that."

"Sorry, I didn't think anyone could hear me," Kim said.

"Approaching jump point," Nance said.

Kim lined the ship up with the icon on her plot display. The *Echo* was racing toward it, and all that was left was to hit the button that would launch them into hyperspace at the appropriate moment.

"Here we go," Kim said, hitting the switch and watching as the dark void of space swirled into the glowing gas of hyperspace.

Chapter 7

Major Le Croix opened his eyes and couldn't believe what he saw. The world, not just Gershwin, but his entire world looked different. There was a crisp nature to his vision, almost like he was watching everything on giant display screens. He was in a large room filled with surgical equipment. There were Krah moving about. As he saw them, targeting areas lit up to show the most efficient means of killing them. They were workers, not warriors. Each one had a surgically added ring around their midsection with various articulated limbs. They looked like strange spider people. The long, delicate-looking mechanical arms had specific functions. Some had tools and were calibrating the surgical machinery. Others had medical implements and were seeing to patients. There were both warriors and workers on the surgical tables and gurneys, and Le Croix was the only human.

"You're awake," one of the Krah doctors said in their grunting language, yet Le Croix heard the sounds translated.

"What did you do to me?" Le Croix asked.

"Chieftain Grubat honored you with enhancements," the doctor said. "You should sit up."

Le Croix expected to be weak, but he sat up easily. His new legs swung off the gurney and hung down to the floor. Looking at them, he felt both excitement and revulsion. His prosthetic legs that replaced his calves, ankles, and feet after being wounded in battle, had been simple devices—arching lower limbs with footpads, which connected to his own legs just below the knee. But what he saw as he looked down after waking up in the Krah medical facility was much more complex. His upper legs were gone, or perhaps built into the new legs. Metal covered the legs, from hip to feet. Large, heavy-looking pistons ran down his thighs, and advanced servos took the place of his knees and ankles. There were feet at the end of his legs, oblong metal paddles with multiple joints.

"Can you stand up?" the doctor asked.

"What the hell did you do to me?" Le Croix said as he stood up. He could feel the power of his new legs. They were strong.

During his basic-training, squats and lunges were a regular part of his exercise regimen. And he'd never felt weak when it came to his legs, but since being wounded, he had struggled with simple tasks like getting up from a chair. It wasn't noticeable to the people around him, but Le Croix felt the extreme effort it took just to get up on his feet. The new legs didn't struggle in the slightest. It felt to Le Croix like he was being held up by two very strong men.

"That's good," the doctor said. "Your body is remarkably adaptable."

"What did you do?" Le Croix asked.

"Gave you new legs, of course. But there was no need for amputation. We mapped your nervous system and used your existing legs to sync your enhancements. They should work perfectly, and in many ways, they are superior to your natural limbs. Running, jumping, and climbing will no longer be taxing to you. You'll be faster and more secure on your feet than ever before, no matter the gravity or terrain. Not to mention that your legs are lethal, which will be advantageous in battle."

"Why would Grubat choose to enhance his enemy?" Le Croix said.

"I cannot speak for the chieftain," the doctor said. "His purposes are his own."

"Can I walk?" Le Croix asked.

"Yes, of course."

"What else did you do to me?"

"We replaced your eyes," the doctor said.

Perhaps it was the translation device being used, or maybe the doctor genuinely felt as if removing a person's eyes was a matter of little importance, but Le Croix felt as if the wind had been knocked out of him. His eyes were gone, but he wasn't blind. It didn't matter that he seemed to be seeing things better than he had before the surgery; just knowing that his eyes were gone made him feel crippled.

"My eyes?" Le Croix said, reaching up to his face.

"And we've added neurological improvements as well."

"What?" Le Croix asked.

His hand felt flesh at his cheek, but a band of metal encircled his head. Running his fingers along the metal, he discovered that it encased his ears and formed a V at the back of his head, with the point just above his neck.

"Think of it as a weapon rack," the doctor said. "You have enhanced hearing, with automatic universal translators. There are neural nodes to control various machine-based weapons or transport devices, along with extrasensory tentacles, if the chieftain should so honor you."

"You mean the tentacles aren't natural?" Le Croix asked.

"They are natural enhancements," the doctor explained. "And many of the systems on our ships are controlled via the neural nodes. Your brain was quite receptive. It is still necessary that you undergo continued testing, but our technology allows for the rejuvenation of body systems. And eventually, replacement. Your normal lifespan is what? Ninety revolutions of your planet around its sun?"

"Something like that," Le Croix said, struggling just to accept what the doctor was telling him.

"With your enhancements, you could easily live five times that long," the doctor continued. "Eventually, you'll need organ replacement, but I see no reason why your flesh can't be biopsied and cloned to produce new organs."

"What are you saying? That I can't die?"

"Of course, you can be killed," the doctor said. "But growing old and dying isn't something you need to worry about. You are of the Warrior caste now."

"Warrior caste," Le Croix said, his mind reeling.

"Go for a walk, but don't go too far. Your mind might require further conditioning to adequately manage the newly enhanced systems."

The doctor moved on, leaving Le Croix standing by the bed he'd woken up on. None of the Krah seemed to fear him. Not that he intended them harm, but he had been a prisoner. In fact, he'd fought a group of Krah warriors. The memories were coming back to him. The pain of his battle was a fraction of its intensity, but the memory of it made him flinch just the same. He had no idea how long ago that had taken place, or what all the Krah had done to him since, but he wasn't worse for wear.

In fact, he felt better than he had in years, certainly more whole than he had since being wounded and losing his legs.

He took a step, expecting it to be difficult. Learning to walk with his prosthetics had taken a significant period of time, yet the new legs were simple to operate. In fact, he felt like *operate* was the wrong word; *use* was a better fit. He could use his new legs just like his natural limbs. They weren't heavy or clunky; they didn't require him to struggle with balance or coordination. He took several more steps, moving through the room on his own. There was no need to hold onto anything to steady his balance. It was as if he had been shackled and someone had cut him free.

He turned toward the door leading out of the room, and he didn't sway or stumble. Walking was effortless. He was walking easily and with more agility than he had ever remembered. Outside the medical facility was a long corridor, but at the end he saw sunlight. He walked toward the exit and had to hold himself back from running.

Everything he saw, his new eyes identified. There were symbols on the doors and signs on the walls that he couldn't read, but his artificial eyes translated everything for him. He passed maintenance hatches, storage rooms, even a training chamber, whatever that was. And then he was outside.

Le Croix could feel the breeze. It was cool and refreshing. The sun was still high in the sky, and there were Krah all around him. Some were even warriors. They looked at him in surprise as he began to jog. His body felt light as a feather, almost like the gravity on the planet had been dialed back, only there was no need to adjust his movements. The legs pumped easily as he began to run. He moved faster and faster, almost without effort, as if he were on a machine that was running for him.

He left the clearing and ran into the trees. No one said anything or tried to stop him. He jumped over fallen trees, large stones, and eventually the river. His new legs were powerful; the sense of freedom was intoxicating. It felt as if he could run for days and days without stopping. But eventually, he turned back and began to walk. Perhaps he could have kept running to escape, but where would he go? He wasn't even on the same continent as the royal city. He might be able to run for hundreds of miles without stopping on his new legs, but he still had to eat and rest. He couldn't swim oceans.

As he walked, he was conflicted. The Krah were alien invaders from another galaxy. He'd seen them capture human vessels with no thought to the people inside, many of whom were killed in the process. They had landed on Gershwin without permission, which was against royal law. And they had taken him prisoner and performed unnecessary surgery on him. Surgery that had been beneficial. If what the doctor said was true, Le Croix would outlive every person currently alive in the galaxy. And what had the Royal Imperium done for him? After serving as a Special Forces officer on multiple missions with complete success, he had finally been wounded. He had lost his legs in service to the Royal Imperium and they had replaced them with stiff metal and pulled him from active duty. Serving General Pershing had been rewarding on some level, but administration was not his forte or passion. He was a warrior. Nothing compared to leading men into battle. Yet they had taken that from him, and the Krah had given it back. The aliens he had come to the Celeste system to fight had treated him better than the humans who had sent him into harm's way.

He was struggling with his inner conflict as he approached the large clearing where Chieftain Grubat had landed his massive ship. Most of that vessel had been taken apart and used to build other structures. And on the far side of the open plain, Le Croix saw a landing craft coming down. He stayed just inside the tree line, watching. The Krah paid him no attention, as if he wasn't a threat or even an enemy, but his training kicked in. He stayed out of sight while watching the newly arrived Krah.

A hatch opened, and a huge Krah came striding out. He was massive, with long headdress tendrils that hung to his waist. Like Le Croix, his legs were metal behemoths and several of his other body parts had been replaced as well. More Krah joined him from the other transports. Three looked like officers, and the rest were less enhanced but looked like hardened veterans. They went to what remained of Grubat's ship, and Le Croix wondered where the chieftain was. A horn sounded, and while Le Croix was certain he'd never heard it before, he recognized it as a beacon to rally everyone together.

Before he knew it, and why he couldn't really say, he went striding out of the woods. All the other Krah were gathering near the remains of the big ship, and Le Croix went with them. Perhaps the doctors had done more than make enhancements, but he didn't feel a compulsion to obey the call of the horn. If he wanted, he could stop, turn back, even run away. But he was drawn to the call on some level. The Krah were warriors, just like Le Croix. They celebrated that fact and had recognized it in him. Perhaps that was something to take into consideration.

Perhaps he wasn't an outsider, or an enemy, but a kindred spirit. They seemed accepting as he approached, and so perhaps it was best if he accepted his place among them.

Chapter 8

The *Modulus Echo* dropped out of hyperspace at the very edge of the Celeste system heliosphere. They were too far away to see the wormhole, Gershwin, or even the activity of the alien vessels. Ben had activated the flux shield before their last jump, and the entire crew waited on the bridge, unsure of what they might find waiting for them.

"Visual scans are clear," Nance said. "There's nothing out this far."

"Best speed into the system," Pershing said.

"Even at our best speed, it will take hours to get close enough to see anything," Kim said.

"Will the shield hold that long?" Pershing asked.

"It should," Ben replied.

He didn't like thinking of the shield having problems again. The aliens had already proven they could follow the *Echo* through hyperspace, and if the flux shield failed, they would have no recourse against the larger, faster vessels.

"Set a course that will take us within range of the ship's video capabilities," Pershing said. "We'll do an extended burn, but shut down all systems when we get in range."

"Plotting a new course now," Nance said.

"Just so that we're all clear," Kim said, "if they come after us, do we run?"

"The mission is to get information on the enemy," Pershing said. "It's possible that after their loss in the Yelsin system that they decided our galaxy isn't worth the losses they'll take. We may find the wormhole unguarded and the system unoccupied."

"We can hope," Duke Simeon said.

"But that's not what you're expecting," Ben said. "Is it?"

"No," General Pershing said. "This wormhole is the only link between our galaxies. Whatever the aliens have planned, they will want to hold this system at all costs. Without it, they have no way of returning home."

"That assumes they want to go back," Magnum said, breaking his usual silence.

"True, but without it, they can't call for assistance," Pershing continued. "They can't be reinforced or get supplies unless they take it from us, and we don't even know if they are like us at all. We've seen nothing but the exterior of their ships."

"We should change that," Staff Sergeant Visher said.

He and his commandos weren't on the ship's bridge, but they loitered in the atrium just behind it.

"In time," General Pershing said. "For now, we need intelligence and time to gather our forces."

"Course is set," Nance said. "Nine hours, twenty-two minutes, to reach maximum visual range."

"Excellent," General Pershing said.

"We should all get some rest while we can," Ben suggested. "We only need one person to man the bridge and we can take turns. I'll go first."

"Very well," Pershing said. "I'll leave the rotation to you, Ben. I'll be back in seven hours."

Kim stood up and stretched. "The ship's on autopilot. But if you need me, just call on the com-link."

"I will," Ben said. "Get some sleep."

"You don't have to tell me twice," Kim said.

"I'll take the next watch," Magnum said.

"Okay," Ben said. "I'll wake you in four hours."

The big man nodded and headed straight for his quarters. The commandos headed to the upper deck, while General Pershing went into the crew lounge. Ben knew the sofa in the lounge wasn't all that comfortable, but he couldn't blame the general for wanting to be close if something happened.

"Will you need me, Ben?" Professor Jones asked.

"No," Ben said with a smile. "Magnum and I will be enough to keep an eye on things. Get some rest."

"Yes...rest. Of course."

Ben watched the older man leave the bridge knowing he was going to work, not to sleep. But the professor was old enough to know when to rest and when to work. He was the only person who could find a way to close the wormhole, if that was even possible. And his work on that problem was more important than any help he could offer on the bridge of the ship.

"Mind if I keep you company for a while?" Duke Simeon asked as he settled into the communications console that the professor usually manned.

"Not at all," Ben said.

They sat in silence for a few minutes. Ben put the ship's speed up on the big display screens on the front wall of the bridge. Nance got to her feet and left the bridge without a word a few minutes later. There was nothing to do but keep an eye on the scrolling video feeds. Ben set the displays to rotate from feed to feed so that every thirty seconds they could look in every direction around the ship.

"Not much to see out here," Duke Simeon said.

"There rarely is this far out," Ben replied. "A few planetoids, maybe. But we'll see some of the gas giants before long."

"You know your way around a solar system," the duke replied. "I suppose you've been doing this a long time."

"Not really," Ben said.

"Is it true you flew through a black hole?"

"Kim was the pilot," Ben said. "But yes, we took the *Echo* through a black hole. It wasn't by choice."

"What happened?"

"We had to jump blind trying to get out of a system under siege and ended up too close to a black hole to escape."

"So you flew through it?" the duke asked. "What made you even think it was possible?"

"I had read the theory," Ben replied. "I can't remember where. Probably in an old science publication from before the Great War."

"I didn't know things like that even existed."

"They do on Torrent Four," Ben said. "Ever been there?"

"I can't say I have," the duke replied.

"There's not much to see. It's a junk world now. Only a few cities and some recycling contractors running rigs in the salvage yards. I grew up there. Found the *Echo* and started rebuilding her. It took a long time, but eventually we got her running, and we ended up in the middle of the fight between the Imperium and the rebellion."

"You joined the Confederacy then?"

"No," Ben said. "But we did some work for them in exchange for Zexum. It was the only way to keep flying."

"Why not just join the Royal Imperium from the start?" Duke Simeon asked. "Surely that would have been easier than refurbishing an old ship like this."

Ben laughed. When he looked at the duke and saw the royal's baffled expression, he only laughed harder. It took a minute to pull himself together.

"What is so funny?" the duke asked.

"You really don't know?" Ben said. "You think we could just stroll into a recruiting office and sign up to work for the Royal Imperium?"

"With your skills, yes," Duke Simeon said. "Kim's a natural flyer. She should have been in the Royal Fleet Academy."

"Oh, she would have if that were possible," Ben said. "For a long time, that was all she wanted."

"What stopped her?"

"You are aware that on class five planets, admission to the academy requires applicants to pass a rigorous skills test, right?"

"It's hard to believe that Kim wouldn't pass it," the duke insisted.

"I'm sure she could have, but to take the test, she needed the recommendation of a citizen of standing and five hundred credits. On Torrent Four, only the exceptionally wealthy had access to the Imperium's schools and programs."

"You're saying that you were too poor to join the Royal Imperium?"

"Too poor, no parents, no legal standing, nothing," Ben admitted. "As far as the Royal Imperium was concerned, we didn't exist."

"I find that hard to believe," Duke Simeon said. "Do you have any idea how much money is budgeted for educational programs on category five worlds?"

"No clue," Ben said.

"If you had it so tough, how'd you learn engineering?"

"My grandfather taught me some things," Ben said. "But mostly I just took things apart and put them back together again."

"You have no formal education?"

"None," Ben said.

The duke looked as if he didn't believe a word Ben had said. It only took a few seconds to pull up the system file on Torrent Four from the ship's computer. The duke scanned it, looking at the photos of the massive salvage fields.

"This is where you're from?" Duke Simeon asked. "All of you?"

"Kim, Nance, Magnum, and I," Ben said. "You really don't know much about the galaxy you rule."

"I don't rule it," Simeon admitted. "I'm the prince's cousin. Until the attack, there was almost no chance of me reaching the throne."

"Do you know about the Confederacy, then?" Ben asked. "Why it exists?"

"I'm learning," the duke said. "They aren't all outlaws and brigands, like I was told."

"Some are, I'm sure," Ben said. "But most are just pushing back against the unjust policies of the Royal Imperium."

"The government can't please everyone," the duke said.

"No, but it doesn't have to burden them either. Do you know what's happening on Mersa Prime?"

The duke looked baffled. Ben couldn't believe that a member of the royal family knew less about the Imperium's activities than he did.

"About the drones?" Ben persisted.

"I'm sorry," Duke Simeon said.

"You're sorry for what's happening or for not knowing what I'm talking about?"

"I have lived a privileged life, I know, but the government is run by ministers who answer to the throne," the duke explained. "I was never privy to those reports. Nor did I try to take on a more direct role. I assumed everything was being handled in a professional manner. Everyone knows about the political maneuvering at court, and in the Fleet, but that doesn't make the system corrupt."

"Well, it is," Ben said. "And I'm not a rebel, not by choice anyway. But I've been to Mersa Prime. I've seen the drones they use to drug the citizens there into complacency."

"You can't be serious," Duke Simeon said.

"I am," Ben replied. "Thousands of drones are launched into the atmosphere and release a gas that was developed for violent offenders in prison. It makes people passive and apathetic."

"Wait, I know what you're talking about," the duke said, his voice rising with conviction. "You're mistaken. Those are weather drones. They help keep violent storms at bay."

"That's the cover story," Ben said. "We came out of hyperspace too close to the planet and dropped right into the middle of a swarm of drones. One even crashed into the *Echo*. Magnum and I had to retrieve it. We ran tests on the contents. There's no question that what it was spraying into the atmosphere was a narcotic. And you can bet when the queen gets there, she'll be drinking bottled water."

"That's all she ever drinks," Duke Simeon said. "You're serious, aren't you? You really believe that the galactic government would drug its own citizens? Mersa Prime is a category one planet, a closed world, with population controls in place. Why in the world would we need to drug the people there? There's not even a hint of rebel sympathy on Mersa Prime."

"Think about it," Ben said. "Maybe the reason there's no sympathy for the rebellion is that the citizens there are all drugged."

"You've believed one too many conspiracy theories, my friend," the duke insisted.

"You'll see," Ben replied. "If you become king, you'll find out the truth. Maybe the royal family isn't behind it, but it is happening. And if we succeed in pushing the aliens out of the galaxy, you'll have to face up to what's going on. When that day comes, remember what you've seen and heard here."

There was a lull in the conversation. They both watched the video feeds rotate on the display screens while they contemplated their own thoughts. For his part, Ben saw that the flux shield was holding steady. He felt some pride in the achievement. The prototype shield could hold up for extended periods of time if it wasn't exposed to heavy fire or debris. And the system used only a tiny fraction of the ship's available power.

"We're not all bad, you know," Duke Simeon finally said. "We're just people too."

"Who?" Ben asked.

"The royal family."

Ben wanted to argue that they profited from the oppressed on a thousand worlds, but he knew it was useless to argue. Instead, he chose to focus on the duke's apparent goodwill.

"Well, your being here does go a long way to changing my perceptions of you."

"How so?" the duke asked.

"You aren't hiding from the fight," Ben said. "I can respect that."

"I've never been in a fight," the duke said. "At least not one that was personal. That business in the Yelsin system was a first for me."

"At least you didn't lock yourself in your cabin," Ben said. "That sort of thing inspires people."

"Let's just hope there are some people left to inspire," the duke said. "The general is concerned that the Fleet isn't responding to her call for help."

"They haven't seen the enemy, but it won't be long until they do," Ben said. "If we don't find a way to stop them here, we'll be seeing them in dozens of star systems."

"You really think that?"

"From what we've seen, they're salvagers," Ben said. "They capture ships and then use them to add to their own vessels. I can relate to that."

"Because you built this ship?"

"Because on Torrent Four, that was how a person survived. You had to learn to find usable gear in the mounds of trash and ruined components. Going through everything piece by piece was slow and unproductive. If you wanted to get the good stuff, you had to keep moving."

"So if the aliens are ship collectors, they'll want to keep moving. Is that what you're saying? They need to find more ships to capture?"

"Exactly," Ben said. "There's not enough here to satisfy them."

"That's a frightening thought," the duke said. "You've given me a lot to consider, Ben."

He stood up and extended a hand. It was a surprising show of respect. Ben stood up and shook the duke's hand.

"You have a fine ship," Duke Simeon said. "I'm honored to be here with you."

"Likewise," Ben said, not sure what else to say.

"I better get some rest while I can. Wake me if there's news."

"Yes, of course," Ben said.

He watched the heir to the royal throne walk up the stairs to the upper deck and wondered if it was possible that he might have actually made a difference in the duke's way of thinking. He sat back down and looked at the time. There were three more hours before he could wake Magnum to take his place. He rubbed his eyes and leaned back in his chair, hoping that his entire watch, and Magnum's to follow, would be boring and uneventful.

Chapter 9

"General," Staff Sergeant Visher said as Pershing made her way up to the galley. "Any news?"

"We'll be in range soon," Alicia Pershing said, filling a mug with hot coffee. She liked it black and almost bitter. Not that she enjoyed the taste, but the hot drink was somehow comforting and stimulating at the same time. "There's no indication from the system that we've been noticed yet."

She put a protein bar into her pocket and went back down to the bridge. Sleeping on the sofa in the crew lounge had been an unnecessary precaution. Their little ship would have been difficult to spot if the aliens were alert and scanning for ships coming into the system, but it seemed like they were lax in their security. She filed that little tidbit of information away, knowing it might come in handy down the road.

Magnum was at his console on the bridge and Kim was just coming out of her quarters as Pershing descended the stairs. Kim stretched and looked up at the general.

"Anything?"

"No," Pershing said.

"I'll grab a bite and be back at my station in a sec."

Pershing nodded but didn't reply. She commanded the crew of the *Modulus Echo* with only the slimmest amount of authority. They all seemed to respect her in their own way, but it was a far cry from military discipline. Normally, even senior officers didn't address her so informally, and the crew members of the little ship were a far cry from officer material. Still, they had their uses, and until they were no longer useful,

Alicia Pershing, acting commander in chief of the Royal Imperium Fleet, would tolerate them.

She looked forward to the day when she had a real army to command again. Not that she ever expected things to be normal, or to have any semblance of what they had been before the Fleet was destroyed. But she knew at some point the alien threat would be contained, the Royal Imperium Fleet would once again dominate the galaxy, and criminals like the crew of the *Echo* would fear the very sound of her name.

"Are we picking up anything yet?" Pershing said as she settled into the chair at her console.

"Negative," Magnum said.

She appreciated that he was thrifty with his words, as if each one cost him something. Unlike Kim, Magnum didn't distract her with unnecessary conversation.

"How close are we?"

"Several light-minutes from the wormhole," Magnum said.

"And we don't have pictures yet?"

Magnum shook his head. They were so far away from the wormhole and Gershwin's orbital plane that their visual scans were ineffective. Pershing looked at the monitor screens built into her console. They were old-fashioned touch screens, but they yielded the information she wanted as soon as she touched them.

The ship's systems were all in the green. The only thing that concerned her was the Zexum level. The tank feeding the fusion reactor was down to a quarter of its capacity. They would need to change it before they were forced to maneuver or jump to hyperspace. The last thing she wanted was to run out of fuel or to have to worry about changing the tanks on the run. It was just one more issue that she wouldn't have to worry about on a military ship. The Fleet vessels had huge Zexum tanks that could power massive warships for months at a time. Not to mention, there were crews whose jobs were to worry about such things so that Pershing was free to focus on strategy.

"Wake the others," Pershing ordered Magnum. "I want everyone on the bridge in ten minutes."

Magnum nodded and left his station. Pershing knew that he and Ben had only gotten a fraction of the sleep she'd enjoyed. Not that sleeping on a stiff sofa in enemy territory was pleasant, but she could sleep anywhere. And despite the stiffness in her neck, she felt better for having gotten some rest. But she couldn't feel bad about the crew not getting more rest. They were a lone, tiny Kestrel class ship in a system with an enemy who almost certainly had more vessels. She hoped she was wrong, but her gut told her she wasn't. They had won a tiny engagement, and at great cost. The war was just beginning. The aliens wouldn't run away after their loss in the Yelsin system. Her destiny was to lead a great war, and the aliens were going to be her nemesis, not a ragtag rebellion.

"Morning, General," Nance said as she slid into her seat.

What the crew lacked in discipline, they made up for in sheer talent. Nance oversaw the ship's systems with ruthless efficiency. In many ways, the young woman was more like the computers she loved than a person. She was too small to be of much use in a fight, but Pershing admired her calm under fire. No matter what trouble they wound up in on the little ship, she maintained her cool, at least outwardly.

"I come bearing gifts," Kim announced as she descended the stairs from the upper deck. "Energy drinks, real fruit, and something called snack cakes. I have to admit, I've already had two and they are delicious."

"Snack cakes?" Nance asked, sounding uncertain.

"They're sweet," Kim said.

The two women were like children in some ways. Pershing had to remind herself that they had grown up in utter poverty in a fringe world where the simplest things like prepackaged snack cakes were a novelty.

"Good morning," Ben said as he approached Kim and Nance. The tips of his hair were wet, and it looked like he'd just scrubbed his face. Probably to help him wake up, Pershing thought.

"Ben, you have to try these," Kim said, her mouth half-full. "They're so, good."

Magnum returned to the bridge and took his seat at the console next to Nance.

"Breakfast can wait," Pershing said. "Let's settle in, people. If we can see the enemy, they can see us."

"Not likely," Kim said. She carried a drink container to the pilot's chair and settled in. "We're drifting, radar's down, running lights are off—it's like we're a ghost in the darkness."

"Never underestimate your enemy," Pershing replied. "Always assume they have the utmost intelligence and capacities, then you'll never be caught off guard."

"Okay," Kim said, sounding skeptical.

"We'll be in max visual range in three minutes," Nance said. "All systems, green."

"Ben, that reminds me," Pershing said. "I want you to change out the Zexum tank now."

"Right now?" Ben asked.

"Yes, I don't want to worry about it."

"Alright," Ben said.

Pershing picked up the note of irritation in his voice, but she didn't care. They weren't friends, and they certainly weren't on a pleasure cruise. She had given the ship's crew more food and fuel than they would see in a year working their odd jobs and smuggling contraband to closed planets. Not to mention she was complicit in covering up the fact that they were responsible for destroying the Royal Imperium Fleet and opening the wormhole that allowed the aliens into their galaxy. She had even given them amnesty for their crimes against the Imperium in exchange for full control of their ship for as long as she needed it. The *Modulus Echo,* with its prototype gravity shield and crew of misfits, was hers to command. Being friendly or polite was not part of the bargain.

Ben headed downstairs, and Pershing turned back to her console where she had a plot of the entire Celeste system pulled up, including their position. It was all based on the Nav Net's projections of each of the system planets and their computer's best estimate of their position before shutting down the engine, radar, and telemetry systems. They were beyond the orbital plane of three of the system's gas giants. Gershwin was the fourth planet from the system's sun, a yellow star. The first three planets were barren rocks, too hot for atmospheres or even liquid water. Gershwin was an oasis among the uninhabitable worlds of the Celeste system, a Goldilocks world with liquid water, breathable air, and thriving flora. Yet, despite the pristine nature of the planet, it was only significant to the Imperium as the private home of the royal family. It had almost no human population and no strategic value. Pershing would have gladly given it to their enemy, but the wormhole just beyond Gershwin's orbital plane made that impossible.

The wormhole bypassed the space between galaxies— space so immense that even traveling faster than the speed of light would take lifetimes to cross. Professor Jones had built a bridge to the alien galaxy at the cost of the Imperium Fleet, and the strategic value of that single passageway through space was incalculable.

"Bring up the wormhole on the ship's cameras," Pershing said. "Maximum zoom."

"I've got it on the main display," Nance said.

The picture was incredibly disappointing. Even at maximum zoom, the display only showed a tiny red glow. According to the Nav Net's planetary position, Gershwin shouldn't be hidden behind the wormhole. But if it was visible it didn't show on that camera's angle.

"That's the best we can do?" Pershing said.

"It's anticlimactic," Kim said. "We can't see a thing from out here. We need to get closer."

"There's a lot of space between here and the wormhole," Nance said.

Pershing wasn't sure if the mousy computer expert was for or against the idea of lighting the engines and flying toward the wormhole.

"It's too dangerous," Pershing said. "The aliens might have stealth technology. We could fly right into a trap."

"We haven't seen that," Kim said. "What makes you think they're hiding?"

"I don't think they are," Pershing said. "But they could be. I'm making decisions based on what's possible, even if it isn't probable."

"Well, then they probably already know we're here," Kim said. "Why are we sneaking around? Fire up the radar and let's see what's going on out there."

"Even with radar, we wouldn't get an accurate assessment," Nance said. "We're too far away."

"Didn't we leave surveillance buoys or something?" Kim said.

Pershing felt as if she'd been slapped. Not by Kim, but by her own failure. She had forgotten about the buoys. The *Deception* had dropped over a dozen on their way to the wormhole. They had picked up one before making their jumps to the Yelsin system, but there were others just floating in the darkness between the worlds, waiting with loads of intelligence to share.

Pershing hit the com-link button on her console. "Ben?"

"Yes, General?" he replied.

"Can we pull the information from the surveillance buoys remotely?"

There was a slight pause. Pershing didn't know if it was because Ben was thinking about her question or doing something else. She could see from her console that the fusion reactor was on standby while he replaced the Zexum tank.

"Yes," Ben finally said. "But we'll have to bring up the radar and point our antenna right at the buoy."

"How long will it take to upload the data?" Pershing asked.

"That depends on the distance, signal strength, and size of the file," Nance said.

"Do it," Pershing ordered. "How much longer do you have on that Zexum tank?"

"Twenty minutes," Ben said. "If I can get a little help."

"I'll send Alpha team to assist," Pershing said.

"Radar is up and running," Nance said.

"I want to know the moment you find one of our buoys," Pershing said.

"It's possible the aliens picked them up," Magnum said. "It's the only tech left in the system."

"Would they really waste time picking up buoys?" Kim asked. "There's not much to them as far as salvage is concerned."

"Oh," Nance said.

"What is it?" Pershing asked. "Did you find one?"

"No," Nance replied. "Not yet. But the energy readings from around the wormhole are off the charts."

"That's normal, right?" Kim asked. "The wormhole emits a power reading."

"It's not the wormhole," Nance said. "It has a bright signature, but it's in the gravitational spectrum. This is different. This is energy, like ship power."

"What do they have in the system?" Pershing asked. "Bring up the radar display."

"We won't have a return on the radar for a while," Nance said. "The power signature is reaching us out here."

"Maybe it's leftover from the Fleet?" Kim said. "Maybe all those ships left residual power in the system."

"No," Pershing said. "There's no wishful thinking in war. The enemy has moved more ships into the system."

"We don't know that," Kim said. "Not for certain."

"I've got a surveillance buoy," Nance said. "Beginning the download."

"We'll know soon enough," Pershing said. She was confident that they would have the intelligence she needed to plan an attack, but she felt a tremor of fear at the thought of what they might find. There was no wishful thinking in warfare, she reminded herself. Chances were high that the aliens were mobilizing every ship they had available and sending them through the wormhole. If Pershing was lucky, the alien ships might be so spread out in their own galaxy that it would take weeks to move a significant force through the wormhole. But Pershing didn't feel lucky, and she certainly couldn't depend on luck.

"Estimated time of retrieval?" Pershing asked.

"Forty-nine minutes," Nance said.

"Start calculating a jump point," Pershing said. "We have to assume they're watching us now. If they send ships in this direction, I want to be able to leave on a moment's notice."

"Where are we going?" Nance asked.

"Make a multijump to the Mersa system," Pershing said. "It's time we gather our forces and push these aliens back where they came from."

Chapter 10

"You need a hand?" Corporal Dial asked.

"As a matter of fact," Ben replied, "I do."

He had the new tank slung over to the fusion reactor, and the floor panels were pulled up, but the Zexum tanks were heavy and hard to control. The *Echo* had a sling and pulley system in the engineering bay to move the heavy equipment. Ben bent down and unfastened the used tank from the reactor.

"What are you doing?" Dial asked. He was followed by three other commandos. They were all strong men and could probably lift the tanks with the sling, but Ben didn't want anyone getting hurt.

"Changing the Zexum tanks," Ben said. "The general wants a fresh tank feeding the fusion reactor before we run into trouble."

"Sounds sensible," Dial said.

"If you can hand me those cargo straps, I'll get this tank ready to move."

"Roger that," Dial said. "Is it true you built this ship?"

"I refurbished it," Ben said as he bent down and ran the cargo strap under the tank that was held on mounts beneath the floor of the engineering bay. "On Torrent Four, there's plenty of scrap and old material to work with. The trick is finding the right components."

"You did that all by yourself?" another of the commandos asked.

"I did the mechanical work," Ben said. "Nance debugged and rebooted the computer systems. She keeps this ship running in perfect order. Okay, let's lift it out."

Corporal Dial used the ratcheting lever to hoist the old tank out of its place beneath the floor panels. The commandos slung it over to the storage compartment that was filled with Zexum tanks. They unhooked the tank and stood it up, while Ben ran the pulley system back over to the full tank that was waiting on the floor beside the open panels.

"What's the word from the bridge?" Dial asked.

"Not much," Ben replied. "We're too far out to get visuals on anything."

"So fire up the radar," Dial said.

"Or doesn't it work?" asked another of the commandos with a chuckle.

"It works," Ben said. He didn't mind the soldiers joking around. He had earned their respect and they had earned his. They took up a lot of space, ate a lot of food, and made a lot of noise on the small ship, but Ben liked having them around. They worked hard, didn't complain, and he felt safer having them on board. "When we turn on the radar, it's like shining a light at the alien ships. They'll see us for sure and know right where we are."

"Ah," the soldier said. "That ain't good."

"No," Ben said. "But we did it anyway just a few minutes ago to find the surveillance buoys. Once we get his tank installed, it might be best if you guys gear up."

"You think the aliens will come after us?" Dial asked.

"I don't think they can afford not to," Ben said. "They'll at least come to investigate. And we know they can follow us through hyperspace. That means making the jump won't mean we're safe."

"Gotcha," Dial said.

They lowered the new tank into position. Dial and his commandos unhooked the straps from the tank, while Ben connected the hose that ran to the fusion reactor.

"Can you guys replace those grates while I get the reactor back online?" Ben asked.

The commandos did as they were asked. Ben got the fusion reactor going and tapped the com-link on his collar.

"Zexum tanks have been swapped out, and the fusion reactor is online, General," Ben said.

"Very good," Pershing said, her voice sounding tiny and far away on his com-link. "Is the shield in good order?"

"Yes, it's holding steady," Ben said. "Almost no power increase over the last eight hours."

"Outstanding," Pershing said. "We've stopped approaching ships. Lock everything down and return to the bridge."

"Okay," Ben said.

"I guess you weren't kidding," Corporal Dial said.

"Unfortunately not," Ben said.

They left the engineering bay and went up to the main deck. Pershing saw her soldiers and gave them orders.

"Wake the others," Pershing said. "I want Duke Simeon on the bridge. Everyone should be in protective gear."

"I'll tell Staff Sergeant Visher," Dial replied, then saluted the general.

Ben was headed to his seat at the engineering console as the commandos hurried up the metal stairs, their heavy boots clanking on the steps. One glance at his console showed all the ship's systems in the green. The big bridge displays showed a video image of space. Ben was sure something was headed their way, but he couldn't see it. The displays also showed a progress bar. The surveillance buoy was halfway through its data transfer.

"General, I have long-range radar," Nance said.

"On screen," Pershing snapped.

The video image changed to a plot of the system. It was a two-dimensional diagram that showed Gershwin, the wormhole, and the space between.

"This can't be right," Kim said.

There were small V-shaped icons representing alien ships. The computer assigned each a number. Ben saw what appeared to be over two hundred alien vessels between the planet and the wormhole.

"Will we have time to identify those ships?" Pershing asked.

"No," Nance replied. "Not if we're leaving the system before that alien ship reaches us."

"How much time do we have?" Ben asked.

"The alien ship will be in missile range in four minutes," Nance said. "We'll be in range of their grappling arms in seven minutes if they continue at their current speed."

Ben glanced at the progress bar. The download from the surveillance buoy showed fourteen minutes remaining.

"I don't want to take any chances that they'll overtake us," Pershing said.

"What happens if the download isn't finished before we leave the system?" Ben asked.

"We'll only get part of it," Nance said. "Some of the files will be corrupted or unreadable."

"If we start running now," Kim suggested, "maybe we can stay ahead of the alien long enough to finish the download."

"We have to stay in line with the buoy," Ben said. "Our receiver has to maintain line of sight."

"And the farther we move from the source, the longer the download will take," Nance said.

"So don't move away from it," Kim said. "We fly toward the alien."

"Why would we do that?" Pershing asked.

Ben could tell that the general was considering all options. She just didn't know if Kim was being serious or just cynical.

"Two reasons," Kim replied. "One, the closer we get, the faster the download. And two, we need to get up to maneuvering speed."

"The alien ships are faster," Pershing reminded her.

"But we're more maneuverable," Kim said. "We don't have to outrun them, just stay out of reach until the download is complete."

"What about our jump point?" Ben asked.

"I'll have to recalculate," Nance said. "But it won't take long."

"Are you certain about the shields?" Pershing asked Ben.

He glanced at his screen before answering. "Positive."

"Very well," Pershing said. "Make your maneuvers, Kim. But I don't want us getting too close. The shield is the last resort."

"But stay close enough that they think they'll get us," Ben said. "Otherwise, they'll slow down and turn with us."

"I've got this," Kim said. "Leave the flying to the big girls."

"What's happening?" Duke Simeon called out as he hurried down the stairs.

Ben turned and saw the royal. His clothes were wrinkled, and his hair was sticking out at odd angles, yet somehow he managed to look roguishly handsome despite having obviously just woken up.

"Sit down and strap in, Your Highness," Pershing said.

Everything seemed to happen quickly. Kim pressed the throttle to their stops and sent the *Echo* shooting toward the alien vessel. Nance changed the bridge displays back to the ship's external cameras. The alien ship seemed to emerge from the darkness of space like a demon materializing from the shadows. It was a big, bulbous craft with an almost insectile design. The articulated grappling arms were reaching for the *Echo*.

"They're trying to lure you in," Nance said. "Those arms are only halfway extended."

"Don't worry, I'm not getting closer than I have to," Kim said.

"Why are we flying toward it?" Duke Simeon asked.

Pershing gave a terse explanation as Ben tapped his com-link and spoke into it quietly.

"Professor?"

"I'm here, Ben."

The old man sounded tired. Ben guessed he'd stayed up working through the break. He was driven, excited by his research, but also pressured by the need to find a way to close the wormhole.

"Looks like we may have some rough flying ahead," Ben warned him. "You might want to put whatever you don't absolutely need into secure containers."

"Oh, thank you," Professor Jones said. "I will do that right away."

"Wooo-hooo!" Kim called out as she suddenly angled the ship up and away from the alien vessel. "Didn't see that coming, did you?"

"The alien vessel is turning," Nance said. "But the space between us is growing."

"I told you we couldn't keep up," Kim said.

"Recalculate the jump point," Pershing said. "They won't give up now that we've challenged them."

"Ten minutes on the download," Ben said.

"They could be in range by then," Nance said.

"I'm counting on it," Kim said. "Set the jump point in this quadrant."

She tapped her display and sent the information to Nance, who began reformulating the jump coordinates.

"Ben, can you shut down one of the wing engines?" Kim suggested. "Make it look like a mechanical problem?"

"I think so," Ben said.

"We'll coast long enough to convince them we're losing power," Kim said. "Be ready to fire the wing engine up on my mark."

Ben was typing commands into his console. The starboard wing engine sputtered, and the *Echo* began a slow, drifting spin. They were still traveling at speed since there was no friction in space to slow them down, but Ben hoped they looked crippled.

"The alien ship is gaining," Nance said.

"How close are we to that jump point?" Pershing asked.

"Two more minutes," Nance said.

"The alien will be on top of us in three," Ben added.

"Don't worry, they aren't doing anything fancy," Kim said. "It looks like they're swinging wide. Probably trying to herd us toward their fleet."

Just the sound of the word gave Ben a sense of dread. All his life, he'd heard stories of the dreaded Imperium Fleet. Until they accidentally led a ship of the line into a black hole, the Royal Imperium had not lost a ship in battle since the Great War. And when the bulk of the Imperium Fleet was lost to Professor Jones's gravity rocket, Ben had felt as if the scales of the galaxy had nearly evened out. But the aliens had built up a fleet of their own. Over two hundred enemy vessels just waiting to raid the more populated systems and do who knew what to the innocent people throughout the galaxy.

"Five more minutes and the download will be complete," Pershing said. "Make it look like we're trying to run."

"Stand by on that engine, Ben," Kim told him.

Ben hit a few keys and tapped some icons on his screen. All that remained was to press one button and the engine would come roaring back to life.

"A little closer," Kim said, coaxing the alien vessel just the way she wanted.

"Jump point is set," Nance announced.

"And just in time," Kim replied. "Now, Ben!"

He pressed the key on his console, and Kim threw the throttle forward. The *Echo* broke out of its drifting spin and turned down in a corkscrew. It wasn't as difficult a maneuver as the ship was capable of, and it only bought them a little distance from the alien vessel, whose grappling arms protruded from the ship in every direction. Ben watched the vessel on his console, changing the feed from the various hull cameras to keep the alien ship in sight.

"We're going the wrong direction," Nance said in her unflappable tone.

"I know it," Kim declared.

The alien ship had shifted its own momentum and was attempting to close on them. But Kim arced back up in a long, gradual maneuver. It took them close to the alien vessel, but it had too much mass to change directions as quickly as the *Echo*.

"Download complete!" Nance said.

"Make the jump," Pershing ordered.

"I'm on it," Kim said.

"There are more ships coming," Magnum said.

Ben looked on his screens but couldn't see anything. The ships were lost in the darkness of space, too far out for the sunlight to illuminate their dark hulls.

"Don't worry, they can eat my dust," Kim said.

"And track us through hyperspace," Pershing said. "Nance, I want new jump points set before we drop out of hyperspace."

"I'll do all I can," Nance said. "But the jump points will be estimates. I'll have to confirm them."

"It's as good as we can do," Ben said.

"Fine," Pershing replied.

"They're sending a dozen ships," Magnum said.

"We'll have to lead them away from the Mersa system," Pershing said angrily. "That will cost us time."

"We don't have a choice," Ben said. "Kim, make the jump."

"Here we go."

The Celeste system, where two hundred alien ships waited and over a dozen were in pursuit of the *Modulus Echo*, disappeared.

Chapter 11

The newcomers were high-level individuals within the Krah hierarchy. No one spoke to Le Croix. He didn't have friends among the aliens. But no one seemed to mind his being there among them either. He was ignored or tolerated—he wasn't sure which.

The newcomers spent nearly an hour just studying the world. Gershwin, or New Krah as his translator said the aliens called it, was an ideal world, one of the few that didn't need terraforming to make it habitable to humans and where people could thrive. Still, the aliens seemed to act as if it were the first planet they had ever been on. They breathed the air, examined the dirt, trees, and sky, and even waded into the river. They were like children full of delight in their new home, which Le Croix found amusing and bothersome at the same time.

A part of the remade soldier disliked the idea of aliens putting down roots in a world that he still felt belonged to humanity. On the other hand, Le Croix was identifying more and more with their culture, especially the idea that a person could take whatever they wanted as long as they were strong enough. He had seen the warriors take tools and even food from the workers, who never challenged or tried to stop them. And more than once, fights had broken out between the warriors over things that seemed trivial to Le Croix. No one ever stopped them. There appeared to be no law or rule against fighting or even killing. More than one warrior's corpse had been carried away after a fight.

Le Croix knew it was only a matter of time before he was challenged. There were ranks or insignias on the aliens, but he knew that those with longer headdress tendrils were of a higher rank or at least more skillful than those with short or no tendrils. He fell in the lowest category. Le Croix had been given new legs, new eyes, and some sensory enhancement, but he didn't have tendrils. He wondered if it was possible to take someone else's after defeating them in a fair fight. Not that he wanted to look just like the Krah. He knew that wasn't possible. He still had human facial features, and his skin was different from the aliens'. But he wasn't searching for a way to escape them anymore, nor was he even looking to find the prince, who had been captured with him. Instead, Le Croix wondered if it was actually possible to find his place among the warriors of the Krah.

Eventually, the newcomers settled down. Camp chairs were brought out, and the three Krah leaders sat under an awning with a view of the river and trees beyond. They spoke with several of the workers and a Yarl that Le Croix had seen but didn't know. Finally, he was called for. He went willingly to see the new arrivals. He was certain they had the power to order his execution, but it seemed unlikely they would since he wasn't resisting and the Krah had already invested a lot of time and energy into the prosthetics—the enhancements, as they were called—they gave him.

"You are a hue-man?" the largest of the newcomers asked.

"I was," Le Croix said. "Before I was gifted with these enhancements."

His words were not translated in any way that Le Croix could see, but the newcomer's grunting language was translated by the neural implants deep inside his inner ear so that he heard his language when the aliens spoke. He assumed it was the same with the newcomers.

"Tell us about your people," said the alien to Le Croix's right. He was a heavy, older-looking Krah warrior with long tendrils.

"Humans are abundant. We have colonized the entire galaxy," Le Croix said. "Most are ruled by the Royal Imperium."

"We have heard of this Royal Imperium," the biggest Krah said.

"How many ships do they have?" asked the third newcomer. "How many warriors? When will they come to defend this system?"

"I cannot say," Le Croix replied.

"Cannot or will not?" the big Krah asked.

"Many were destroyed when the wormhole was formed," Le Croix said.

"What is this…wormhole?" asked the heavyset Krah.

"The portal you traveled through to reach this galaxy," Le Croix said. "It is surrounded by fire."

The three Krah nodded in understanding.

"The rest of the Royal Imperium Fleet was scattered," Le Croix admitted. "It is uncertain who will lead them, and if the others will obey. I cannot say how many are left, or when they will return, because I do not know."

"I am Warlord Racca," the big alien said. "This is Warlord Tusgar."

The heavyset Tusgar growled but nodded. Le Croix wasn't sure what to make of the gesture. It wasn't friendly, but it didn't seem to be menacing either.

"This is Warlord Oligar. He will be taking control of this world. You are to serve him."

Oligar looked ancient in some ways. His skin was dark and crisscrossed with scars, yet the muscle beneath was undeniable. His eyes, which were not enhanced, seemed bright.

"Serve?" Le Croix asked.

"You have been accepted in the Warrior caste," Racca continued. "Chieftain Grubat gifted you with enhancements, but he has been tasked with responsibilities off-world. You are now a Yort. That is less than a trooper, but higher than a slave. What is your name?"

"I am called Le Croix."

"You will be challenged, Yort Le Croix," Racca said. "That is the way of the Krah. The strong thrive, and the weak serve."

"I am not weak," Le Croix said.

"Perhaps," Oligar replied. "But you are ignorant of our ways, as we are of yours."

"Serve Oligar, and do not deceive him if you hope to gain rank and reputation," Racca said. "You will be protected as long as—"

Le Croix cut the huge alien off. "I don't need protection."

"If you interrupt a warlord again," Tusgar said, "you'll be ripped to pieces for disobedience."

"Forgive me," Le Croix said. "I am still struggling to find myself."

Oligar stood up. He moved slowly, not trying to hide his actions in any way. Reaching back, he made a fist and drove it hard into Le Croix's stomach. The human doubled over. Normally, such a blow would have driven him to his knees, but the artificial legs held firm. Le Croix gasped for breath, but he didn't retaliate as the old warlord returned to his seat.

"You are forgiven," Oligar said.

"Take your time, Yort Le Croix," Racca said. "Yours is a big galaxy. There will be plenty of time for fighting. Find yourself and serve Warlord Oligar. You may yet earn a place in the Krah Empire."

"Sit behind me," Oligar ordered. "We may yet have questions for you, Yort Le Croix."

He moved around the three warlords. There were no chairs behind them, but there was a stool. Le Croix sat, watching as other Krah came to report.

The workers were busy, building structures from a hydropower plant downriver to barracks for the warriors and workers. The warriors were sent to explore the land. Some hunted the local wildlife, harvesting animals to be used as food. Others reported of the terrain they explored. The timber was thick, and the wildlife abundant, which didn't surprise Le Croix, who knew the world had been protected for centuries and had only a tiny human population.

Eventually, word was brought to the warlords about a ship. A holographic projector created an image of the ship that hovered in the air in front of the warlords. The warrior giving the report tried to answer their questions, but it was clear he didn't know much. Le Croix felt sick seeing the ship. It had a thick central section and two wings with engines on their tips. He recognized the ship immediately and felt guilt over his betrayal. Not that he had told the Krah anything about the

Royal Imperium that they didn't already know, except perhaps that most of the Fleet had been lost. That fact might make them more aggressive. Le Croix didn't know if he could betray General Pershing. She had been good to him, but she hadn't given him new legs.

"Do you know this ship, Yort Le Croix?" Oligar asked when the warrior making the report could give no more information.

"Yes," Le Croix said, feeling sick but making his decision. He was with the Krah. They had helped him more than his own people and accepted him as one of their own. If he tried to fight, he would just be killed. If he held out on his new masters, they would punish him. No one was coming to save him, and if he cooperated, he had a chance to build a new life.

"Well?" Racca asked.

"That is a Kestrel class ship," Le Croix said. "An old vessel, but enhanced."

"How so?" Oligar asked.

"It has a special shield," he admitted. "It uses gravity waves. It's impenetrable."

"A worthy adversary," Racca said. "Why was it here?"

"I cannot say for certain," Le Croix said. "But my best guess would be to study you."

"Who commands this vessel?" Racca asked.

"That would be Brigadier General Pershing," Krah said. "She is a great tactician."

"Does she command more ships?" Oligar asked.

"She will. They will gather their forces and come here to stop you."

Tusgar chuckled. "Many have tried. All have failed."

"I would not underestimate her," Le Croix said.

"How many ships will she bring?" Racca asked.

"As many as she can. Like I said, the Royal Imperium Fleet is scattered."

"We should return to our ships," Tusgar said. "This system must be protected."

"Hochum holds the system," Racca said. "Oligar controls this world. Our task is to assess the star map."

Le Croix felt another wave of guilt as the aliens tapped into the Navigation Network. He had seen most of the technology, and the device used to hack into the human system was different from anything he had seen them use.

"Do you recognize this map?" Oligar asked him as the galaxy replaced the *Modulus Echo* on the holographic projector.

"I do," Le Croix said. "It is our galaxy."

Racca stood and waved his hands, expanding the hologram until it filled the space beneath the awning. The sun was going down, and the sunlight was waning, which only made the hologram appear brighter and clearer.

"So many worlds," Racca said. "Do your people have a foothold in every system?"

"Most," Le Croix admitted. "Not all stars have planets, and some are uninhabitable. But those that are have humans dwelling on and around them. Others have space stations."

"It is true your people fight with projectile weapons?" Tusgar asked.

Le Croix nodded. "Guns, both projectile and focused light. Our ships carry missiles and fire laser cannons."

"It is because they have so much," Oligar said, waving a mechanical hand at the hologram. "It has made them soft."

"Wasteful cowards," Tusgar said. "We will crush them."

"You both miss the point," Racca said. "They have people on a thousand worlds. They outnumber us. If we are not careful, we will be defeated."

"You speak truth," Oligar said.

"Not all humans are fighters," Le Croix said.

"Slaves, then," Tusgar insisted.

"There are too many," Racca said. "We could be overrun."

He tapped on a star and the holograph changed to a single system. There were nearly twenty planets in the system, each with several moons. A large space station also orbited the system star.

"What is this system?" Racca asked Le Croix.

The Nav Net listed the star system. The warlord's question made Le Croix wonder if the enhancements worn by the big warriors weren't translating written text for them.

"That's the Dennab system."

"Does it have a habitable world?" Racca asked.

"Yes," Le Croix explained. Halpha Seven is what we call an old world, or a Goldilocks planet, because it required no terraforming before humans could live on it."

"What is the population?" Racca asked.

"Four billion, I suppose."

He was surprised at the response from the warlords. They acted as if he had struck a painful blow.

"Four billion?" Oligar asked.

"On the planet," Le Croix said. "The moons here and here, Lucida and Argru, are both inhabited, with probably another billion combined. And the Dennab station houses several hundred thousand. It's a solar collector, which generates energy from the star."

"Now do you see?" Racca said. "These humans are spread across this galaxy in numbers we cannot comprehend."

"Magnificent," Tusgar said. "Our conquest will be legendary."

"Or short lived," Oligar said.

"This task before us is not impossible," Racca said. "But let us not forget that Chieftain Grubat lost ten ships before we arrived."

The other warlords growled, and Le Croix had to hide his surprise. Perhaps the Krah weren't as strong as he thought. Doubts began to erode his resolve.

"We cannot be lured into haste by the vast wealth before us," Racca continued. "What good is a thousand ships if we do not have the warriors to man them?"

"Or the workers to reshape them," Oligar added.

"Perhaps we do not even need them," Tusgar said, waving a hand as dusk colored the landscape in a purple hue.

"What we need is time," Racca said. "If we can hold this system, more Krah will come to this galaxy."

"There are not enough Krah," Oligar said. "The humans in one system outnumber us."

"But unlike other races, they can be enhanced," Racca said. "They are not all cowards. Some will make fine troopers, perhaps even Yarls, one day."

"You would make the humans Krah?" Tusgar asked.

"It is one way, not the only way," Racca said. "We must begin to think differently if we are to rule this galaxy. Time to plan, and to grow is what is essential now. I will speak to the other warlords personally."

"I will come with you," Tusgar said.

Le Croix watched them leave. Oligar remained in his seat until the others were gone. Then he drew a curved dagger from his belt. For a moment, Le Croix was certain the warlord was going to drive the blade into his guts, but after a moment, the Krah turned the knife and handed it to him handle first.

"You will need this, Yort Le Croix. Use it wisely. We cannot afford to lose you."

He left Le Croix under the awning, and despite the warm temperature on New Krah, Le Croix felt a chill.

Chapter 12

Hyperspace felt like a breather to Ben. It wasn't safe. Hurtling through space faster than the speed of light was a dangerous endeavor to say the least, but at least they couldn't see the alien ships pursuing them.

"They can't outpace us," Kim argued. "How would they know where we're coming out of hyperspace?"

"That doesn't mean they aren't right behind us," Nance said.

"We'll find out soon enough," Pershing said.

Ben could see the worry on her face. She was a proud, older woman, and not one to concern herself with beauty. That said, she wasn't ugly by any means, but there were lines around her eyes and across her forehead that seemed to be growing deeper. Fear had a strong effect on aging, he supposed. And whether any of them admitted it or not, they were all afraid. Perhaps their fears were different, but they were real.

The aliens were completely unknown. There was no way to guess if they kept prisoners from the ships they captured. They hadn't bothered retrieving or opening the emergency pods that held the royal family. That fact alone made Ben fear that they would murder or jettison any people they might incidentally capture when they took over a human ship. Perhaps hardened warriors like General Pershing didn't fear death, but she feared defeat, submission, and loss of freedom and importance. Ben just wanted to make sure his people, and his ship, weren't captured or destroyed.

"So we stay at the first jump point," Ben said. "For how long?"

"An hour," Pershing said. "Maybe two. If the aliens are following us, we'll know it by then."

"And if they are following us?" Kim asked.

"Then we lead them away from the Mersa system to someplace where we have an advantage."

"Like an asteroid field," Ben said. "There, big ships can't maneuver like we can."

"Oh, that's bold," Kim said. "But nothing too dense. I can fly through a storm without getting wet, but why take that kind of chance?"

"Look into it," Pershing said. "We need some way to shake their pursuit. A nebula might do the trick. If they use advanced radar or energy tracking, the radiation of a nebula might hide our tracks."

They spent an hour debating possible sites. Nance put the most likely candidates into the navigation computer, but they couldn't calculate jump points until they were out of hyperspace. Ben sliced up an apple and munched on the fruit while they finished their first run. The flux shield was holding up well. It had less than ten percent residual energy gathered by the swirling gravitational waves. They were safe up to fifty percent, but somewhere between seventy and eighty would cause the swirling waves to collapse back down on the *Echo*. Ben didn't like to think of his beloved ship imploding, or what that would do to his friends.

"Exiting hyperspace in one minute," Nance said.

Ben glanced around. Everyone was focused, even Duke Simeon. As soon as the ship dropped from hyperspace, they would search for any sign of the enemy. They were like gazelles whose only defense from the big predators of the jungle was speed. The alien ships were faster, but the *Echo* was more agile. She could change direction more quickly than the larger alien ships, which made her hard to catch one on one. But if a dozen alien vessels dropped out of hyperspace behind them, it would be difficult to get away.

"Here we go," Kim announced from the pilot's seat. "Three, two, one, mark!"

The big bridge display was split into four video feeds, one from each side of the ship. They had come out of hyperspace in a vast stretch of nothing. They were in between star systems and light-years from the nearest celestial body. Kim had the engines at full throttle, and Ben knew they were racing away from the position where they had dropped from hyperspace, but without a point of reference, it felt as if they weren't moving at all.

"Radar?" Pershing asked.

"Nothing yet," Nance replied.

"Ben, how's our shield holding?"

"It's doing fine," Ben said.

"Alright," Pershing went on. "Now we wait."

The hour passed slowly. They stayed on the bridge, monitoring the vast emptiness around them, but there was nothing to see. The alien ships didn't follow them, which was a relief, but the difficult part was not knowing what might happen at any moment.

"We've been here an hour," Nance said.

In truth, they had been flying nonstop since coming out of hyperspace. Ben guessed that they were several thousand miles away from their original drop zone. If the aliens followed them exactly, they would be far behind the small Kestrel class ship when they came out of hyperspace.

"Calculate a jump point to the Mersa system," Pershing said. "We've wasted enough time."

No one argued. And while it was frustrating to wait around for nothing to happen, Ben was glad they hadn't been followed. He also understood the general's need to know her enemy. They just didn't have the resources to capture one of the alien vessels, which in his mind was the first step to learning about the aggressive beings from another galaxy. He also knew that it might be impossible to communicate with them or learn anything about them.

Space exploration had been an era of anticipation. For centuries, mankind had spread through the galaxy, expecting to find intelligent life at any moment, but had been always disappointed. That era had led to the belief that mankind was truly alone. They were the only intelligent beings on a thousand inhabitable worlds. If life existed somewhere else in the universe, it was not in the Milky Way galaxy. The lack of life hadn't slowed mankind's growth or discouraged the colonization of the galaxy. There were still parts of the outer arms that had yet to be explored, but the hope of finding life had faded.

Professor Jones's gravitational theories had been proven in a shocking manner. His concept of opening a portal to another part of space was sound. In fact, it had worked better than anyone had expected, opening a tunnel from one galaxy to another. But while mankind was alone in the Milky Way, other intelligent life obviously existed in its sister galaxy, and they were actively using the wormhole to spread into mankind's territory.

"Jump point is set," Nance said.

"Very good," Pershing replied. "Drop the shield, Ben. There's no need to waste energy while we're in hyperspace."

Ben tapped a few buttons on his station, and the flux shield wound down.

"It's down," Ben said.

"Just in time," Kim replied.

They jumped into hyperspace again, and Nance put a large timer on the bridge display. The journey from their position to the Mersa system would take over ten hours. As the mottled glow of hyperspace filled the displays, Ben sat back, feeling the stress drain away.

"Another successful jump," Kim said. "Time for some food. Who's with me?"

"Me," Ben said.

"Is three a crowd?" Duke Simeon asked.

"Not at all," Ben replied. "Magnum's coming too."

The big man glanced up, nodded, and rose from his console.

"Let's check in on the professor," Pershing said. "I want a report on his progress."

"I'll tell him," Ben said.

The group of four slowly climbed the steps to the upper deck. They were all tired. The stress of their run in the Celeste system and through their first mini jump had taken a toll. Ben was happy there was enough time to sleep.

"You look tired," Kim said softly.

"I am tired."

"Too tired to hang out a bit?" she asked.

"No," he replied. "I'll check on the professor and then join you in the galley."

"Sounds good," she said.

The Special Forces commandos were lounging in the galley and observation deck. Some played cards, others talked quietly over drinks. Ben was so turned around, he didn't know if it was morning or evening, but a large ale, some food, and a good night's sleep sounded perfect to him.

As the others headed for the galley, Ben circled around the observation platform that took up the middle of the ship's upper level. Around the sides were the ship's staterooms, and Ben went immediately to the one occupied by Professor Jones. His short knock was answered immediately.

Ben knew he looked tired, but the professor looked frazzled. His hair and beard were sticking out in different directions, there were dark bags under his eyes, and he seemed jittery.

"Ben, Ben, it's good to see you, my boy," the professor said. "Come in, please. Find a place to sit. Just don't move anything important."

The guest rooms on the *Echo* were small. A bed filled half the space. A small table with two stools, a video display, and a personal storage locker took up most of the rest. The bathroom facilities were tiny, but having privacy on a starship was a luxury in and of itself. Other than meals, a passenger could stay in their quarters with no need to ever come out. The queen had done exactly that for most of her time on board.

"I don't know what's important or not," Ben said. "Do you?"

"It's all important," Professor Jones said. "I just haven't put it all in order. This is like a puzzle, Ben. A 3D puzzle with many layers and no guide. But I will solve it. There has to be a way to close the wormhole safely."

"You need to get some rest," Ben said. "This can wait."

"The general needs an update. I suspect that's why you're here."

"She can wait too," Ben said.

"No, no, that won't do. I'll tell her myself. And then I'll get some rest. Maybe just a nap."

"A shower, a meal, and then at least six hours of sleep," Ben said. "That's what we both need. I'll bring you some food if you like."

"No, I'll join you. I just need a minute to arrange my research and tidy up a bit."

"We're in the galley," Ben said.

He left the stateroom and returned to the galley. The *Echo* had a small, but well-appointed galley, with ovens and coolers. The space was well designed, but only large enough for a single person to work in. Kim was busy putting different kinds of food onto serving trays. Magnum was leaning against the wall with a drink in one hand, watching. And the duke was in the galley pulling food from the ovens.

"Just in time," Kim said. "Duke Simeon is cooking."

"The duke cooks?" Ben asked.

"I took a cooking class or two," Simeon said. "The culinary arts are a great way to impress women."

"Like he needs to work at it," Kim scoffed.

"A title only goes so far," the duke replied.

"I can't even imagine," Ben said.

The food was delicious. A fun mix of spicy meat, fresh greens, and several creamy sauces to dip soft, warm bread into. Professor Jones joined them, as did Staff Sergeant Visher and Corporal Dial.

"Has the general shared any info from the surveillance drone?" Visher asked.

"No," Ben said.

"What more do you need to know?" Kim said. "The aliens have over two hundred ships in the Celeste system, and probably more coming all the time."

"So it's war, then," Dial said. "I hate fighting in space."

"Fighting anywhere is not good," Professor Jones said.

"Sometimes it can't be avoided," Magnum said.

"Spoken like a true warrior," Visher said raising his glass to the big man.

"The question is, can we summon enough ships to fight them all?" Ben asked.

"Don't ask me," Kim said. "I don't know anything about the Royal Imperium military."

"Most people don't," Visher said. "It's like government. All the highest-ranking officers are political appointees, regardless of their leadership abilities."

"Including General Pershing?" Ben asked.

"No, she's the real deal," Dial said.

"Spec Ops is the only branch politicians won't touch," Visher said. "Pershing rose through the ranks on merit."

"But will the other ship commanders follow her?" Kim asked.

"They should," Duke Simeon said.

"In a perfect world, maybe..." Visher said. "My experience is that a void in power upsets the whole applecart. Every greedy politician and ship commander will want to ensure they get top billing."

"You think the Royal Imperium will fracture," Ben said.

Visher nodded, while Duke Simeon looked aghast.

"What is this? Fractured? You mean civil war?" the duke asked.

"Look, the systems with heavy rebellion influences will almost certainly secede," the staff sergeant explained. "Some of the systems with strong military garrisons will be tempted. It's the perfect opportunity for a power-hungry politician to point to the Imperium, say it's broken, and declare themselves the Grand Pooh-Bah of their little coalition of planets, moons, and space stations."

"And those groups will have enough military strength to hold out," Kim said.

"Even if their aim is just to give themselves political clout when things get back to normal," Visher continued, "a person who says they can deliver planets and military assets will be able to demand just about anything they want."

"Fantastic," Ben said sarcastically.

"I think you all misjudge the people's love for the royal family and the stability of the Imperium," Duke Simeon said.

The rest of the group laughed. Ben felt bad. The look on the duke's face revealed that he earnestly believed that people loved and revered the royals. Unfortunately, Ben knew otherwise.

"That's cute," Kim said, patting Duke Simeon on the back.

"I'm sorry, Your Highness," Staff Sergeant Visher said. "I've served in the Royal Imperium military all my adult life. I'm as loyal as they come, but we have to put away the propaganda and be honest with one another."

"I am being honest," Duke Simeon replied. "Why wouldn't the people heed our call for help?"

"Because you're not the king," Corporal Dial said. "Not officially."

"And that's enough of an excuse for many to do what they think will profit themselves the most," Ben said. "Besides, we're talking about the people in power, not the masses. The staff sergeant may be loyal to the Royal Imperium, but if his superiors aren't, there's not much he can do."

"And that's the thing," Staff Sergeant Visher said. "I don't think most people will do anything until they know for sure which way the wind is blowing."

"Bastards," Kim said.

"Hey, if we could, we would drop you all at the nearest inhabited planet or station and fly far away from here," Ben admitted.

"Can't say I blame you," Dial said.

"But you're needed," Duke Simeon said. "Your presence here is an example to every capable shipmaster that fighting the aliens in the Celeste system is the right thing."

"We're not here because we're needed," Kim said.

"The general pulled us in because of the flux shield," Ben added. "We turned over the specs, but there's no way she could have one installed on a regular ship any time soon. So she cut us a deal."

"People will do what's best for them," Staff Sergeant Visher said. "Including the ship commanders, regardless of the queen's request to follow General Pershing into battle against the aliens."

"It doesn't help that the aliens haven't attacked any other system," Corporal Dial said.

"You want them to attack the innocent?" Duke Simeon said.

"No, of course not," Dial said. "But there's hardly anyone to report what's going on. I'm betting half the Fleet thinks the news about the wormhole and aliens is all some kind of hoax."

"I've known good soldiers who served their entire career and never left the first post they were assigned to," Visher said.

"It's hard to care about something that is far away and doesn't seem to affect your life in any tangible way," Ben agreed. "Until we escaped Torrent Four, what the Royal Imperium did was of almost no concern to us. And if I'm being honest, I didn't even know you existed, Your Highness."

"You didn't study the royal family as a child?" Duke Simeon asked.

"We didn't even have schools," Kim told him. "Our boy Ben here is self-taught."

"And how'd you learn to fly?" the duke asked.

"Training programs and virtual reality, mostly," Kim said.

"That's impressive," Visher said. "Most people can't make the change from simulators to the real thing."

"I raced kites too," Kim said. "I think every pilot should do it."

"Kites?" Dial asked. "You mean you were hanging from a kite and racing other people?"

"Through canyons," Ben said. "It's dangerous."

"Sounds insane," Visher said.

"Maybe it is," Kim said. "But when you love something, you have to find a way, right?"

She looked at Ben, and he felt his face flush a little.

"Besides," Kim went on, "the key to kite racing is merging with the rig. Your body becomes part of the aircraft in a way. I wouldn't want anyone to race who didn't want to, but flying a kite is the best way to learn how to move and think about flying."

"And she would know," Professor Jones said. "She is the first person ever to navigate through a black hole."

"Maybe," Kim said. "But no one will ever know that."

"Why not?" the duke asked.

"Because they're outlaws," Corporal Dial said. "Badass smugglers living on the fringe."

"No, it's because the command staff denied that it took place," Visher said.

"We don't have permits," Ben admitted to the duke. "We're not registered."

"Just wanted in a dozen systems," Corporal Dial said, sounding like a commercial for a holo-flick.

"Things have changed," the duke said. "The Fleet is scattered, the king is dead, and I'm on a smuggler's ship trying to stop an alien invasion."

"Sounds like the plot of a good book," Visher said.

"I'd read it," Kim said with a smile.

"Thank you so much for the food," Ben said, pushing his plate back and getting up. "But I'm due some downtime, and I'm taking it before things get even crazier."

"I'll take care of this," Magnum said, pulling Ben's plate over to his side of the table. "Get some rest."

"I will," Ben said.

"We all should," the professor said.

"Time for some PT," Visher declared. "Corporal, let's round up these yahoos and head downstairs."

"Roger that," Dial said.

Kim and Ben ambled down the stairs and across the atrium to the door outside his quarters.

"You coming in?" Ben asked.

"Actually, I was going to give Nance a break," she said.

"You're a good friend," he told her.

"You let us sleep earlier, so now it's your turn. But I'll be here when you wake up."

"Can't wait," Ben said.

They kissed, then Ben went into his room. His quarters were neat, but the bed was ruffled from his nap earlier. He pulled off his clothes, took a quick shower, then climbed into his bed. On the little table by the bunk was a chrono. He set the alarm to sound in eight hours, then hit the button that shut off the lights to his room. The crew quarters were in the wing sections of the Kestrel class ship, and there were skylights over his bunk. Ben looked up at the swirling glow of hyperspace. His eyelids felt heavy, and soon he was asleep.

Chapter 13

The priests were on a private barge that was being towed behind the *En'Galla*. Seven more Krah ships accompanied them. Five were explorers whose shipmasters were eager to prove themselves by capturing human ships and thus increase their reputation and their wealth. Given enough time and opportunity, chances were good that they could capture enough ships to double their vessels in size while still making enough offerings to rise from mere Yarls to chieftains.

The sixth was a colony ship, long and segmented. It looked like two dozen ships linked together. The colony ships housed the Krah young and were the official domain of the highest rank. Alpha Vistol commanded the colony vessel and would oversee the Krah settlements on their new home world. Guarding the colony ship was a Krah Destroyer with multiple weapons including projectiles that could be launched against other ships or rained down onto planets.

It was an impressive convoy, even if it was led by explorer vessels and a disgraced chieftain. Yet even the mass of Krah ships in the human galaxy near the portal didn't compare with the majesty of the planet. Grubat had seen many things in his lifetime and experienced many victories in battle. Yet nothing compared to the sweetness of standing on the planet he had named New Krah, with its wide-open spaces, clean air, abundant resources, and wildlife.

"Father," Yarl Cherbak said from the shadows to the side of the *En'Galla*'s command center.

Grubat stood at his customary place on the observation deck, watching as the convoy moved toward the ring of fire that marked the portal to the new galaxy. He turned and looked at his son. The weight of his mistakes was like thick chains wrapped around his head and shoulders. The sins of the father were borne by his children, and Cherbak deserved more. It had been Grubat's plan to give his son more responsibility, but it seemed Cherbak was ready to surpass his father. Grubat could see the look of challenge in his son's eyes. He wouldn't do it on the *En'Galla*. To stamp out the shame of his father's failures, Cherbak would need to kill him with as many witnesses as possible.

"You summoned me?" Cherbak said.

"Yes," Grubat replied. "I have made a decision."

"I stand ready to hear it, Chieftain."

Grubat knew a lie when he heard it. It was taking all of his son's strength not to let his resentment through in his words. Grubat was proud of that. He had raised a proper warrior, one who could control his emotions and didn't let his desires dictate his actions. Cherbak had a strategy for redeeming himself, and he would wait for the proper time to act rather than give in to his feelings at that moment.

Cherbak's tendrils were writhing in an almost angry fashion. They betrayed his son's true feelings, but there would be time to warn Cherbak about that later.

"When we return to New Krah, I will turn over the *En'Galla* and her crew to you."

"But you are our chieftain," Cherbak said.

"Not anymore. I lost that right when I failed to foresee Yarl Hassik's treachery."

Grubat noticed that his son didn't argue the point. It was like an open wound. The pain of that failure was intense and hadn't dulled with the passage of time. He had done what the warlords ordered him to do. When he returned to the Algonny Outpost, he had found the temple stripped bare and the collection of ships waiting to cross over into the new territory opened up by the portal. The priests had converted their rectory into a barge. There were no engines, but it could be towed by a starship, which is why it was being pulled by the *En'Galla*. Grubat was delivering the priests to the new Krah home world, which they would consecrate. The colony ship would be disassembled and landed with the massive crew to form the first true Krah city in the pristine world. And despite his role in everything, Grubat would not be remembered or honored. The taint of his failure colored everything, from his reputation as a chieftain to his relationship with his son.

"What will you do, Father?" Cherbak asked.

"I will serve on New Krah," Grubat replied, "however I am needed."

"I will escort you down myself," Cherbak said, his tendrils shivering. Grubat couldn't tell if the shiver was from anticipation or fear.

"My failure was not weakness, Cherbak. Fighting me may not have the result you desire."

"I desire only to bring glory to my name."

"And if you lose?"

"If I lose, I'll be dead," Cherbak said. "Either way, I won't have to live with the shame I see in the eyes all around me."

"I will not hold back, Cherbak. I am of the Warrior caste."

"As am I."

The younger Krah turned away without permission. It was insulting, a complete lack of respect, yet it didn't surprise Grubat. Nor did he force his son to show the proper respect.

"We are entering the portal, Chieftain," Yarl Quissi announced.

Grubat growled and turned back to the large windows. Outer space and the light of stars disappeared, and they began the journey that would take them to their new home. The more Grubat thought about the human galaxy, the more he realized it was where the Krah could thrive. The galaxy they had conquered was low on resources. It had nothing left to give them, and while it had made them strong, the human galaxy would provide the space and means to grow powerful beyond measure.

Grubat had seen the star map the humans used. There were thousands of star systems, hundreds of which could support the Krah immediately. And once they had taken the secrets of terraforming from the humans, they would make even more worlds to colonize. There would be no need to control their numbers any longer. New Krah alone could support the entire empire. They would have the resources to build mighty cities and even greater space stations. The humans would serve their Krah overlords, and the mighty Krah Empire would reign supreme. Grubat only hoped he could live long enough to see it.

In time, they would master the secret to opening portals to new galaxies. Once the humans were crushed under the enhanced heels of the Krah, they would spread to other galaxies until the entire universe was theirs to command. The thought of that ultimate glory made Grubat tremble all over. He could feel destiny calling him. There would be many challenges ahead, but he had always been victorious in battle. And Yarl Hassik's treachery had taught him one valuable lesson—he couldn't trust anyone. His way had been to lead by example and reward his Yarls who showed initiative. He would have to change to command more fear. In time he would rise again. He would shake off the shame of his failures and make his mark on the human galaxy.

The trip through the portal didn't take long, and the convoy of ships passed through without trouble. On the other side, in the human galaxy, the ships made their way through the assembled vessels and into orbit around the planet.

"Prepare the landing craft," Grubat ordered Yarl Quissi.

"All of them?" Quissi asked.

"Yes, we will ferry the priests down to the planet's surface," Grubat said. "Send them word to prepare."

"As you wish, Chieftain."

Grubat looked out the windows, gazing around at the beauty of space filled with Krah ships of every class. And below them all, lit with the golden light of the nearby star, was New Krah. A vibrant, pristine home world waiting to receive them all. It would be the last time he saw the beauty of the new galaxy from such a vantage point. Then he swept from the command center with complete confidence.

It crossed his mind to order his son to stay on board the *En'Galla*. If Cherbak didn't go down to the surface with Grubat, he couldn't challenge his father in a fight to the death. But he had never turned away from a fight, no matter how distasteful. Grubat was a warrior, and battle was his home. If his son felt that fighting him would relieve some type of pain or humiliation, Grubat wouldn't hold him back.

At the landing craft, Cherbak was waiting.

"Will you pilot the ship down yourself?" Grubat asked.

"Yes."

There was no mention of the honorary title of chieftain, or of the more intimate title of father. Grubat had mated with Cherbak's mother long ago. The young Krah were raised on colony ships and separated into castes as they reached the development age. Cherbak had been appointed to the Warrior caste, trained with the other younglings until he was ready to become a Yort. They didn't find each other until Cherbak was a trooper and was on track to become a Yarl with piloting skills. There was no doubt Yarl Cherbak had potential. It would be a pity to waste it on a needless challenge, but Grubat refused to counsel his obstinate son. If Cherbak couldn't see the futility of challenging his father, he wouldn't bother trying to change Cherbak's mind.

"We will dock with the priests' barge," Grubat ordered.

"Yes, I know."

"Very good. Proceed."

The landing craft detached from the *En'Galla* and drifted over to the barge using only basic thrusters. The docking procedure didn't take long, and when the air lock opened, Grubat found the high priest and a group of his subordinates waiting.

"We are ready to see this new world," the high priest announced.

"Come aboard," Grubat answered. "We will proceed immediately."

The priests filed in, filling up the small ship. They strapped themselves into seats as Cherbak lifted off the barge and began the trip down to the surface. Grubat stood behind his son, holding onto a handle mounted to the ceiling. He braced himself as the ship bounced through the planet's atmosphere. Cherbak didn't make the descent easy for him. The landing craft rolled over as they descended until the ship was upside down. Grubat held himself securely, pushing up onto the handle and gripping the deck with his enhanced feet.

Eventually, they turned right side up, and the air smoothed out. The landing craft had only small windows. Grubat could see white flashes as they passed through clouds and blue sky, but the grandeur of the planet was still hidden. They passed over a range of jagged mountains as the landing craft continued to descend. Grubat saw snow-covered peaks and eventually the evergreens that clothed the lower portions of the mountains.

A few minutes later, the landing craft circled the clearing where Grubat had landed the *Nog'Deit*. His ship was stripped down to almost nothing, but it was surrounded by new structures, and there were resources from the planet being gathered as well. Grubat saw logs neatly stacked together and piles of large stones. It all seemed to be happening so fast that Grubat couldn't help but accept that his future was bright.

The ship settled onto the ground, and the priests all stood.

"Welcome to your new home," Grubat said.

The side hatch folded down, creating a ramp, and the priests filed out. They were normally stoic, reserved individuals, but Grubat watched them gaze at the beauty of the planet in awe. It was midday, the sun was bright, the sky was clear, and a light breeze ruffled the leaves on the trees that towered around the clearing.

The high priest turned back to Grubat, who had given them space before following down the hatch.

"It is magnificent," the high priest declared.

"And ours for the taking," Grubat said with a little bow.

The priest had surely heard of his humiliating failure and did not give Grubat the recognition he felt he deserved, but he saw the gratitude in the priest's eyes. Warlord Oligar appeared from around the ship, his arms spread wide.

"Welcome to New Krah," he said in a booming voice.

The warlord and high priest continued speaking, but Grubat was surprised to see the human, Le Croix, following behind Oligar. The human looked sleek and powerful with his new enhancements, and it appeared that he had accepted his place among the Krah. Gifting the human warrior with the enhancements had been a gamble, but it appeared that his intuition was well placed. Le Croix must have shared information with the warlords in exchange for a new place with the old warrior who had been given command of the planet.

Grubat knew that Oligar would be replaced soon by Alpha Vistol. What that meant for the human, Grubat didn't know. But the warlords had seen what Grubat had first envisioned, a human-Krah hybrid who had much to offer the Krah as they battled a new enemy.

Grubat walked down the ramp and approached Le Croix. The human looked well enough. The enhancements had been a success and hadn't strained his physical body too much.

"Le Croix," Grubat said.

"Chieftain Grubat," the human replied. "Welcome back."

"You have taken to the enhancements, I see."

"They serve me well."

"And whom do you serve, Le Croix?"

"I am a Yort in Warlord Oligar's service."

"Then you have fared well, Yort Le Croix."

The human looked uncertain but didn't reply. His body stiffened noticeably, and Grubat sensed danger behind him. A quick turn revealed Cherbak, stripped to the waist, a tor'ax in each hand. The priests were watching, as was Warlord Oligar. Cherbak threw one of the axes to the ground in front of Grubat.

"I challenge Chieftain Grubat," Cherbak said loudly.

More warriors were gathering, forming a circle. Grubat started to bend down and pick up the ax. It was the traditional way of accepting the challenge of a rival, but before he could reach the weapon, Le Croix darted around him and picked it up first.

"I will stand in Chieftain Grubat's place," Le Croix said.

Cherbak growled, but the highest-ranking warrior was Warlord Oligar, who held up his hand to stifle the murmurs of the crowd.

"Chieftain Grubat, do you accept Yort Le Croix as your proxy?" Oligar asked in a rumbling voice.

"Let me do this for you," Le Croix said. "For both of us."

Grubat was torn. He had no desire to fight his own son to the death, but defeating a Yort, especially one of another race, wouldn't satisfy Cherbak.

"He won't be happy until he kills me," Grubat said.

"Let me prove myself to you," Le Croix said. "I owe you that much."

Grubat looked to Warlord Oligar and nodded, then stepped back. Le Croix turned to face Cherbak, who snarled angrily.

"When I'm through with your pet, Father, I'll finish you," Cherbak said.

"As you wish," Grubat agreed.

Chapter 14

"One minute to the exit window," Nance said.

"Ben, stand by to raise the shield," Pershing said. "Kim, let's be ready for evasive maneuvers."

"Roger that," Kim said in a mocking tone.

They dropped out of hyperspace in the Mersa system fearful of what they might find, but there was no sign of the enemy.

"We're being hailed by Space Control," Nance said. "I didn't even know that was a thing."

"It's standard emergency procedure," Pershing replied.

"Because of the attack on the Celeste system?" Duke Simeon asked.

"No," Pershing said. "Officially, it's due to the fact that Mersa is a closed planet."

"Doesn't help that we don't have a transponder code," Kim said.

Ben looked at the radar display on his console. They were five thousand miles from Mersa Prime. At cruising speed, it would take them two hours to reach orbit, but between them and the planet were four large ships.

"What are those things?" Ben asked.

"Drone control ships," Pershing said. "They must be here delivering more of the atmospheric drones."

"The ones with mind control gas?" Kim asked.

There was a moment of silence on the bridge. Everyone knew what was on the drones, but Pershing and Duke Simeon refused to admit it.

"The Royal Imperium has a docking station here," Pershing said. "Looks like the *Romulus* and the *Artimus* are resupplying."

"Are those battle cruisers?" Nance asked.

"They are," Pershing said. "Although I'd be surprised if they're willing to leave this station."

"Why's that?" Duke Simeon asked.

"Because it's safe here," Kim said.

"Because two capital ships are required protection for a class one star system," Pershing said. "Put the message from Space Control on speaker."

Unidentified vessel, this is Mersa System Space Control. Please turn on your transponder and state your business. If you do not respond, you will come under fire. Over.

"They don't mess around," Kim said.

"Their job is to stop smuggling ships like this," Pershing said.

"Should we raise shields?" Ben asked.

"Negative, stay on this course and don't do anything without a direct order from me."

"Yes, ma'am," Kim said.

"Patch me through to Space Control," Pershing said. "Mersa System Space Control, this is the R.I.F. flagship, *Modulus Echo*. We bring news from the Celeste system. I repeat, this is Brigadier General Alicia Pershing, commander in chief of the Royal Imperium Fleet, on her flagship the R.I.F. *Modulus Echo*. We have Duke Simeon on board as well. Requesting permission to make orbit. Over."

The response was almost immediate. *R.I.F. Modulus Echo,
shift to heading four-niner-seven and proceed to Mersa station.
Over.*

"Is that good?" Kim asked.

"It's neither good nor bad," Pershing said. "Nance, can you
bring up the information on the space station?"

"Here it is," Nance replied.

She was as quick and efficient as the computer she loved.
Ben glanced at the information. The space station was run by
Admiral Alphonse Benning and had its own wing of interceptor
spacecraft. Ben knew that interceptors were larger than fast-
attack fighters and carried heavier weapons, but they weren't as
fast or maneuverable. Most of the station was given over to
logistics and supplies, and most of the soldiers stationed there
weren't fighters.

"A.B. is old school," Pershing said. "Mersa is his home
world, and he's a stickler for protecting it."

"What's that mean for us?" Ben asked.

"It means we have our work cut out for us," Pershing said.

Two hours later, they slipped into the guest docking bay.
Ben's hands were sweating. He told himself that General
Pershing was the commander in chief and that she would
protect his ship and crew, but he couldn't help but wonder if
Admiral Benning would respect her authority. Before General
Pershing recruited them, the *Modulus Echo* was the most
wanted ship in the galaxy. For all Ben knew, there could a
squad of soldiers waiting outside the air lock to arrest them all.

"Relax, Ben," Kim said.

She had piloted the ship into the station dock as smoothly
as anyone could ask. Nance was running systems checks, and

the general was preparing to disembark with Duke Simeon and Staff Sergeant Visher. Ben stood at the railing looking over the cargo bay. It was encouraging to see all the crates of supplies. There was more food on the *Echo* than Ben had ever seen in one place before. He had a storage compartment crammed full of Zexum tanks, and with General Pershing on board, the *Echo* was the most important vessel in the Royal Imperium's vaunted fleet. But he couldn't help but worry.

"Can't," he replied. "Too many variables."

"This isn't math. You can't reduce human behavior to some archaic formula."

"But wouldn't it be great if you could?" Ben said.

"We did our job," Kim said. "We're safe. It's time to relax a little. Let's have a drink, lounge around in our most comfortable clothes, and maybe take in some holo-programs from Mersa."

"You think Tolliver's down there somewhere?" Ben asked.

"Most likely," Kim replied. "Although he may be locked up in a Security Force detention cell along with the others."

"It makes me wonder," Ben said. "Do you think we're making a difference?"

"We're making a difference, Ben. Even if it's only for ourselves."

"Okay," Ben said. "I'll get the drinks, and you find something to watch."

"Now you're talking," Kim said.

Chapter 15

The two warriors circled each other. Le Croix had been in enough battles to know that Yarl Cherbak intended to kill him. The tor'ax was blade heavy and offered no protection for his hand. It was an offensive weapon only, which meant speed and evasion were Le Croix's only means of defense.

Yarl Cherbak had one enhanced leg and one enhanced arm. Metal ran up the entire right side of his body, from his foot to his shoulder. His headdress tendrils were moving in a jerky fashion, and the scowl on his face revealed his anger. Le Croix knew about anger. It could drive a person to accomplish more than they thought possible, but in a fight, it could drive a person to overcommit and make mistakes.

The Krah warrior feinted, then dropped back, watching to see what Le Croix would do. The human was on the balls of his artificial feet, ready to move but staying calm. He looked almost relaxed and didn't react to Yarl Cherbak's feint. The big Krah switched the tor'ax to his left hand and twirled it in a circle. In response, Le Croix drew the curved dagger that Warlord Oligar had given him. He didn't know if using the second weapon was against the rules. Watching the other Krah fight, he saw that some used weapons, while others didn't. Yarl Cherbak scowled at the sight of the curved blade, but none of the other Krah seemed surprised or outraged.

After a few moments of sizing him up, Yarl Cherbak charged Le Croix. He kept his tor'ax low, obviously intending to knock the human off his feet with a blow from his empty but enhanced hand. Le Croix waited until the last second, then spun to the side. He let his momentum spin him around and drove the butt of the dagger into the Krah's lower back. Le Croix felt thick muscle, but the blow landed hard, and the handle of the dagger had a small, weighted pommel that gouged into the Krah's flesh.

The blow drove Cherbak forward, and the Yarl roared in anger and fury. He replicated Le Croix's spin, lashing out with the tor'ax, but the human had already moved out of range. He walked casually away from his opponent, with his back exposed. Le Croix didn't have the extrasensory tendrils that might have warned him of danger from behind, but he was no stranger to a fight and knew how to read his surroundings. At first, the tendrils of the spectators writhed eagerly, but when they stiffened straight out from the scar-faced warriors, Le Croix dropped to the ground and rolled over his shoulder.

Cherbak had rushed straight at him, his tor'ax held high. When Le Croix dropped to the ground, the Krah didn't know what to do. He tried to stop his charge and shifted toward Le Croix, hoping to chop down and kill his opponent in one massive blow. But the human was a canny fighter, and with his enhanced legs, he felt whole again for the first time in years. He swung his own tor'ax down in a vicious chop that severed the front half of Cherbak's enhanced foot.

The wound, while far from fatal, sent a shock wave through the Yarl. He jumped back from Le Croix, but was off-balance. His tor'ax came down in a clumsy swing that was easy to avoid, and Le Croix slashed at the Yarl's forearm. The curved dagger caught Cherbak just below the elbow and slashed deep into his flesh. The tor'ax fell from his hand, and the big Yarl screamed in pain.

Le Croix could have charged in to finish the fight, but instead he moved back, staying alert for danger. He knew it was only a matter of time before he was challenged, and he wasn't sure that the Yarl would be his only opponent in the fight.

The Krah were shouting now, whooping and cheering. Some were even calling his name, but Le Croix ignored them. He wasn't fighting Cherbak to impress anyone. And while he had no idea how important family relationships were to the Krah, he didn't want to kill Cherbak if he didn't have to. He had heard the Yarl call Grubat his father. Perhaps it was a mistranslation, but Le Croix didn't want to take that chance.

Cherbak bent down and picked up the tor'ax with his enhanced hand. The scowl of anger was gone from the big Yarl's face, replaced with a look of intense concentration. Le Croix was as strong as most men, but he had no doubt the Krah were stronger. The warriors were big boned and thick with muscle, yet surprisingly quick and agile. Cherbak moved toward him with more care, brandishing the tor'ax in his good hand, while his left arm hung at his side, slick with blood.

It was Le Croix's turn to feint. He juked to his left, then spun back to his right, lashing out with the tor'ax and following it around with the curved dagger. But Cherbak had moved out of range, and instead of striking at Le Croix, he chopped his tor'ax at the human's heavy ceremonial weapon. The ax heads connected, and Le Croix felt the impact vibrate up the metal handle of the weapon. It sent a jab of pain up his arm, which caught him off guard. He realized he'd have been better off just dropping the weapon, but he held on, enduring the pain that almost cost him his life.

The unexpected jarring pain consumed his attention for a second, and in that second, Cherbak moved in. He stabbed at Le Croix, thrusting the flat top of his tor'ax straight into the human's face. The blow sent him reeling backward, his vision narrowing to a tiny slit. Cherbak seemed far away, and for another second, Le Croix didn't know what was happening. But then his senses returned, just as the Yarl raised his heavy weapon to split the human's skull. Le Croix realized he couldn't escape the blow. The Krah warrior expected him to try and dodge the powerful chop and stood ready to adjust his attack to catch the human and end the fight.

But Le Croix did the one thing Yarl Cherbak didn't expect. He jumped toward the Yarl, driving himself forward on his powerfully enhanced legs. Le Croix lowered his head, driving it into Cherbak's chin. He felt the strong right arm of the Yarl come down onto his shoulder, and the tor'ax slipped from the Krah's hand as he was knocked backward. Le Croix's ears were ringing, and he could feel a knot forming on top of his head, but Cherbak was down on the ground, disarmed and completely vulnerable.

Le Croix threw himself forward, bending at the knees and landing with all his weight on Cherbak's stomach. The wind blew out of the Yarl's lungs. And with a strong but carefully aimed blow, Le Croix slammed the butt of the dagger into the side of Cherbak's head. The Krah's eyes rolled back in his skull, revealing the bloodshot whites of his eyes. The alien's body stiffened, and the headdress tendrils went lax.

The crowd had gone silent, and Le Croix wasn't sure what to expect. For a moment, he didn't move, waiting for an attack that didn't come. He had been a prisoner, then a guest among the aliens. But with his victory over Chieftain Grubat's son, Le Croix had been fully accepted. He wasn't a Krah, but he was of the Warrior caste, none could deny it. His body had accepted the enhancements, and he was a dangerous foe in a fight.

Le Croix reached out and took hold of one of Cherbak's headdress tendrils and pulled. It released easily from the headdress, almost as if in submission to him. Le Croix rose to his feet and looked around. There was admiration on the faces of the Krah, especially Warlord Oligar. Le Croix slipped his dagger back into a sheath that was mounted on his enhanced thigh, then picked up Cherbak's tor'ax. He carried the weapons over to Chieftain Grubat and handed them over.

"I spared his life," Le Croix said, realizing for the first time that he had a bleeding gash across one cheek and on his nose.

"I am grateful," Grubat said.

Le Croix moved toward Warlord Oligar. Together with the high priest who had just recently arrived, they left the scene of the fight. The spectators were dispersing too, and Le Croix felt the postfight fatigue set in. It was less from the exertion of the battle and more a result of the adrenaline being filtered out of his bloodstream.

"You did well," Warlord Oligar said.

"Indeed," said the high priest.

"Let me connect your tendril," Oligar said.

He held out a hand that was metal. The old warlord was more metal than flesh. Both arms and legs were enhanced, as was most of his body. He looked like a robot with a Krah chest and head. Both of Oligar's eyes, like Le Croix's, were enhanced, and he had long tendrils that hung from his headdress almost to his waist.

"You could have taken them all," the high priest said as Le Croix dropped onto a low stoop. "Why only one?"

"I wanted to leave him a reminder," Le Croix said. "Not a humiliation."

"There is no shame in losing a good fight," Oligar said. "He's lucky you showed mercy."

"Ah, mercy," the high priest said. "A character flaw, perhaps? Or maybe a weakness to use against the humans."

"He was Chieftain Grubat's son," Le Croix said.

"That matters not," the high priest said.

"But Grubat gave you the enhancements," Oligar said. "A generous thing to do."

"It was."

"But surely he did it just to see if it was possible," the high priest said.

"Doesn't matter," Le Croix said. "He could have killed me, but he didn't. He could have left me locked in a cage, but he didn't. Showing his son mercy was the least I could do to repay him."

"An interesting point of view," the high priest said. "The reports I have received said the humans were cowards who didn't fight with honor."

"I believe it is true in some cases," Oligar said as he threaded the tendril into an empty slot in Le Croix's metal headband. "But we shouldn't underestimate the humans. They are capable fighters and they outnumber us."

"The gods will aid our victory," the high priest said.

"Are the gods in this galaxy?" Oligar asked with sincerity. "We are far from home."

"The gods rule the entire universe," the high priest said. "Who do you think opened the portal between our galaxy and this one? It was the gods, I assure you. They have seen our conquest and opened new opportunities for us."

Le Croix wanted to point out that it wasn't a god who opened the wormhole, but an experimental weapon that wiped out most of the Royal Imperium Fleet. Instead, he kept his mouth shut and wiped the blood from his face. His cheek burned from the gash, but he ignored the pain. He knew it was only temporary. Instead, he focused on the sudden sense of anticipation he felt. It was as if he could smell something tangy, but it wasn't an odor. He could feel the emotions of the two Krah in front of him. One was ambitious and arrogant; the other was slightly afraid. It was like he was able to taste their emotions, and while he had no idea how or why, he realized it was an incredible advantage.

"Go and see the surgeons," Oligar said. "Let them see to that gash on your face. Then get some rest. You've earned it."

Le Croix stood and bowed. "Thank you, my lord."

"You are blessed by the gods," the high priest said. "I look forward to your exploits, Yort Le Croix."

"He has a tendril," Oligar said. "He is a trooper now."

"Trooper Le Croix," the high priest declared. "I approve!"

Le Croix left the little awning and walked toward the skeletal remains of the ship that Grubat had landed on Gershwin. Le Croix had once been a prisoner on that ship, but most of it was gone, salvaged to create something new. That thought reminded him of the *Modulus Echo*. He couldn't help but feel a pang of shame that he had joined the aliens, yet they had given him what the Royal Imperium never could. Despite the gash on his face and the painful lump on top of his head, Le Croix felt good. He felt strong and whole. In fact, he felt stronger than he had ever felt before, thanks to the Krah. He might feel shame that he had turned against the Royal Imperium, some might even say against his own race, but he didn't regret it. He was a warrior again, and in his mind, nothing was better than that.

Chapter 16

"No," the queen said in an icy tone, which made it clear she would not change her mind on the subject. "Both ships are needed here."

"Your Majesty," Admiral Benning said with more patience than General Pershing thought possible. "Mersa station is home to an entire squadron of interceptors. It is more than enough—"

"And Gershwin had more than half the Royal Fleet," the queen argued, cutting the aging admiral off. "Yet we were still left undefended. If Mersa Prime is to be the new capital, I insist that the *Romulus* and the *Artemis* remain on station. You can have whatever other ships you want, but not those."

General Pershing wanted to argue, but not as much as she wanted to slap some sense into the unreasonable royal. She was a fool, Pershing thought, if she believed two battle cruisers could protect the system from over two hundred alien ships. But even as acting commander in chief, she couldn't defy the queen.

"We must take the fight to the aliens," Pershing said. "I cannot do that alone."

"So rally more Confederate ships," the queen said. "Let them take a turn defending the galaxy if they're so hellbent on being in charge. Let's see how they like it."

Pershing had mixed feelings about the rebels. For years she had fought them. They were like an infestation. As soon as she wiped out one secret base, another sprang up. The rebels would fight until it was costly, then slip away, hiding in plain sight, reforming their terrorist operations from a new base. She hated them, yet she couldn't deny that they had answered her call for help. The group of rebel fighters had even sacrificed their ships to defeat the aliens. She hoped they would continue to help in the cause, but it was past time for the Royal Imperium to step up.

"What have you heard from our summons?" Pershing asked Admiral Bennings.

"Very little, I'm afraid," he said. "If help is coming, they did not broadcast their intentions."

"This is unacceptable," the queen snapped. "There are reports that several systems are declaring themselves independent from the Imperium. I want those military leaders here to answer for their treasonous actions. I'll have their heads to decorate the palace walls."

Pershing knew that Mersa Prime had a royal palace. Most of the old worlds did. But the queen was smart enough to know that she would just be a place holder in the palace. She wasn't the king, and officially she had no say in the defense of the Imperium. But with her husband's death still unverified, she could make demands that would be taken seriously, as long as she was visible. Once she was out of sight, those in charge could put her wishes to the side, so she remained where she could leverage the most power. At the moment, that was Mersa station.

"One war at a time," Pershing said, matching the queen's frostiness. "The priority is stopping the aliens and regaining control of the Celeste system. As long as the wormhole remains open, we are vulnerable."

"Has your scientist devised a way to close the passage between our galaxy and the aliens?" Benning asked.

"Not yet," Pershing said. "But an armada of ships positioned around the wormhole would be just as effective. We can destroy anything coming through."

"If your intelligence is right, and there really are over two hundred alien ships," the queen said, "the point is merely academic. We don't have the firepower or the resources to stop that many vessels. Find another way, General. We cannot lose more ships if we are going to defend ourselves properly."

Pershing heard the accusation veiled in the queen's words. Pershing knew there was nothing proper about war, especially one with an alien race they knew nothing about, but arguing semantics wouldn't help.

"If there's nothing more..." the queen said. It was a dismissal and Pershing resented it, but she wasn't in a position to defy the queen.

"As you wish, Your Majesty," Pershing said with a bow. Her jaw was clenched so tightly it hurt, but she got the words out.

Pershing turned for the door of the station commander's quarters where the queen had ensconced herself upon arriving in the Mersa system. Pershing had no idea where Benning was keeping himself, but his unseating was the least of her worries. The fact that he had sided with Pershing over the queen would probably result in his early retirement so that the royal could bring in a commander who would do whatever she wanted.

Benning started to follow Pershing out, but the queen called him back.

"Admiral, a word," the queen said.

Benning stiffened. Pershing saw a shadow of a frown cross the admiral's face. She didn't blame him. The queen was an irrational woman wielding too much power for her own good. In an effort to retain the control that made her feel safe, she was making decisions that put her in danger. And the fact that it also endangered the entire galaxy angered Pershing, but there was nothing she could do about it. As long as the queen insisted there was hope of finding her husband or son, power within the Royal Imperium would not shift to a new ruler. And the void left by an absent king would make the entire Imperium vulnerable to the dissidents she had spent her life fighting.

As the old saying went, the patients were in charge of the asylum, and if they had their way, the Imperium would not survive. On the way back to the *Modulus Echo*, General Alicia Pershing, acting commander in chief, tried think of a way to combat over two hundred alien ships. She had almost no resources. Her Special Forces troops on Yelsin Prime wouldn't be able to help. She didn't even have a transport vessel to move them into the appropriate star system.

Mersa station was a military installation and as such was spartan in the extreme. Crossing through the air lock back into the *Echo* felt to Alicia Pershing like she was moving back onto a luxury yacht. The ship was old, but it was designed with comfort in mind. Despite years of neglect, Ben and his crew had painstakingly restored the old ship, and while nothing on board was new, everything was clean.

She was halfway up the stairs from the cargo hold when Duke Simeon and Ben appeared above her. Both men looked expectantly at the general, which only soured her memory of the meeting with Admiral Bennings even further.

"Well?" Duke Simeon said.

"We were refused," Pershing said, walking past the two men and continuing up the next flight of stairs toward the galley.

"Refused? How is that possible? You're the commander in chief of the Royal Fleet."

"And Queen Ultane has taken control of the Mersa system and all its resources," Pershing replied.

"So, what does that mean?" Ben asked.

"It means we need a new plan," Pershing replied. "How do you fight a war with no resources?"

She had reached the galley and poured herself a small cup of strong liquor. The drink had a medicinal feel and helped calm her frayed nerves. Ben filled three mugs with ale, and they sat down together at the long table in the middle of the *Echo*'s elevated observation deck. Pershing was struck again by the simple elegance of the ship. The round chamber was neatly arranged, and light from the space station filtered in from the skylights above them.

"What about the rebels?" Duke Simeon asked.

Pershing looked at Ben. "I'll reach out," he said. "I know a guy that might have some information for us down on the planet."

"There is no resistance on Mersa Prime," General Pershing said.

"For good reason," Ben replied. He looked as if he was about to say more, but suddenly he stood up.

"What's wrong with him?" Duke Simeon asked.

"I've got it," Ben said. "It's brilliant."

"What are you talking about?" General Pershing asked.

She was growing accustomed to Ben's strange intellect. He was undoubtedly a genius, but completely untrained. His mind worked differently than other people's, and his breakthroughs came suddenly at odd moments. Still, if he had an idea, she would listen to it. A general without an army wouldn't accomplish much.

"The drones," Ben said. "We can use the drones."

"Drones? You mean..." Duke Simeon couldn't bring himself to speak the truth out loud.

General Pershing knew that the weather drones had been misused on Mersa Prime. She hadn't known it before Ben and his crew told her, but she did know the lengths to which her predecessor would go to get his way. She started doing the math in her mind, but she couldn't get past the glaring problem the drones presented.

"The drones aren't military equipment," Pershing said.

"The drone ships and operators aren't military?" Ben asked.

"Yes, the ships and the operators are under my command, but the drones themselves have no weapons. They're weather drones."

"Okay, so we weaponize them," Ben said.

"You want the drone pilots to fight the aliens?" Duke Simeon asked.

"Not like a fighter pilot would fight," Ben said. "There are over two hundred alien ships in the Celeste system, right?"

"At least," Pershing said. "Although they may have begun to venture out to other systems."

"So we weaponize the drones. It doesn't have to be complicated," Ben said. "Essentially, all we want is for each of the drones to explode on contact."

"You'll make them into missiles," the duke said. "Will they have enough power to destroy the alien ships?"

"Not just one," Ben said. "But if we swarm them, we could do some real damage. How many drones do we have?"

"Each of those drone operator ships should have between two and four thousand drones," General Pershing said, warming to the idea. "They go into the upper atmosphere and detonate to release payloads of chemicals that disrupt storm formations."

"Right," Ben said. "So we replace their payloads with something that will react to the detonation with more force."

"Such as?"

"It could be anything," Ben said. "We used hydrogen tanks to destroy the captured ships in the Yelsin system."

"Mersa station has munitions for re-equipping battle cruisers," Pershing added. "The queen can keep her ships, but we will take the weapons."

It was a brilliant plan, Pershing admitted to herself. If she deployed the drone ships in just the right way, the drones could overtake most of the alien vessels before they knew what danger they were in. It would take careful coordination, but it was possible. The logistics would also be difficult, and there was no time to waste.

"I'll give the orders," Pershing said. "Ben, the *Echo* needs to be ready to leave soon. Make sure you have everything we need."

"What will our task be?" Duke Simeon asked.

"We go in first and scout the enemy again," Pershing said. "The drone ships will jump to a safe distance at the edge of the system, and we'll direct them to their final positions."

"Why not just send them straight into the alien vessels?" Ben asked.

"Because once our drones begin to detonate, the aliens will realize the danger," Pershing explained. "We don't have enough ships to surround them completely, but if we deploy the drones carefully, we can cast a wide net and destroy as many of their vessels as possible."

"I'll make sure we're ready," Ben said. "Can you people spare a few missiles?"

"Whatever the *Echo* can handle," Pershing said.

"We have racks on each wing for missiles," Ben said. "Five each. And if could store some extras in the cargo hold, it wouldn't hurt."

"I'll have it done," Pershing said. "Get your people ready. Your Highness, with your permission, I'll see to the arrangements."

"Of course," Duke Simeon said.

"Ben, if you really know someone in the system who can find out if the Confederates will help us, that would be useful too," Pershing said as she headed for the stairs. "We can strike a blow to the aliens with the drones, but we can't hold the system with them. Not for long."

"I'll send him a message," Ben said.

"This is so exciting," Duke Simeon declared.

"I'm glad you think so," Ben remarked. "Personally, I think danger is overrated."

Pershing smirked. The two men were behind her and couldn't see the look on her face, and for that she was grateful. Danger was like a drug to her. She needed it. She needed to be tested, to see exactly what she was capable of. And the aliens were proving to be a more difficult problem than she expected. They would be her greatest challenge, and the measure against which she would be judged by history.

Chapter 17

Ben sat at his console, with a direct communications link down to the planet. Kim, Nance, and Magnum were clustered behind him. The feed from Mersa Prime was displayed on the big screen across the bridge, but the camera that would show Ben was mounted on his console.

The screen was blank for a moment, but then Toliver's face appeared. He was an older man, but he had proven himself strong and capable on their trip from the sprawling Brimex Solar Systems space station in the Skopes system. That adventure, one of their very first missions after fleeing Torrent Four on the *Echo*, seemed like it happened in a different life. The group of older rebels from Mersa Prime had been thrilled to finally get passage home. Unfortunately, the Royal Imperium's security forces had set an ambush for the group. Some had been killed giving the *Echo* a chance to escape.

"Oh, how the mighty have fallen," Tolliver said. "I can't believe you're working for the Imperium."

"Hello, Tolliver," Ben said.

"How's kicks, you old pirate?" Kim said.

Tolliver chuckled. "I believe you are the pirate, my dear. I am well. How are the four of you?"

"We're alive," Ben said.

"And still flying," Kim added.

"It's good to see you again," Nance said.

"It's good to see you too," Tolliver said. "As you can guess, we've been busy here. The discovery of the Imperium's nefarious activity with the drones was not well received. At least it wasn't until after we got the drugs out of the systems of the people who were willing to trust us."

"That's water under the bridge now," Ben said. "The Royal Imperium is broken and we have a bigger threat."

"The rumors are true, then?" Tolliver asked.

"Yes," Ben said. "Aliens from another galaxy have arrived."

"The enemy of my enemy is my friend," Tolliver said. "Only, there are so many enemies, it's hard to keep track."

"True enough," Ben said. "But for now, we've been given an opportunity to do something that will pay dividends in the future. General Pershing is in charge now, along with Duke Simeon of the royal family. They've offered amnesty for any rebels willing to help them fight the aliens."

"Sounds like they want us to sacrifice our warriors to do their job," Tolliver said.

"That's true enough," Ben said. "But with over half the Imperium Fleet destroyed, we have to pull together to defeat the aliens and secure our galaxy."

"I can see the wisdom in that," Tolliver said. "The Imperium is splintering. We've heard rumors of systems declaring independence."

"That's right," Ben said. "And once the aliens are defeated, every world will have to decide what their future will be. I can't guarantee that the Imperium will allow independence, but the duke had agreed to hear the grievances against the Imperium. Amnesty now and a seat at the table when the fighting is over—that's better than we could have expected from the Imperium, even if the rebellion had been strong enough to threaten their power."

Tolliver didn't answer right away. Ben could see that he was sitting down, and a large window behind him showed the lights of a large city in the darkness. Tolliver looked concerned, but Ben could tell he was thinking about things.

"I'm not sure how I can help," the older man finally said. "What little resistance we had was weak and scattered. A few people might be willing to help with your fight, but I can't promise anything."

"We don't need fighters," Ben said. "Not from Mersa Prime. What we need is a way to communicate with the rebel leaders. My source is refusing to help."

"Holt is a fool," Tolliver said. "All he cares about is what will benefit him and his aims."

"You can say that again," Kim chimed in.

"He offered us a small group of rebel ships," Ben said. "But the aliens are merciless scavengers. They capture any ship they can and don't care what happens to the crew."

"We had to sabotage the rebel ships in the Yelsin system," Kim said. "But it worked."

"We took out nine alien vessels there," Magnum said, speaking for the first time.

"A victory, then," Tolliver said.

"But at a high cost," Ben said. "We don't have a lot of resources to keep up the fight. The general has a plan to retake the Celeste system, but we need help to hold it."

"And fighters to go down and retake Gershwin," Nance said.

"The aliens have taken the planet?" Tolliver asked.

"That's what we think," Ben said. "Can you get word to the Confederacy? They should have heard of General Pershing's offer of amnesty in exchange for help. What we need is a reliable liaison."

"I suppose that's me," Tolliver said.

"If you're willing," Ben replied.

"I'm willing to help you," the older man said. "Of course, I'll help, but I'll need time."

"Send word that anyone willing to take the general's offer should come here, to Mersa Prime." Ben said. "If we haven't returned by the time they arrive, the general will leave instructions."

"Fair enough," Tolliver said. "Does she know who I am?"

"No," Ben said.

"We would never reveal your name to the Imperium," Kim said.

"But they could trace this call," Tolliver said. "That's okay. I'll be your liaison, and you can share my information with the general. I'll have to cut ties with my people down here, but that doesn't amount to much at any rate. You just make sure that you stay alive, Ben. All of you are welcome here once this is all over."

"That's generous of you," Ben said.

In truth, he wondered if they would be welcome anywhere once the fighting was over. If they could defeat the aliens, and that was far from a foregone conclusion, he feared that General Pershing would fail to keep her promises. But he couldn't let that fear keep him from doing the only thing that might save the *Echo* and her crew from being hunted as criminals.

"Don't worry," Kim said with her usual bravado. "I'll keep them alive."

"I'm sure you will," Tolliver said smiling. "I wouldn't say no to another trip on the *Echo*. She's a special ship."

Ben agreed completely. "Then it's a deal," Ben said. "Once this is all over, we'll take you wherever you want."

"Agreed," Tolliver said. "Take care."

"You too," Ben said.

The big displays went blank, and Ben sat back in his seat.

"It was good to see him," Kim declared. "He looked well enough."

"Let's just hope we didn't get him into trouble," Ben said.

"You don't trust the general's offer?" Nance asked.

"I trust her, but she isn't in charge here," Ben said. "I don't trust the queen."

"Tolliver can look after himself," Kim said. "And if the Confederates have any sense, they'll take the general's offer. But we need to focus on us right now."

"The Imperium workers are loading missiles onto our wings right now," Magnum said.

"We'll get the extras loaded into the cargo bay," Ben said. "Let's be ready to leave as soon as the general is back on board."

"When will that be?" Nance asked.

"I don't know," Ben admitted. "Any time, I guess."

"You think her plan will work?" Kim asked.

Ben didn't bother pointing out that it was all based on his idea. He wasn't looking for glory or recognition. All he cared about was keeping his friends and his ship safe.

"It has to," Ben said. "There isn't any other choice."

Ben and Magnum left the bridge together. Magnum, as usual, was quiet, but Ben always felt better when the big man was with him. It wasn't just about feeling safe—Magnum wasn't Ben's bodyguard—they were friends. And unlike his other friendships, there didn't need to be a lot of words spoken between them. Magnum was content to let Ben take the lead in most things, but when Magnum stepped up, Ben gladly stepped back.

At the bottom of the stairs, Corporal Dial was waiting for them. He and the other commandos had been working nonstop since the general decided to put Ben's plan into action.

"Looks like we're parting ways," Dial said. "We've been assigned to the three drone ships to help oversee weaponizing the pods."

"At least we'll know the drones are ready," Ben said.

"It's been a pleasure working with you," Dial said, shaking Ben's and Magnum's hands. "I don't often see such competence outside the military."

"Thanks, I guess," Ben replied with a grin.

"Be safe," Magnum added.

"Yeah, you too," Dial replied. "A supply ship is linking up with the *Echo* as we speak. I did a check on the plastic sheeting. She's still airtight, so you shouldn't have a problem."

"Thanks," Ben said, knowing he would check the temporary barrier to hold the ship's atmosphere in place.

"Till we meet again," Dial said.

He picked up his gear and headed for the air lock. Ben watched him go. People came and went, that was part of life on an interstellar ship, but the *Echo* seemed almost empty without the Spec Ops team. And he wondered briefly about Major Le Croix. Ben hadn't known the officer well, but he had led the team on their rescue mission…and sacrificed himself to the enemy. Yet the rest of the platoon continued on, never missing a beat. It felt wrong somehow, but Ben knew the mission was the most important thing. They had to stop the aliens, then they could grieve.

"Let's check that plastic again," Ben said. "Better safe than sorry."

Magnum nodded. It only took a few minutes, and by the time they finished checking the plastic barrier, the supply ship was ready to deliver the crates of missiles. Ben and Magnum watched as the *Echo*'s rear hatch lowered and a floating sled glided in with six rectangular crates stacked neatly on a pallet. A soldier brought the load in and set it on the deck. Ben couldn't identify his rank, but he looked young, and with only a single stripe on his uniform, he was maybe a new recruit. He looked bored as he lowered the sled. It was a big load, each crate was wide enough to hold a coffin, and Ben could tell they were heavy too. The sled used small repulsors to help move the heavy loads. Each of the crates was labeled Royal Imperium Military Munitions.

"Strange to see so much government equipment on the *Echo*," Ben said.

"Almost like we're an Imperium ship," Magnum agreed.

"There's not much room, but we should move those missiles onto the other side of the barrier," Ben said. "Let's stack them up by the air lock."

The job took longer than Ben expected. Each of the crates weighed several hundred pounds. They were forced to dial back the *Echo*'s artificial gravity to be able to move the heavy containers. Each one held four of the long missiles that were almost as big around as a grown man's thigh. Fortunately, they weren't armed, and the explosive chemicals that would make them detonate upon impact were kept in separate chambers inside the rocket-powered weapons. Ben felt safe enough having them inside the ship, and if they had to load them onto the *Echo*'s wing mounts, it was good to know they wouldn't accidentally detonate if he bumped one into the ship.

"Is there anything else that needs to be done?" Kim asked as Ben and Magnum returned to the bridge.

"No," Ben replied. "The missiles are all squared away. We have plenty of Zexum and food."

"All ship systems are green," Nance added.

"As soon as the general gives the word, we can go," Ben said.

"When she says jump," Kim remarked, "we say how high."

"It's a job," Ben said.

"You don't feel like we're betraying the Confederacy?" Kim asked. "I'm not judging, just wondering where everyone stands."

"We never joined the Confederacy," Ben said. "We took on some jobs from them, but we have always been independent."

"Maybe," Nance said. "Maybe not."

"We never would have gotten off Torrent Four without them," Kim said.

"Until the aliens came through the wormhole, we were criminals in the eyes of the Imperium," Magnum added.

"True, but that doesn't mean we were rebels," Ben said. "Don't forget, Holt and his friends used us too. They plastered the video footage of the battle in the Bannyan system all over the galactic network, and boasted about our ship as if we were one of their own."

"Doesn't that mean something?" Kim asked.

"No," Ben replied. "Look, I don't like the Imperium any more than the rest of you, but look at how things stand now. We have more fuel, more food, and more weapons than ever before."

"Because we're part of the government system that treated us like dirt all our lives until they needed us," Kim said.

"True, but this is an opportunity that only comes once in a lifetime," Ben continued. "We did our part for the rebellion. Now we're doing what we need to do to make sure we have a future. Confederacy or Imperium doesn't matter if the aliens take over."

"What if they aren't planning to?" Nance asked. "There's no news that they're spreading. Maybe they just want Gershwin. We could let them have it and live in peace."

Ben wished he could believe Nance, but he knew leaving the aliens to control the wormhole was a bad idea. They knew nothing about the aliens. And with control of the Celeste system, they could bring anything through the passage between the galaxies. It was too big a risk, and Ben felt a sense of obligation for having opened the wormhole in the first place.

"I don't think so," Magnum said.

"You don't think they might just want Gershwin and nothing else?" Nance asked him.

"I don't think we can live in peace," Magnum replied.

"Look," Ben said, "whatever our feelings about the aliens or the Imperium, the indisputable fact is, this job is best for the four of us. Without it, we're outlaws."

"But the general might get us killed," Kim replied.

"Anything is possible," Ben said. "But I doubt she wants to put us in danger. She's the commander in chief, after all. She can't take too much risk."

"Under different circumstances, I would agree," Kim said. "But she's desperate, and the aliens are unpredictable."

"So we have to watch out for ourselves," Ben said.

"Minimize the risk as much as possible," Nance added.

"And hope her plan works," Kim said.

"It should," Ben said.

"Does anyone else feel like we're starting a fight with a monster?" Kim asked. "We might be biting off more than we can chew, even if the Confederates pitch in and help us fight."

"At least this way we can live with ourselves," Ben said.

"Living is what I'm talking about," Kim said.

"The general is on her way," Nance announced. "She and the duke will be on board soon, and she's sent word to leave for the Celeste system as soon as possible."

"So we're doing this?" Kim said. "Last chance to cut and run."

"You would really abandon the general and give up our immunity?" Ben asked.

"I'm not saying it's a good idea," Kim replied. "Just that it's possible."

"We could hide somewhere," Nance said, thinking about the idea. "Maybe with the war, the Imperium wouldn't even bother looking for us."

"I don't think I can do that," Ben said. "We might be able to hide in a fringe world, but we'd have to get rid of the *Echo*."

"We could trade her for another ship," Kim said.

"And we would always be looking over our shoulders," Ben said. "I want a better life than that."

"Okay, I'm not against sticking around," Kim said.

"It's probably for the best," Nance added.

Ben saw that Magnum gave him a nod, and Kim blew him a kiss before she swiveled her pilot's chair around to face the big bridge displays.

"Do we have a jump point?" Kim asked.

"On screen," Nance said.

"Let's double-check and make sure we aren't still connected to Mersa station," Ben said.

"All clear except for the docking arm," Magnum said.

"I've sent word to Space Control," Nance said. "We're cleared to depart once the general is on board."

"I'm here," Pershing said as she and Duke Simeon came up the stairs from the cargo hold.

"Docking arm is free," Magnum said.

"All clear ahead," Nance added.

"Alright, back into the void," Kim said.

"Ben, raise our shield," General Pershing said. "We're going straight to the Celeste system and I don't want to drop out of hyperspace with our defenses down."

"Okay," Ben said, typing at his console.

"So long, civilization," Kim said.

"Shield is spinning up," Ben said. "We'll be at full strength before Kim makes the jump."

"Good," the general said. "It's time we take the fight to the enemy."

"Transition to hyperspace in thirty seconds," Nance announced.

Ben glanced at his display. The monitor was built into his console and showed the flux shield at eighty percent. The system had to get the flow of gravity spinning around the ship before increasing the gravitational power to full.

"Let's make some history," Duke Simeon said.

"I just hope we don't become history," Ben said quietly to himself. "Flux shield is ready."

"Alright, people," Kim said. "Here we go."

Chapter 18

The gash had been cleaned and sealed with some type of flesh glue. Across the medical facility, which was really just a single room deep in the belly of Grubat's old ship that was being scavenged piece by piece to build a sprawling Krah settlement, a worker was repairing the damage to Yarl Cherbak's foot. Le Croix had chopped off the front half of the warrior's artificial foot, but the worker had no trouble repairing the damage.

With his face cleaned and tended to, the surgeon began to study the junction between Le Croix's enhanced legs and his torso. The artificial limbs joined his body at the hips. His lower legs had been amputated by Royal Imperium surgeons, but the Krah workers who had created his prosthetics had built them on top of his existing upper legs. They were metal, yet they responded to his will just as if they were his own flesh. He knew the Krah had somehow tapped into his nervous system to make the artificial legs so responsive, and he wasn't really even curious as to how they did it. He was just thankful to feel whole again.

"You fought well," the surgeon said. "It seems the enhancements are effective."

Le Croix heard the surgeon's grunting language, but it was overlapped by the translator built into the headdress that covered his ears.

"Yes," Le Croix said, knowing his language was likewise translated by some hidden device in the worker's own enhancements.

"Any pain?"

"None," Le Croix said.

Actually, his face was throbbing with pain, and his body was aching from the fight and ensuing exhaustion, but he was sure the worker was referring to his legs.

"There seems to be some blistering here," the surgeon said, shining a light where the metal legs stopped and Le Croix's own flesh started. "Probably chaffing from your battle."

"Should I be concerned?"

"No," the worker said.

Le Croix stood up, and the worker, who was still bent over him, was forced to stumble back. All his life, he had been looked over and bypassed as little more than a pawn in the political games of the Royal Imperium. He was an officer, but that amounted to little in the class structure of the galaxy where fortune and fame were valued above all else. But in the Krah culture, warriors were at the top of the hierarchy, and he found that he liked it that way. The surgeon had skills far beyond what Le Croix could understand. The worker was part artisan, part engineer, and part doctor, yet he was far below the warriors, whose only skills were to fight.

Le Croix left the medical bay and found his way outside. After spending most of his life in military vessels and space stations, he had come to view the world he found himself in much the same way that Grubat did. Like many of the other warriors, Le Croix preferred to sleep outside, in the open air. The temperature dropped at night, but the Krah built fires and wrapped their bodies in thick blankets.

Overlord Oligar had quarters in a long building that was still being constructed. It would be the home of the Krah of highest stature in the settlement, and the warlord was obligated to stay there, but Le Croix joined a group of warriors sleeping outside. He wrapped himself in a blanket and stretched out on the ground beside the fire.

Smoke rose into the air above him, but Le Croix could still see the stars. Unlike the other warriors beside him, the human knew what lay out there in the vast reaches of the galaxy. Conquering his fellow humans held little interest to Le Croix, but the respect of the Krah did. If he had to kill people to gain more of it, then he would do so. He had no idea how far a foreigner could rise in their ranks, but he was determined to find out.

The next morning, Le Croix's nose was filled with dried blood, and his mouth tasted like ash. He needed something to drink. He rolled on his side, coughing as a ship's engine roared to life somewhere in the camp. He got up slowly, letting the blood drain from his head where his face was throbbing from the gash. He couldn't help but wonder if his nose had been broken as well. It certainly felt painful enough.

"We are wanted, Le Croix."

The human turned and found Grubat standing behind him. The chieftain had long tendrils, which waved back and forth almost as if they were defying gravity.

"We are?" Le Croix said, his voice a croak.

"Alpha Vistol has arrived," Grubat said. "Soon the ships in orbit will begin their hunting. We must present ourselves and find out where we will be of greatest service."

"What about Warlord Oligar?" Le Croix said, looking for something to drink.

"He has returned to his Thralldom," Grubat said. "Come."

They walked across the wide field. At some point, they passed a group of workers preparing food. Le Croix was given a metal bottle with water inside, and a bowl of gruel. There was meat available, but his teeth ached from the fight, and Le Croix was content with the soft food, which helped clear the foul taste from his mouth and gave him strength.

Eventually, they came to a transport. It was little more than an open platform, with repulsor-type engines. The two warriors got on, along with a few workers, one of which took control of the vehicle. They rose straight up in the air, the transport making almost no noise until they were above the trees. Le Croix could see for miles. The forest was vast, and to the north, mountains were visible in the distance.

They flew at speed, the wind buffeting their bodies. There was nothing to hold onto. The workers huddled on the floor of the platform, but Grubat stood tall, his arms folded across his chest. Le Croix did the same, letting his enhanced feet grip the platform. It felt strange to be flying in what seemed to be contrary to all thought of personal safety, but it was exhilarating at the same time. Eventually, they came to a wide plain at the foot of one of the mountains that rose up in a vertical cliff where a river spilled down in a sparkling waterfall. Along the base of the mountain, several ships were carefully arranged. They were of different sizes and shapes, and unlike Grubat's vessel, they weren't being torn apart to build new structures.

"Alpha Vistol? Is he the leader of the Krah?"

"A leader, yes," Grubat said. "Alpha is the highest class. You were Yort, the lowest, before defeating Yarl Cherbak earned you the rank of trooper."

Le Croix processed what he knew of the Krah. They were a strict class society, with three different castes: Warrior, Worker, and Priest. He knew the most about the warriors, but very little of the other castes. For the warriors, there were ranks within their caste: Yort, Trooper, Yarl, Chieftain, Warlord, and Alpha. As the transport descended, Le Croix wondered once again how high a human might rise in their hierarchy.

As soon as the transport landed, Grubat marched toward a glistening black ship, half the size of an Imperium battle cruiser. It was an intimidating vessel and could easily carry over a hundred Krah comfortably, depending on what its purpose was. As they approached, a hatch opened, and the high priest who had been with Warlord Oligar came outside.

"Alpha Vistol will see you shortly," he said. "He bids you to wait here."

Grubat bowed slightly, and the priest hurried back inside the ship. Le Croix turned and looked over the land. They were high enough to see for a long way. The waterfall flowed in a wide, shallow river that meandered across the plain and disappeared into the forest. The air was cooler near the mountain, and unlike the other Krah camp, it was quiet.

"How many worlds are like this, Trooper Le Croix?" Grubat asked.

"Few," Le Croix said honestly. "Most of the inhabited worlds are polluted and home to millions of humans."

"But there are more like New Krah?"

"There are some," Le Croix said. "Owning an entire world is rare, but not unheard of. Most are held by wealthy families or by naturalist societies trying to preserve a world's native species."

"And they have breathable air and acceptable living conditions?"

"Some do," Le Croix said. "It depends on what you consider acceptable. Many inhabited worlds only have small areas that are fit for life. Others have large cities built underground or in protected bubbles on the surface."

"Your kind must value the Worker caste above all others," Grubat said.

"I suppose," Le Croix said.

"I could live here forever," Grubat said. "It is far superior to the worlds I come from. There are none so pristine or so well adapted to the Krah as this."

"What about your home world?" Le Croix asked.

"It was destroyed by war," Grubat said proudly. "We have lived among the stars ever since, pillaging the inferior races of our galaxy. But in this new place, things are different."

The hatch behind them opened without warning. Le Croix and Chieftain Grubat both turned at the same time. Alpha Vistol appeared from the dark ship. The Krah leader was almost entirely enhanced. The alpha's body was all robotic, and only his head appeared to be flesh, although most of it was covered with a richly appointed headdress. Instead of hanging tendrils, his extrasensory limbs looked like antlers rising upward above his head. When he spoke, his voice was gravelly and made Le Croix wonder just how old the alpha was.

"Chieftain Grubat, I have heard your name spoken," the Krah leader said.

"It is an honor, Alpha Vistol," Grubat said with a full bow.

"And you must be the human trooper that High Priest Alwain has been telling me of. How are you called?"

"Le Croix," he said, imitating Grubat's deep bow.

"And our enhancements seem to fit you well," the Krah leader said. "But tell me, why have you turned against your own kind?"

"Humanity is strong," Le Croix said. "I was a warrior in their great military, but when my legs were damaged, they cast me aside."

"He was given the simplest enhancements," Grubat said. "It was disgraceful."

"And it was your idea, Chieftain Grubat, to enhance a hue-man."

Occasionally, the Krah uttered words that were new to their vocabulary, such as Le Croix's name, and the word *humans*. In those instances, Le Croix's translator didn't bother to say the word, and he heard it naturally from the Krah.

"After Trooper Le Croix was tested," Grubat said, "I set four Yorts in his path. He defeated them in unarmed combat but sustained an injury in the process. I deemed him worthy of enhancements, and it was a good opportunity to see how our technology would be incorporated by their smaller, frailer bodies."

"And the experiment was a success," Alpha Vistol said. "High Priest Alwain says you defeated a Yarl in single combat."

"Yes," Le Croix said.

"Our enhancements seem to have been advantageous," the Krah leader said.

Le Croix bowed again, feeling suddenly self-conscious about the blistering around his hips where the metal was bonded to his flesh.

"Very good," Alpha Vistol continued. "It seems we have much to learn from each other."

"It would be my pleasure," Le Croix said.

The Krah began to talk, making plans, while Le Croix stood nearby, listening. His heart was conflicted, his body ached, and a strange itching began around his hips. Le Croix didn't move, not even to scratch. He could feel the slow, viscous fluid deep in his sinuses shifting, and his tendril picked up feelings of eager anticipation wafting through the air like a light fragrance. He could attack the alpha, but he would almost certainly be slaughtered. And even if he were successful, it wouldn't stop the Krah invasion. Gershwin had fallen, the Celeste system was theirs, and soon they would venture out across the galaxy. It was a foregone conclusion that General Pershing would rally the Imperium Fleet, but Le Croix couldn't guess who would be successful. And if he had to pick a side, he decided that he would stay with the Krah. They had honored him and given him status, while the Royal Imperium had sidelined him after he'd made a great sacrifice on their behalf.

Perhaps that made him a traitor, he couldn't say. It was almost as if the choice had been made for him, and all he could do was live with it. But at least he was living as a full man, a warrior in his prime once more. It was something he hadn't even been able to dream of before he was captured by the Krah, and he refused to give it up. He would fight and die for them, if necessary, but at least he would go the way he always imagined, fighting in battle surrounded by his brothers in arms. The Krah saw things differently. They did things that seemed strange. But fighting was fighting, and while they used different weapons and tactics, Le Croix knew how to wage war.

And he would make a name for himself—one the Krah revered and humanity feared.

Chapter 19

The trip through hyperspace was uneventful, but as they neared the Celeste system, the tension increased significantly.

"Last checks," Pershing reminded her ragtag crew of mercenaries.

"Two minutes until we emerge from hyperspace," Nance said.

"Flux shield is in the green," Ben said.

"Missiles are armed," Magnum said.

"Just remember, we can't fire them while the shield is up," Ben added.

"I won't forget," General Pershing said. "This isn't my first time commanding a starship in battle."

She couldn't believe the crew of the *Echo*, which had been the most wanted felons in the galaxy until she graciously granted them all immunity, would presume to tell her how to run the ship. But until she had more resources, she would tolerate their presumptions and coddle their precious egos. Her destiny was bigger than her need for respect.

"I wish there was more I could do," the duke said.

"We're a big crew on a small ship," Pershing reminded him. "And our job is to observe and direct the battle, not fight it. But trust me, Your Highness, the galaxy will know who was here this day. Your name will be at the top of the list. Putting yourself between the enemies of humanity and the people you rule will not be forgotten."

It was an unnecessary reminder, at least in her mind. Of course, the duke would take credit for the victory—there was never any doubt about that in her mind, but she stroked his ego just the same. She needed him on her side if she were to have any chance of winning over the commanders across the galaxy who still had ships and troops at their disposal. Being commander in chief of a military without ships and very few soldiers wouldn't do her any good.

"Approaching the exit vector," Nance announced.

"It's about time," Kim said. "I'm dying of boredom here."

"No one is dying," Ben said.

"Let's stay focused," Pershing reminded them.

"Three, two, one," Nance counted down.

Suddenly, the glow of hyperspace was replaced with the deep black of the Celeste system. They had come in right above the system star, which was below and behind them. In the distance, the fourth planet, the royal home world of Gershwin, seemed to glitter against a starry backdrop.

"Maximum zoom on all forward cameras," Pershing said.

The view on the big displays changed. They were too far out to see everything clearly, but there were still a lot of ships around the planet.

"Alright, let's pick up visual scanning. Report anything that moves," Pershing said.

The crew, all except for Kim, who was piloting the ship as it slowly crept toward Gershwin, searched the ship's exterior camera feeds. They couldn't risk giving their position away by using traditional radar, and they would have to get closer if they were going to direct the probe ships into position.

"All clear," Ben said.

"Me too," Nance added.

"I've got nothing," Duke Simeon said.

"Clear," Magnum said.

General Pershing had seen nothing on the cameras she had assigned herself to search. And that was the biggest relief. She had been afraid they would come out of hyperspace and fall under immediate attack. The probe ships need them to guide them into position. The plan she had concocted with Ben's help would only work once. Surprise was their only advantage, and once the aliens knew that the probes could be weaponized, they would avoid them at all costs.

"Okay," Pershing said. "Let's head deeper into the system. Continue visual scanning. I want the shields up until I give the order. We're not looking for a fight. And I don't want to attract attention until the probe ships arrive."

"Any idea when that will be?" Kim asked.

"They were being loaded with munitions when we left the Mersa system," General Pershing said. "That shouldn't have taken more than an hour."

Of course, an hour under her watchful eye could easily stretch into three or four hours once she was out of the system. And the probe ship commanders were not the cream of the crop. Being assigned to a ship full of weather drones was as low as a military officer could get. One of the commanders was fresh out of officer training; the other two were what she called pity appointments. They were politically assigned commanders who had proven themselves inept for any other duty. Still, they had accepted her orders and would surely arrive at some point. Patience was a big part of warfare, and she had learned to be still and wait for reinforcements long ago.

They did a short burn to build speed, then cut the main drive and let their momentum carry them into orbit around

Webber, the second planet in the system. It was a dark, green ball of murky gasses in a stormy atmosphere, but it was close to the same position in its orbit as Gershwin in relation to the system star, which gave the *Echo* a perfect point of view.

"Let's count those ships," Pershing said. "Get as many logged onto your computer as possible."

"That's difficult to do without radar," Nance said.

"Do the best you can," Pershing said.

"Looks to me like some of the ships have left the system," Kim said.

"They could be hidden on the other side of the planet," Ben said.

"Or maybe they went back through the wormhole," Duke Simeon suggested.

There were times when General Pershing thought the duke stated the obvious just to feel like he was part of the conversation. And it grated her nerves that the crew was having a conversation as they spied on an enemy that vastly outnumbered them. Normally, she would have ordered them to keep their opinions to themselves—the crew of the *Modulus Echo* had no discipline.

"Wouldn't that be nice?" Kim said. "Maybe they don't like it, and they're going home."

"I show more ships arriving through the wormhole," Nance said, bursting the bubble of naive optimism.

The other thing bothering Pershing was the fact that the fleet of alien vessels had spread out around the planet. They seemed more intent on guarding Gershwin than holding the wormhole. She made up her mind to bring in two of the probe ships close to the ring of fire that marked the passage between the galaxies. The third would approach from the opposite side of Gershwin.

They circled Webber for more than an hour before the probe ships arrived at the edge of the heliosphere. They sent a tight-beam communication toward Webber. Pershing had guessed that the aliens wouldn't pick it up as long as none of their ships were between the second and third worlds in the system. Fortunately, it appeared as if all the alien ships were massed around Gershwin.

"Probe ships are here," Nance announced. "Waiting for approach vectors."

"Send them," Pershing said, having given the coordinates to Nance while they waited.

The reply was sent via another tight-beam communication, and once it had been sent, Kim took them out of orbit.

"Start moving us toward Gershwin," Pershing announced. "Ben, drop the shields, but make sure it's ready to go when we need it."

"You got it," Ben said.

"Magnum, bring your missiles online," Pershing ordered. "Once those probe ships make the short jump from the outer reaches of the system into their positions around Gershwin, things could get dicey fast."

"Roger that," Kim said. "I could use some action."

Pershing had heard soldiers with prebattle jitters. Some joked, others prayed, and some got themselves hyped up as if war were just a game. Kim was feeling the tension, as was everyone else on the little ship's bridge. The professor up in his cabin was the only passenger on the *Echo* who didn't have a clue what was going on.

Pershing knew the stakes, and she felt the pressure not just to win a victory but also to turn the tide of the war. If she could retake the system, shut down the wormhole, and take out the alien ships, the war could be won almost before it even began. And while part of her wanted a protracted conflict where she would be tested and her strategies studied for centuries into the future, another part of her wanted to wipe out the enemy with nothing but three probe ships and an old transport ship.

"Looks like we've been seen," Kim said. "Three of the ships are breaking orbit and heading this way."

"Time until they reach us?" Pershing asked.

"Twelve minutes at this speed," Nance said. "Less if they accelerate."

"Magnum, I want you to target three missiles at each of the ships. Prepare for a rapid fire at maximum range," Pershing ordered. "Ben, stand by on that shield."

Both men acknowledged her order, but Pershing's attention was on the big display screens. The probe ships had just come out of their microjump and were close to the wormhole. Pershing saw several ships react to their sudden presence.

"Now," Pershing said. "Release your probes now."

The commanders of the probe ships had the simplest of orders. They were to jump to their assigned locations and immediately release their total load of probes. From the safe distance, the probe operators on board the ships would send the weaponized weather drones hurtling toward the alien fleet.

"Radar up," Pershing said. "Have they released their payload?"

"Yes," Nance said. "And the third ship just arrived on station."

"Outstanding," Pershing said.

She felt a wave of confident hope, even though the probes were too small and too far away to see. They were a mass of death, a deadly net that would soon descend on the aliens.

"We're in missile range," Nance said.

"Fire!" Pershing ordered.

The missiles jumped from the Kestrel class ship's wings and sped through space. Pershing was forced to divide her attention between the missiles and the probes.

"That's nine," Magnum said.

"Power down the weapons," Pershing ordered. "Raise shields."

There was a moment of silence as they waited to see what would happen in the first real battle with the alien fleet. It was a long pause, pregnant with anticipation. And then the first probes reached the alien ships and the real war began.

Chapter 20

Kim pushed the throttle to its stopper and pointed her toes down on the foot pedals. The ship, which was already speeding toward the alien ships, began to rise. At that same time, explosions popped in the distance. They couldn't be heard, but the flashes were visible.

"The probes are working," Ben said.

Kim could hear the eagerness in his voice. It wasn't excitement regarding the death of the aliens, but the hope that his plan would work. More and more little flashes of light were visible.

"Bring up the radar-enhanced plot," General Pershing ordered.

Kim knew the general was used to having real-time three-dimensional imaging, but they had to settle for a two-dimensional display. Kim saw thousands of little dots hurtling toward the alien armada. One of the red V-shaped icons glowed yellow, then disappeared.

"Got one," Duke Simeon said triumphantly.

Kim knew that one wasn't nearly enough to stop the aliens. There were almost two hundred ships in orbit around the planet. Kim noticed that the three rushing toward the *Echo* were altering course to track Kim's new trajectory. She waited a few seconds until they were fully committed to tracking her, then pushed both her heels back on the pedals, rotating the wing engines. Flying came naturally to Kim, and the differences between space and atmospheric flight didn't pose a challenge to her as it did to most pilots. She knew that just rotating the engines wouldn't get her the desired result. There was no gravity pulling the ship downward and no friction to stop her inertia. That meant she had to angle her wing engines so that the *Echo* made an arcing dive without losing momentum and giving the approaching aliens ships an advantage.

"The missiles are in range," Magnum said. "Going active."

"Look at that," Ben said.

The big display screens were taken up by the radar-enhanced plot, but on Kim's console displays, she quickly flipped through the camera feeds on the *Echo*'s outer hull. In the distance, she saw the alien ships extending their grappling arms. They looked like sea creatures with dozens of tentacles. The arms reached for the missiles as the warheads shot toward them. There were multiple flashes as the missiles exploded, destroying the grappling arms but not causing any damage to the alien ships. Eight of the nine missiles were intercepted, but one got through. It impacted the leading alien ship and blew a gaping hole in the vessel's bulbous front section. Gas and debris flew out of the ship, which immediately lost speed and began to slowly rotate end over end.

"One got through," Duke Simeon crowed.

"The other two are slowing down," Nance said.

"They're afraid," the duke announced.

"Ben, shields up," General Pershing said.

Kim kept on her downward trajectory. The alien ships were still pursuing, but had slowed so that they didn't get any closer. They didn't try to match the *Echo*'s maneuverability either, but they began to slowly turn so that they would be behind the small ship.

"Shield is spinning up," Ben said.

"The alien fleet is moving," Nance said.

A glance at the plot proved the computer expert true. Kim could see that two-thirds of the alien ships were turning and moving toward the far side of the planet. On the plot, the third probe ship sat quietly on the opposite side of Gershwin from the other Royal Imperium ships. The fleet was moving toward them, oblivious to the danger that was being disgorged from the probe command ship's belly.

"They're bunching up," Ben said.

"What choice do they have?" Duke Simeon declared. "If they run, we'll take the system."

"And they haven't seen the other probe ship," General Pershing said.

There were more and more flashes as the red V's indicating the alien ships turned yellow and disappeared from the plot.

"Shield is up," Ben announced.

"Looks like the one we hit is out of commission," Kim said.

The damaged alien vessel continued to spin, the hole in her nose section vented gas and debris that looked almost like a living organism that was bleeding from an open wound.

"Fourteen ships have been destroyed by the probes," Duke Simeon said.

A second later, Kim saw flashes of light from the other side of the planet. The tiny probes impacting the alien ships that thought to take shelter behind the Royal home world couldn't be seen exploding on the plot. Only the alien ships flared a golden yellow before disappearing, but Kim could see the explosions on her console, which still showed the ship's exterior camera feed.

Nothing happened quickly in space, and the aliens didn't pilot their ships in neat formations, but it was clear that panic was setting in. The aliens seemed to be fleeing in all directions.

"We need more firepower," General Pershing said.

"They're down twenty ships," Duke Simeon said.

"That's only a fraction of their forces," Ben replied.

The *Echo* was getting closer to Gershwin's orbital plane, but they were still a solid hour away from the planet itself. They could see some of the red V icons on the display turning orange as they were damaged. The enhanced radar was gaining more and more information on the alien ships. More were destroyed by the probes every second, but the majority was fleeing.

"It looks like someone is getting control of their fleet," Nance said. "All ships are moving into this quadrant."

A square on the upper right side of the plot started blinking green. Kim could see Gershwin in the middle of the display, and the wormhole was slightly lower than the planet and to its left.

"General," Duke Simeon said. "We're being hailed."

"By the aliens?" Pershing asked in surprise.

"Oh no, sorry," the duke said with a chuckle. "It's Commander Varner on the probe ship *Tempest*.

Kim didn't have to look back at the general to know Pershing was frowning, yet she didn't rebuke the royal, who had obviously stumbled in his attempt at running the communications console.

"Put him through," General Pershing said in a slow, deliberate manner.

Modulus Echo, this is the Tempest. We've exhausted our supply of probes and await your command. I repeat, we're out of probes and the enemy is on the run. What are your orders, General?

"Stay on station, Commander Varner," Pershing said. "How many probes do you have still under your command?"

We've got maybe three or four hundred, the officer replied. *But we can't recapture them. The probes will detonate on contact.*

"I'm aware of that fact, Commander. I want your surplus probes positioned in front of the wormhole. Can your operators manage that?"

Affirmative, General. We'll begin re-tasking the drones ASAP.

Kim couldn't count how many alien ships were left. Her best guess was that half of the enemy fleet had either been destroyed or disabled. There was debris all around the planet. Getting to or from Gershwin would be a dangerous task for a long time unless the Royal Imperium had some way of clearing the space of the floating debris.

The other two drone command ships reported in. General Pershing kept them on station, but ordered them to set jump points in case the aliens attacked. The drone ships were defenseless vessels, and there was no need to keep them in harm's way, but as long as the aliens feared them, they were useful where they were.

Suddenly, three more ships appeared on the plot.

"General," Nance said in her customary calm tone. "Three ships just entered the system. "Transponders show them as the *Everest*, the *Andromeda*, and the *Romulus*."

"I guess the queen changed her mind," Kim said.

"Incoming message," Duke Simeon said, trying to sound more professional. "Tight-beam transmission from the *Everest*."

"Put it through," Pershing said.

General Pershing, this is Admiral Dietz on the queen's flagship, the Everest.

There was a slight pause, and Kim realized that something odd was happening. She'd studied the Royal Imperium Fleet in preparation for the Flight Academy test she'd never been able to take. But the queen's flagship was new to her. Obviously, Queen Ultane was taking full advantage of her husband's untimely death, and like any good politician, she was snatching whatever power she could get her hands on.

Can you give us a sitrep, General?

If Pershing was angered by the strange turn of events, she didn't show it. The *Echo* was in no immediate danger, and Kim couldn't resist turning to see the look on the general's face.

Pershing didn't reveal a thing. She had the perfect poker face. It was like a mask, hiding her feelings perfectly.

"We have used the weaponized weather drones to clear the space around Gershwin," Pershing said. "But the aliens are regrouping."

Looks like you've got two bogeys on your tail.

Kim thought she heard an almost taunting tone to the admiral's voice.

"They're pacing us," Pershing replied. "Undoubtedly hoping to push us into a trap."

Stay on course, Admiral Dietz ordered. *The Romulus is moving into an intercept position.*

"Very good," Pershing replied.

The intercept position was actually forty miles above the *Echo* but well within the battle cruiser's laser range. The alien ships didn't deviate and continued pacing the *Echo*. Kim saw that the aliens were almost exactly halfway between the *Echo* and the *Romulus*.

Kim had the alien ships on her display and watched as the *Romulus* opened fire. The Royal Imperium battle cruiser had a variety of weapons, but the laser cannons were by far the deadliest. A missile could have crossed the twenty-mile distance between the ships in a matter of seconds, but the lasers crossed the empty space in less time than it took Kim to blink. Fat flashes of white light lit the alien vessels like lightning. The grappling arms were less effective in blocking the lasers, which were powerful enough to vaporize the spindly articulated arms and blast straight through to the alien ship's hull. The lasers scored long gashes on the alien ships' hulls. They didn't have the kinetic force of missiles or torpedoes, and the lasers didn't cut all the way through the thick hulls of the alien ships, but they turned the outer portion to slag.

"Direct hits," Nance said.

"The aliens are still coming," Ben added.

"No, they're running," General Pershing said. "Kim, take us hard to starboard."

Kim pushed the joystick to the right and angled her foot pedals in opposite directions. The chatter from the bridge of the *Romulus* could be heard over the bridge speakers.

Spin up tubes four through eight. Target the sides where we took out their grappling arms.

Kim watched as four torpedoes were launched. They shot out of the large warship like old-fashioned bullets from the dark muzzle of a gun and were almost immediately lost in the darkness of space.

"Are they following us?" Kim asked.

"Negative," Pershing said.

"Looks like they're breaking for the rest of their fleet," Nance said.

"They won't make it," Magnum said.

The next several seconds seemed to drag by with extraordinary slowness. The alien ships increased speed. Metal was dripping from the sides of their superheated hulls. The *Romulus* was left behind as the alien vessels tried to flee. The *Echo* was gaining distance too, moving back toward the trio of Royal Imperium ships.

Stand by for torpedo impact in three, two, one...

Suddenly, the alien ships exploded. Each blew in two stages as they were hit with the torpedoes. The ships kicked upward and broke in half, then both halves blew up in a spectacular display of fire, sparks, and glistening debris.

"General," Nance said. "The alien ships are leaving the system."

"Track their trajectory," Pershing said. "We've tipped our hand too early."

"We didn't want them to run?" Duke Simeon asked. "We've won."

"We've taken the system, but they still have over a hundred ships," Pershing snapped. Kim could feel the anger radiating from the general and wisely kept her mouth shut. "We can't track them through hyperspace the way they can follow us. That many ships could ravage half the galaxy before we eradicate them."

Kim saw the danger the alien ship posed. They were blinking out of the system as they jumped into hyperspace in twos and threes. Kim could see that they were moving in the same direction, which hopefully meant that they would stay together instead of jumping to a hundred different systems where it would be impossible to stop most of them.

"The only thing in that direction is the Crossini system," Nance said. "And it's three days away at our top speed, General."

"Odds are, they're jumping to a blank point in space," Pershing said. She leaned forward and hit the transmit button on her console. "*Tempest*, this is General Pershing. I want you to jump to the Crossini system and scout the enemy fleet. Do not engage. Just observe and report."

Modulus Echo, this is the Tempest. We are a drone-operating vessel. Spying on the enemy is outside our parameters.

"I'm changing your parameters. Get to Crossini and tell us what you find."

Belay that order, Admiral Dietz said. *All ships, stand down, by order of Queen Ultane.*

"Admiral Dietz, I am the acting commander in—"

I know who you are, General, and while I respect your experience on the command staff, quite frankly I'm surprised that you would even try to command the Fleet. You're not even a naval officer. At any rate, that is all water under the bridge. The queen has named me commander in chief of the Royal Imperium military.

"And so it begins," Duke Simeon said.

There were no more enemy ships in the system, and the *Echo* was far from the debris that might endanger them. Kim swiveled around to look at the general, who showed no sign of emotion.

"Should we do something?" Ben asked.

"Negative," Pershing said. "The queen is most likely on the *Everest*, and this has become a political game now."

"I should say something," Duke Simeon declared.

"No," Pershing told him. "Not yet. Better to see what we're truly up against before we commit ourselves to action."

"But the queen is using Admiral Dietz to stay in control of the Imperium," the duke said in frustration.

"Indeed," Pershing replied. "And the admiral is using her to advance his own career. It's just a game to them, and one they'll play regardless of the consequences to the galaxy."

"And we're just going to let them?" Kim asked.

"For the moment, we wait and see," Pershing said.

I believe we should have a strategy session, Dietz said, his voice loud over the bridge speakers. *I'm assuming you don't have holo-projection capabilities on that little ship, General. Why don't you join us on board the Everest, and we'll make our plans now that we've taken the Celeste system back.*

Kim wanted to point out that the admiral and his trio of battle cruisers hadn't really done much of anything. It was Ben's idea to use the weather drones against the aliens. And as much as Kim resented General Pershing, the woman had devised the strategy that won back the system. But it didn't surprise Kim one bit to see another politician showing up at the end of the battle and taking credit for the victory.

On the other hand, if General Pershing wasn't in charge anymore, Kim hoped that meant they could be discharged from service as well. The *Echo* wasn't a warship, and Ben had given over the plans for the flux shielding to the engineers at Brimex Solar Systems. They should be able to take their amnesty and leave, unless Admiral Dietz decided not to honor the agreement General Pershing had made with them. Kim didn't like to think about that. The last thing she wanted was to be arrested after risking her life and their ship to help the Royal Imperium. Still, they couldn't take any chances, and Kim started typing a message to Nance. Just being close to three Royal Imperium battle cruisers made her nervous enough. And if they had to run, Kim wanted to be ready.

"Of course, Admiral," Pershing replied over the ship's communications system. "We will dock with you momentarily. Kim, take us to the *Everest*."

"You're sure?" Duke Simeon asked.

Pershing nodded. Kim swiveled back around and took control of the *Echo*. The *Everest* was behind them. The large battle cruisers were slow in real space, and Kim was forced to fly back to them.

"We're being directed to wait for a tractor beam," Nance said.

"That means they're taking us inside their ship," Ben said.

Kim heard his nervous tone and knew exactly how he felt. Once they were in the hangar of an Imperium warship, they would be at the mercy of the government who wanted to see them humiliated and destroyed.

"What should we do?" Kim asked.

"Whatever they say," Pershing replied in the same even tone she had given orders with during the battle.

Kim looked over her shoulder at Ben. He didn't look nearly as confident as he usually did, but he nodded. Kim wanted to run. It seemed ludicrous to willingly give control of the *Echo* to anyone else, but they had to trust General Pershing. She had given her word, and they had given theirs. If the Royal Imperium decided to double-cross them, there was really nothing they could do about it.

"Dropping the shield," Ben said.

"Moving into position," Kim added, hoping that they would survive the encounter to fly again.

Chapter 21

"We've retaken the Celeste system," Admiral Dietz said calmly. "The rest is really just a mopping-up exercise. You saw how our weapons made short work of the alien ships."

General Alicia Pershing stood near the admiral and the queen, who were talking in front of a row of holographic images of the commanders on board the other Royal Imperium ships. She could read the tension on their faces. It wasn't that they disbelieved Admiral Dietz, but she knew they were afraid. Six ships couldn't hope to hold the Celeste system if the aliens returned, nor could they hunt down the alien fleet that had fled the system. And a scan of the planet indicated a strong alien presence on Gershwin as well. Duke Simeon watched from the edge of the projection field, too keyed up to stand still.

"I never doubted your prowess in battle," Queen Ultane said. "That's exactly why I chose you to be the new commander in chief of our military forces."

The queen looked directly at Pershing when she made the announcement about Dietz being her pick for CIC, but it wasn't a surprise. The admiral had already let that cat out of the bag. And Pershing didn't find the queen's behavior shocking in the least. She was a petty woman, a narcissist to be sure, perhaps even a sociopath who used people in a vain effort at control. Pershing let the announcement roll right off. It didn't matter who was chosen to command the Royal Imperium military, not when Pershing was destined to be at the center of the conflict with the alien forces. Her belief in herself was all that mattered, and Pershing had no doubts there whatsoever.

"I've sent word to the rest of our forces regarding the best tactics for defeating the aliens," Admiral Dietz continued. "All that remains is for the Royal Imperium to hold fast. We shall be the rock they beat themselves against until they are no more."

If he expected cheers from the other commanders, he was disappointed. They stood at attention, looking nervous. Pershing couldn't tell if they disagreed with Admiral Dietz and were just too scared of the queen to speak up, or if they were just terrified of the aliens.

"Admiral," Pershing said softly. "Your strategy is flawed and doomed to failure."

Dietz whirled around, facing Pershing for the first time. His face was red and she knew he was embarrassed. Perhaps he thought it best if she voiced her concerns in private, but he wanted to be in charge of the Royal Imperium's military and he would have to learn to deal with criticism.

"I beg your pardon," he said angrily. "Do you really think it appropriate to speak to the commander in chief this way?"

"I think we don't have the luxury of foolishness," Pershing said. "Not after Admiral General Volgate destroyed over half the Fleet in his foolish quest to detain a single, nonmilitary vessel."

"You're referring to the fiasco that led to the capture of the royal family," Dietz said. "How could Admiral Volgate know that an alien race from another galaxy was planning an attack?"

"He couldn't," Pershing said. "But we do. And we can't waste time or resources in subduing that alien force. If the enemy armada had dispersed in different directions, I might agree with you. Our capital ships are a match for the aliens in equal numbers."

"Equal numbers?" Queen Ultane said in a haughty tone. "Did the *Romulus* not just destroy two alien ships with almost no effort?"

"You mean the ships that were tracking the *Echo*?" Pershing said. "The two ships that didn't evade or try to fight back? Well, if the encounters with the aliens were all that simple, I would agree with Admiral Dietz, but let's not fool ourselves. The aliens are learning about us, and they have over a hundred ships in their fleet."

"We have even more," Dietz snapped.

"Do we?" Pershing asked. "The Royal Imperium is fractured, and most of the capital ships spread across the galaxy are hesitant to join us here."

"There is no need," Dietz said. "As I stated, I have sent word regarding the best strategy and tactics to deal with the aliens. When they appear in occupied space, we'll destroy them."

Pershing shook her head in pity, and it was the commander of the *Romulus* who came to her aid.

"Admiral," Commander Washburn said. "We can't stop a hundred of their ships, not without considerably more firepower."

"They would be foolish to attack with all their strength at once," Dietz said.

This time Pershing couldn't hold back her laughter. Dietz was a political appointee, not a tactician. He was naive and in way over his head. But Pershing's deriding laughter infuriated him. He stepped close to her and raised his hand to strike her, but Duke Simeon grabbed his wrist.

"Control yourself, Admiral," he snarled.

"It's okay," Pershing said. "I have insulted our commander in chief, and for that I apologize. But surely you don't really believe the alien fleet will just run around the galaxy without any sort of strategic plan, do you? The most important resource in the entire galaxy to the aliens has to be the wormhole. It's the only way back to the galaxy they call home, and the only way for their reinforcements to arrive."

"But they left the system," Dietz said. "We won."

"We struck a blow, no doubt," Pershing agreed. "But the battle for the Celeste system is far from over. I suspect they jumped only a short distance away."

"And how can you know that?" Queen Ultane asked.

"She doesn't know," Dietz said angrily. "Don't forget she ordered the *Tempest* to the Crossini system in hopes of following the aliens."

"I wanted the probe ship to check on the Crossini system because it is the only system along the aliens' last known trajectory. Odds are against them going there for several reasons, not the least of all because it is so far from the wormhole, but we have to know where they are. If I'm wrong about their tactics, and they don't make multiple jumps to evade us, then I want to know what they would do in the Crossini system."

"You can't have it both ways," Dietz said. "You can't fault me for expecting the aliens to attack after you ordered a ship to track them in doing that very thing."

"Arguing isn't helping," Duke Simeon said. "We need a sound plan for holding the Celeste system."

"I have just given it to you," Admiral Dietz proclaimed.

"We can't hold the system with just a handful of ships," Pershing said. "The aliens will return, and when they do, we'll be vastly outnumbered, even with reinforcements."

"Has anyone seen the aliens stand and fight?" Dietz said. "They're cowards. They won't fight us."

"Actually, we have intelligence that shows the aliens capturing our military and civilian vessels," Pershing continued. "I haven't seen them fire conventional weapons, but that doesn't mean they can't. And even if that technology is outside their usual tactics, it won't take them long to capture a military ship and use our own weapons against us."

"They would lose ships in the process," Dietz replied, but Pershing could tell he hadn't considered the prospect of the aliens using human weapons to fight back before.

"Perhaps, but we don't know anything about them," Pershing said. "It's possible that losing ships is acceptable to them."

"They might even be able to replicate our technology," Commander Washburn said. "They have committed forces to Gershwin, and they jumped inside our galaxy. Odds are, they have access to the Nav Net. It wouldn't be hard to find weapons schematics online. For all we know, they're building them as we speak."

"So what are you proposing?" Dietz said. "That we go after them? That's madness. We don't even know where they are?"

"No, we can't pursue them yet," Pershing said. "What we need is intel. I would position the *Everest,* the *Andromeda,* and the *Romulus* around the wormhole to stop more ships from crossing into our galaxy. And I would send a commando team down to the planet to gather intel on the aliens themselves."

"We don't have a Spec Ops team available," Dietz said.

"Actually," Pershing said, "we do. I had them on the *Modulus Echo* but split them up on the probe ships to help weaponize the drones."

"We don't have transports for getting them to the surface of Gershwin," Dietz said, anxious for any reason to reject Pershing's plan.

But the queen knew better. She lowered her head, realizing that her puppet was outmatched. Duke Simeon cleared his throat and stepped forward.

"Actually, we do," he said with a stern gaze. "As the rightful heir to the throne, I suggest that you put General Pershing in charge of the Celeste system's defense, while you and the queen go on a recruiting tour to get our ships back under our command."

Pershing saw several of the other commanders nod in agreement, but they weren't courageous enough to speak their minds. It was just another failing of the Royal Imperium's policy of giving command assignments to politicians who didn't have the first clue about warfare. She knew they would follow her lead because she was competent, which made them think she would keep them alive. But the real problem was their unwillingness to speak out against a superior for fear of losing favor and being passed over for promotions to prominent government posts.

"No," Dietz said. "I am commander in chief of the Royal Imperium military. I'm in charge."

"For now," Duke Simeon said.

"Honestly," Queen Ultane snapped, "there is no difference between the strategies. Surely you all see that."

"I agree," Admiral Dietz replied. "Let's not let petty jealously distract us from our mission to defend the Royal Imperium at all costs. General Pershing, gather your commandos and find a way to get them onto the planet. I will see to the placement of our ships."

He pressed a button and the holograms faded away. Pershing was about to leave the room when Dietz stepped close and blocked her way. She thought he might try to attack her again, but the man was a politician. He had a round belly that hung over the waistband of his uniform and thick jowls that bulged over the collar of his jacket.

"You have one job, General," he whispered.

Pershing held her breath so that she didn't have to smell the hot air that puffed into her face from the admiral's warning.

"Keep that buffoon away from Her Majesty," Dietz continued. "He has no place in the royal dynasty."

"Actually, with the king dead and the crown prince missing —"

"Don't argue with me!" Dietz hissed. "We are no equals, General. And don't ever try to embarrass me again. I'll throw you out of the service. Don't forget that."

"I'll do my best," Pershing said through clenched teeth.

The admiral smiled, gloating over her. But she knew he was just another political hack that would be easily replaced when he inevitably failed. Her duty was to persevere the political merry-go-round and ensure that her troops were not harmed by harebrained strategies. They were depending on her. In fact, the entire galaxy was depending on her. And she couldn't let them down no matter what.

Chapter 22

"I don't like it," Kim said.

Ben wasn't surprised, and he didn't disagree. Being on the Imperium ship was unpleasant. But if they'd wanted to take the little crew captive, they could have done it already.

"Let's just try to stay calm," Ben said.

The bridge was more tense than it had been with the aliens chasing them or in the battle at the Yelsin system.

"I am calm," Kim insisted. "But I don't have to like it. They could surround us at any second, and even if I could get off this flying rat trap, they could catch us with their tractor beams."

"It isn't going to come to that," Ben said.

"If it does," Magnum spoke up, "we'll need a distraction."

"What would happen if you spun up the flux shield while we're still on the *Everest*?" Kim asked.

"We would cause a lot of damage," Ben said. "And get killed in the process."

"Better dead than in an Imperium prison where they torture you for no reason," Kim said.

"Guys, I've got a message from Tolliver," Nance said.

Ben was thankful for the distraction, however small. None of them had left their stations on the bridge since the *Echo* had been taken aboard the *Everest*. They watched the technicians working in the hangar bay. There were only a few, and they all looked bored. If they were putting on a show to lull the crew of the *Echo* into believing they weren't being watched, they were fantastic actors.

The hangar was a massive space inside the lower section of the *Everest*, and there were at least twenty fast-attack fighters lined up neatly on launching racks. Ben guessed that the entire squadron could be launched before the flux shield could spin up to full power. Even if they could get off the *Everest* and evade the tractor beam and heavy weapons, they couldn't outrun a squad of fast-attack ships. Like it or not, they were helpless to resist the Royal Imperium forces. They had no choice but to trust General Pershing.

"Great," Ben said to Nance. "Can you put it on the big screen?"

Nance rolled her eyes and hit a few buttons on her console. Tolliver's face appeared on the big forward displays. He smiled and began talking, his voice booming from the bridge speakers.

"Hello, all. I hope this finds you well," Tolliver said. "I have good news. The Confederate forces are interested in the general's offer. They're a little hesitant, though, as you might suspect. None of the Imperium forces searching for them or guarding their worlds have shown any signs of standing down. So to test the offer, the ground forces from Gemli in the Lebbanon system have volunteered for a trial run, so to speak. They have weapons and will fight for General Pershing provided she sends a transport to pick them up. That's two hundred soldiers, so you'll need something bigger than the *Echo*. Still, it's a start. The commander's name is Lawrence, and they have orders to report in on the conditions. If things go well, I'm sure the other worlds will volunteer as well.

I hope this helps. It may not be as much help as she needs right off the bat, but it's more than nothing. Let me know if I can do anything else. I suppose you know the queen named a new commander in chief, an admiral named Arnold Dietz. I'm not sure what that means for the four of you, but I'm hoping it's all good. Stay safe out there. Send word when you get this."

The image of Tolliver froze, and the bridge fell silent. Ben was about to speak when the doors on the hangar slid open and General Pershing came walking toward them. Ben couldn't help but feel relieved. She wasn't surrounded by guards or leading a platoon of soldiers to arrest them. Instead, she and Duke Simeon came into the hangar alone and crossed the cavernous space toward the *Echo*.

"Looks like it's time to go," Ben said.

"It's about time," Kim said.

"All systems are ready," Nance said.

"Once the general and Duke Simeon are on board, notify the *Everest*," Ben said. "They may have procedures for leaving the hangar."

"Or maybe they never want us to leave again," Kim said, but she gave Ben a wink.

The large rear hatch was open, and Ben watched the general and the duke enter. The plastic sheeting that was sometimes used to seal off the ship had been pulled down, and there was nothing blocking Ben's view over the railing of the atrium.

"They're on board," Ben said, walking back to the bridge. "Let's seal the cargo hatch, and I'll get the artificial gravity running."

"What's our status?" General Pershing asked as soon as her head cleared the top of the stairs.

"I'm ready," Kim said.

"All systems are green, and the *Everest* has been alerted," Nance added.

"The cargo hatch is closed," Magnum said.

"And the artificial gravity is up," Ben said. "We're ready to go."

"Then go," Pershing said. "We've wasted enough time here."

The *Modulus Echo* left the Royal Imperium battle cruiser under its own power. The Kestrel class ship was old, but she was graceful. Kim flew the *Echo* out of the *Everest*'s hangar without a hitch and quickly outpaced the big capital ship.

"Looks like everyone is headed for orbit," Kim said. "Is that where you want us?"

"Actually," Pershing said, "we need to dock with the drone operators and pick up Alpha team. We've been cleared to begin reconnaissance of the aliens on the surface of the planet."

"That might be a problem," Nance said. "The entire world is surrounded by debris. It's going to be like flying through an asteroid field just to reach the upper atmosphere."

"I love a challenge," Kim said.

"What about our shield?" Pershing asked. "Won't it be strong enough to get us through?"

"If we can avoid enough debris, it should," Ben said. "The movement of the gravity field was designed to cast off lasers or missiles, but too much matter will only get caught in the flow and overload the system."

"We're getting people down to the planet one way or another," Pershing said. "And the *Echo* is the only ship capable of atmospheric flight, so that means we're getting through the debris field. Nance, plot a course to the drone ships. Ben, go get Professor Jones and let's put a plan together."

"Why's it so important?" Kim asked. "There's not a lot of people on Gershwin. And if we can't get down to them, then surely they can't come up to attack us."

"I'm not worried about an attack from the aliens on the planet," Pershing said. "But I'm desperate for intel on who they are and what they want. I have a feeling that the fleet didn't run far. They'll be back soon to regain control of this system."

"And Admiral Dietz has no clue what he's doing," Duke Simeon said.

"If they come back," Ben said, standing up from his console on the bridge, "we won't be able to stop them, will we?"

"Even with the Imperium warships?" Kim asked.

"We've been lucky so far," Pershing said. "Surprise and desperate measures have won the minor skirmishes we've fought so far. But the aliens have to be learning. And they know the only way home is through the wormhole. I suspect they'll adapt to our tactics, perhaps even build weapons of their own. Either way, until we can get a lot more ships of our own in the system, we're vulnerable."

Ben left the bridge and headed to the upper deck, where Professor Jones had hidden away in his quarters while he worked tirelessly to find a way to close the wormhole. It seemed like at every turn, no matter how hard Ben tried, things just got worse, not better. They were successful in chasing the alien fleet out of the Celeste system. But although Ben's plan to use the weather drones against the aliens had been a success, and they had destroyed dozens of the enemy vessels, they had no confidence that the aliens wouldn't return in overwhelming force. Not to mention that in the process, they had flooded the space around the system's only inhabitable planet with so much debris that getting to it would put them right back in danger.

At the professor's door, which was open, Ben could see that every flat surface, including most of the deck, was covered with data. There were personal data pads, e-book readers, computation displays, and even old-fashioned paper, all covered with complex mathematical formulas and information on gravity from research done all across the galaxy.

The professor himself looked harried. His clothes were wrinkled and his hair was askew, but his eye twinkled. It was clear to Ben that the professor was doing exactly what he wanted to do, which was dive deep into the mystery of gravity.

"You looked concerned," Professor Jones said as Ben approached his quarters.

"I am," Ben said. "We have a new problem."

"They are stacking up, eh?"

"It's like they're drawn to me," Ben said. "Pull up the bow external camera feed."

The professor had to search a little to find the display controls. The old ship had wall-mounted displays that still worked in most of the passenger cabins. He toggled through a few of the exterior camera feeds and stopped on a view of Gershwin. They were far enough away that the planet looked smaller than a marble, but it was well lit by the system star. The normal blues and greens, laced with traces of white clouds, were muted, and light reflected off the thousands of bits of floating debris that were spinning around the planet.

"What has happened?" Professor Jones said.

"Well, the good news is our plan to use the weather drones against the aliens worked."

"It worked too well, I see," the professor said. "That is the debris from the battle."

He pointed to what appeared to be a cloud around the marble-sized world.

"I don't know how many ships they lost, but at least twenty percent of their fleet," Ben said. "Add that to the thousands of weather drones we launched against them, some of which haven't detonated yet, and we have basically a very crowded minefield."

"True," Professor Jones said. "But most of the debris is caught in the planet's gravity. In time, it will condense down and form a beautiful ring."

"How long with that take?" Ben asked.

"Only a few decades," Professor Jones said.

"That doesn't help us now," Ben said.

"Do we need to go to the planet?"

"Yes," Ben said. "Before the aliens come back."

"Then we do have a problem," the professor said.

"Think we can find a way through the debris?"

"Anything is possible. But let me warn you, Ben. Once we commit, there is no turning back."

"What do you mean?"

"I mean that field is in constant motion," the professor warned. "If we get halfway through and decide it's too dangerous, we can't just change our mind. There is no turning back."

Chapter 23

Grubat watched as the fire in the sky continued. It was strange, and something he had not witnessed before in his time on the planet. The day had begun normally enough. The chieftain was preparing his Yarls for a trek into the forests and mountains around Alpha Vistol's settlement. Suddenly, a few hours before the evening meal, the sky was filled with what looked like fiery comets. Most streaked across the sky, spewing dark smoke, but burning up completely before reaching the ground. As evening approached, the fire around the objects became more visible, but the firestorm continued seemingly without any decrease in the number of objects streaking across the heavens.

It came as no surprise when Alpha Vistol summoned Grubat to the high chamber. Unlike most Krah, even the decorated warlords like Racca, alphas had entire ships to themselves. They were grand strategists with immense wealth, more powerful than even the high priests. In space, they commanded super ships that were actually long trains of different ships linked together. Among the many linked vessels, the young were raised before being assigned to a caste and sent away to learn their craft. At the front was the alphas' personal quarters, a single ship that was the sole domain of the alphas, called the high chamber. To be invited inside was a great honor, and since landing on New Krah, Alpha Vistol had used his ship as the official headquarters for the invasion.

From his ship, Alpha Vistol could command not just the ground forces but also the ships in orbit. Grubat had heard that

Alpha Vistol had approved the sending of explorer ships to several of the closest systems. Once they returned, a grand strategy would be devised to lay claim to the new systems and the wealth of technology from each. It was an effort to keep the Krah from squabbling with each other over who had the right to pillage the human settlements. Yet it seemed that something strange had happened above them. Something that had surely affected the ships in orbit. Grubat couldn't say for certain how many Krah vessels had come through the portal, but there were more than he had ever seen in one system before.

At the entrance to Alpha Vistol's ship, two powerful-looking Yarls stood guard. Their presence was symbolic, meant to send a message to anyone looking to disturb the alpha.

"I have been summoned," Grubat said as he approached.

"Alpha Vistol awaits you inside, Chieftain," one of the Yarls said.

Grubat nodded. He was their superior, but his authority had been diminished to the crew of just one ship. As soon as Yarl Cherbak was well enough, he would take them into space to join the conquest, while Grubat led a tiny group of warriors to explore the new world. It would have been horribly shameful to have lost so much of his wealth and following if Grubat hadn't become so enthralled with the planet. He no longer cared for riches or status. To return to a crowded spaceship would be torture in his mind. He would gladly sacrifice his station among his people for the chance to live the rest of his life on New Krah.

Walking into the alpha's ship was both exciting and stifling. The ship smelled of cleaning supplies and recycled air. It was completely different from the wide-open spaces outside the ship. It seemed small and cramped somehow, even though it was the exclusive home of just one person. The corridor led straight back to what was essentially a throne room—a large, empty space with only a single ornate chair where Alpha Vistol sat. From that seat, which could rotate, he could pilot his vessel and the entire train of other ships that were tethered to his. But with the ship separated from the others and no longer flying, the room had become a fancy audience chamber from which the alpha commanded the Krah.

Grubat dropped to one knee and bowed his head.

"You summoned me?"

"Yes," Alpha Vistol said. "You have seen the fiery signs in the sky above?"

"I have."

"What are the people saying it is?"

"No one knows," Grubat said. "Some think perhaps it is from a geologic event spewing fiery projectiles."

"That is incorrect," Alpha Vistol said. "What do you think it could be?"

"The only thing that makes sense is a meteor shower, but that cannot be."

"Because?"

"Because our ships would be in danger," Grubat said. "And they would have spotted the meteors approaching long before they reached the atmosphere."

"Astute," Alpha Vistol said. "And yet the truth is even more unbelievable."

"My lord," Grubat said. "I do not understand."

"Our ships were attacked," the alpha explained. "Many were lost. What you see are the remnants of over forty Krah ships that were destroyed by the hue-mans."

"That cannot be," Grubat said softly.

Yet he knew it to be true, not just from the look on the alpha's face but also from the distress he sensed radiating from his leader and the fact that the humans were more resourceful than any race the Krah had ever encountered.

"Did they bring a vast army?" Grubat asked.

"No," Alpha Vistol said. "In fact, only a few ships challenged our fleet. Yet they released thousands of smaller craft, ships no larger than a trooper's kit of personal belongings."

"Thousands?" Grubat asked.

"It is so. The warlords sent word before being forced out of the system."

"What did the small vessels do?"

"Just what your Thralldom encountered," Alpha Vistol said. "The small vessels flew with reckless abandon straight into our ships. There were so many they could not all be stopped, and each one was rigged to explode on contact. More than half of the fleet took damage, and many were lost."

"What incredible waste," Grubat said. "I can scarcely believe it."

"Yes, it is unfathomable," Alpha Vistol said. "What is more, we are now cut off from the fleet and from the portal that links to our own galaxy."

"We must retake the system," Grubat said. "We have underestimated the humans for too long."

"Indeed," Alpha Vistol said. "Which is why we must begin taking defensive measures."

"You think the humans will come here?" Grubat asked.

"Sooner or later, it is inevitable," Alpha Vistol said. "I have sent word to your camp to move all their resources here. As the ranking warrior on the planet, you shall be in charge of the defenses, reporting directly to me."

"As you wish, my lord," Grubat said.

"The fleet hasn't gone far and will return soon. I will coordinate their efforts as best I can, but for now, we are blind to what the hue-mans are doing in the system. I want defensive works built around this settlement. We must protect the young at all costs."

Grubat knew that Alpha Vistol was right. After centuries of controlled procreation to keep from overburdening the Krah's spacefaring vessels and outposts, the need for more warriors and workers was greater than ever. With the new planet to call home, they could grow their numbers exponentially. And if what Trooper Le Croix claimed about the galaxy was true, they could multiply throughout the new galaxy for centuries without worrying about running out of resources.

"I will see to it," Grubat said.

"See that you do. Every warrior is yours to command," Alpha Vistol said. "I only ask that you share your plans with me."

"Of course, my lord."

"And keep Trooper Le Croix close. He may be of great help to us in understanding our new enemy."

"He will be," Grubat said, "or he will die."

"It is the way," Alpha Vistol said. "You are dismissed."

Grubat bowed again, then left the ship. It felt good to be outside again. Night had fallen, and from their elevated position, he could see out over the forest. The light from the fragments of the lost ships in space above them lit the night with a spooky, wavering glow.

Grubat returned to where his small group of warriors had been making preparations to be away from the settlement for several days. There was meat roasting over a firepit. He heard muted voices and knew exactly what they were all discussing. Telling them of the human victory would be difficult, but they had to know the truth. The warriors were strong, but defeat was practically unknown to the Krah.

He supposed they would have to get used to the idea that the humans presented a danger greater than they had ever faced. Grubat knew from speaking to Trooper Le Croix and studying the human star map that if they joined together, they could easily defeat the Krah. Time was the key to true victory in the new galaxy. If the Krah could hold the system, and increase their numbers, they could eventually match the humans. A careful expansion would be the best strategy. The Krah would chafe at the very idea of limited raids, but they needed time, and as long as the humans didn't consider them much of a threat, it was possible that they could hold the system long enough to build their forces.

As he approached the fire where the meat was roasting and filling the air with a rich aroma, he waited for a few seconds, letting his Yarls and troopers gather in close.

"I have news," he told them. "But first, send someone to find Trooper Le Croix."

Chapter 24

Kim used the *Echo*'s thrusters to position the ship next to the *Tempest*. It was the last of the three drone operator vessels they were docking with. Most of the commandos were already on board and looking at their equipment under the stern gaze of Staff Sergeant Visher.

The *Tempest* extended a docking tube that suctioned onto the side of the *Echo*, covering the air lock and making a secure tunnel for the last of the soldiers to pass through.

"The *Tempest* is extending the docking tube," Nance said. "Stand by."

"The first time was fun, but now I'm just bored," Kim said.

She was watching her monitors closely to make sure nothing compromised the procedure. If they were moved away from the *Tempest* by some outside force, the docking tube would tear and the soldiers attempting to cross from one ship to the other would die. And if something pushed them into the larger drone ship, the *Echo* would be damaged, perhaps even destroyed. She portrayed cool confidence, but inwardly she was hypervigilant.

"Corporal Dial and Private Felix are crossing over," Duke Simeon announced from the comms station.

"Air lock is cycling," Nance said.

It was a neat operation. The *Echo* wasn't a military ship, yet they were carrying out their tasks with precision and efficiency. That made Kim proud. Over the ship's com-link, Magnum reported from the cargo hold.

"They're on board," he said.

"Air lock is sealed," Nance said. "The *Tempest* can retract the boarding tube."

"Roger that," Duke Simeon said. "I'll tell them."

Kim knew that Nance could have handled the communications with the *Tempest*, but the duke was eager to play a role in the handling of the ship. She wasn't sure if he was learning anything or just pretending. Most children pretended to be members of the royal family, so maybe the duke pretended to be an officer on a fighting ship. Kim couldn't be sure, and the *Echo* wasn't like a battle cruiser. The Kestrel class vessel was built to operate with a crew, or under the right conditions, a single person. Nance had further enhanced that ability by linking all the computer systems together.

"We're clear," Nance said.

"Great," Kim said. "I'm heading toward Gershwin, but I'll find a spot to wait for the general before entering the debris cloud."

Kim swiveled the *Echo* around using her thrusters, then engaged the main drive as she flew away from the drone ship. It was like a huge container in space, which was essentially what it was. There were people on board, over a hundred members of the crew that consisted mostly of the drone operators who controlled the small unmanned craft via remote control. But the ships were built to carry and store thousands of drones. There was nothing sleek or graceful about them. The *Echo*, on the other hand, was both classic and fierce at the same time, with long sloping wings that made her look like a bird of prey.

They flew without incident to a point in space where Nance had discovered the least amount of debris. From the ship's external cameras, it looked like a trash field. Most of it was smaller than a dinner plate, but there was so much of it that it turned into a cloud.

General Pershing, who had been giving her commandos instructions, finally returned to the bridge and took her seat at the navigation console. Ben and the professor weren't far behind.

"Good, you haven't started yet," Ben said.

"We were waiting for you," General Pershing said. "What's your recommendation?"

"That depends on Kim," Ben said.

"Me?" Kim replied in surprise.

"Yes," Ben said. "Because we can't use the flux shield."

"And why not?" General Pershing asked.

Ben stepped back, and Professor Jones cleared his throat before speaking.

"Are you familiar with the old sport of baseball?" he asked. "It's a children's game now, but in the distant past, it was played professionally by adults."

"That's the game where one person throws a ball and the other hits it with a stick," Pershing said.

"Exactly. Unfortunately, it illustrates our dilemma perfectly," the professor explained. "As you know, the shield around the *Echo* is not static. Think of it like a fan. When something hits it, be it a missile or a floating piece of space junk, it doesn't merely bounce off. The motion of the gravity stream spins it away with much greater force, just like a ball being struck by a bat."

"And that's a problem because?" Pershing said.

"Because there's so much debris, and it's all in motion. If we fly in and start shooting the junk around, the entire cloud could become unnavigable," Ben explained.

"Each piece of junk that came in contact with the shield would be hurled at much greater speed and force," Professor Jones added. "Those pieces would impact others, sending them colliding with still more, until the entire cloud was out of control."

"But wouldn't the shield protect us?" Pershing asked.

"Perhaps," Ben said. "But it would be like getting shot a thousand times at once. I can't promise the shield would hold up to that type of bombardment."

"And setting off that kind of motion in the debris cloud would make it too dangerous to leave the planet if we succeeded in getting through," Professor Jones continued. "We couldn't leave again, and no help could get to us."

"That's unacceptable," Pershing said.

"Precisely, which leaves us with two options. The first is the safest, but takes the most time. I propose the battle cruisers move in close and use their tractor beams to pull the debris away from the planet."

"We don't have to move all the debris," Ben said. "Just enough to open a corridor that ships could safely pass through."

"How long would that take?" Pershing asked.

"Days," Professor Jones said. "Maybe weeks. It depends on how efficient the crews of the battle cruisers are."

"What's the other option?" Duke Simeon asked.

"Kim could try to fly through the cloud without shields," Ben said. "I've charted a course based on what the radar was able to pick up. It's dangerous, but it should be possible. She's a hell of a pilot."

"Ah, thanks," Kim said.

Pershing leaned back in her chair, pressing her fingertips from one hand onto the fingertips of the other.

"Either way," Ben continued, "the battle cruisers could work to clear the field."

"Time is the one variable we cannot count on," Pershing said. "We have to get to the planet."

"Looks like your lives are all in my capable hands," Kim said jokingly. She held her hands up and made them shake as if she were unsteady.

"This isn't a laughing matter," Pershing said.

"She can do it," Ben urged. "It's risky, but I trust her."

"Me too," Nance said without a second's hesitation.

"No risk, no reward," Magnum said.

"Wait a second," Duke Simeon said, pointing at the bridge display. "You aren't seriously suggesting that we fly into all of that with no shields."

"I am," Ben said.

"That's suicide," he snapped. "And don't forget, you have the future king on board your ship. Let someone else go."

"That's precisely the point," Pershing replied. "We're the only hybrid ship available. No one else can get the commandos down to the surface."

"So they wait," Simeon said. "What good is one squad going to do down there anyway?"

"The aliens aren't even on the same continent as the royal residence," Nance said. "From what we can tell, they aren't using aircraft to move across the surface."

"We aren't going to protect the people down there," Pershing said. "The goal of the insertion team is to capture some of the aliens."

Kim felt a stab of terror.

"Capture them?" Kim said. "As in bring them on this ship?"

"Yes," Pershing said.

"That is aggressive," Ben said. "Why?"

"If any of you can think of a better way to study our enemy, I'm open to suggestions," Pershing said.

"If we could hack into their computer systems," Nance volunteered, "we could mine a ton of data."

"Assuming they use computers the way we do," Pershing responded. "And how long would that take?"

"Too long," Ben replied quietly.

"Look, my people will observe and report, but there's only so much we can learn that way," Pershing said. "What we need is full interrogation of the enemy. I have to know how they think, what they value, and why they're here. Anything short of that will leave us vulnerable."

"So you're going to torture them?" Kim said, an angry tremble in her voice.

"Torture is a last resort," Pershing said.

"But it's not off the table," Ben replied.

"Anything that can get us closer to total victory is on the table," Pershing replied. "None of you hesitated to destroy the alien ships that are now scattered between us and Gershwin.

How many aliens died in that attack? We don't know because we simply know nothing about them other than they aggressively hunt any ship that comes within range. We have to know more. How adaptable are they? Why don't they have weapons on their ships? How do they think? Have they all come through the wormhole, or are there millions more that could come pouring into our galaxy at any moment?"

Kim didn't know what to say. She didn't like the idea of capturing an alien. Sure, she wanted to win the war, if that's even what it was. She wanted to be through, to have the Royal Imperium personnel off the *Echo* and the freedom to live their lives again. But if she was being honest with herself, she didn't want any part in handing someone, even an alien, over to the Royal Imperium to be interrogated. There were rumors of torture that haunted her dreams. It was the reason they had resorted to using the gravity rocket against the Royal Imperium Fleet in the first place. Better to die than to be kept alive in a torture chamber to be cut and sliced and tormented for years just to please the royal family.

"I don't like it," Kim said.

"It doesn't matter what you like or dislike," General Pershing said. "Our deal hinges on the fact that until this war is over, you will follow my orders. We get our people safely down onto the planet, and they'll do the rest."

"Can you do it, Kim?" Ben asked.

"What? Fly through the debris cloud?" Kim replied. "You know I can."

"Then make your preparations. I want us in atmo as soon as possible."

Kim wanted to refuse, but that would put them right back where they started—in danger of the Royal Imperium torturers. Even if they could manage to kill the general, there was no way they could take out an entire squad of Special Forces commandos who were armed to teeth. They could die trying, but that alternative didn't appeal to Kim either. The only option that gave them hope was following the general's orders.

"I guess it's their fault for coming here in the first place," Kim said as she settled into her pilot's seat. "Ben, would you be a doll and get my helmet?"

"Sure," Ben said.

"We all need emergency space suits on," Pershing said.

"Suit up and strap in," Kim said with a chuckle. "This is going to be fun."

Fifteen minutes later, they were ready. The commandos were strapped into the emergency jump seats, which were really just a metal bench that folded out from the wall of the cargo bay, with safety netting and harness straps. Everyone but the professor was on the bridge, and they all had space suits on with helmets. Working the ship's controls in thick boots and gloves wasn't easy. Kim preferred the feel of the joystick in her bare hand, but that couldn't be helped.

"Everyone is ready," General Pershing said. "You may proceed."

"Here we go," Kim said as she eased the main drive throttle forward and flexed her feet up and down on the wing control pedals.

She had positioned six display screens around her monitor, the most her console would support. They were like windows, each with a camera feed from the hull's exterior. Three showed the space in front and to either side of the ship. The fourth monitor, which was positioned on an articulating arm above the others, showed the space above the *Echo*. The fifth and sixth monitors showed feeds from below and behind the spacecraft.

The cloud of debris took focus the closer they flew. Kim could see areas littered with small pieces of debris no bigger than her fist, and many were as small as credit markers. Between the clouds were larger portions of the destroyed spaceships and drones. A grappling arm that looked more like a snake than part of a spaceship. A portion of a hull that had once been part of another ship that was captured, then converted to the alien vessel that had snatched it from its original owner.

To Kim, it seemed like the vast salvage fields of her home world of Torrent Four had suddenly been transported to the space around the pristine world of Gershwin. All her life, she'd heard stories about the royal planet—the wide-open spaces untouched by human civilization, the air and water so clean that no filtration was needed. Yet, to Kim, it all seemed tainted, first by the greed and hypocrisy of the royal family, then by the aliens and their ruined starships that littered the space around Gershwin.

Kim spotted the body of one of the aliens floating through space as the *Echo* dodged a jumble of wrecked components tumbling along together.

"Take a look at that," Kim said, her voice tense with the stress of dodging the floating junk all around them.

She was doing her best to follow the yellow line on her forward monitor. It was the route Ben had plotted through the debris field, but it wasn't perfect. There were large pieces of space junk that would destroy the *Echo* floating into their path on a regular basis that required Kim to keep the ship moving. She used her feet to rotate the Kestrel class vessel, which spiraled around the debris as much as possible, diving up and down and to either side whenever necessary.

"Is that a body?" Ben asked.

"Looks like it," Duke Simeon said. "But no legs."

"Can we get it on board?" Pershing asked.

"We don't have a tractor beam," Ben replied. "Someone would have to go out and get it. There just isn't time. It's too dangerous for the *Echo* to stay in place."

"Zooming in to get a better look," Nance said.

"Just don't adjust my cameras," Kim said. "I need them just like they are."

"Roger that," Ben said. "Your six cameras are off-limits."

"It looks humanoid," Duke Simeon said.

"Are those tentacles growing out of its head?" Nance asked.

It was hard for Kim not to look at the alien, but she had to keep scanning her dedicated camera feeds. Staying on the golden line that was superimposed on her main display wasn't easy, and dodging the debris made it even more challenging.

Occasionally, they were forced to fly through some of the swirling clouds of dust and tiny particulates. It was eerie hearing the metal hit or scrape across the ship's hull. Sweat had formed on Kim's forehead, and she worried that it might cause her emergency helmet to fog up, but there was nothing she could about it. She couldn't even risk letting go of the controls to take it off. If it began to impair her vision, she would have to ask Ben to help her with it.

"Two arms," Ben said. "The proportions make it look as if it had legs of some sort."

"But they weren't blown off," Nance said. "The stumps look scarred, but surgically corrected."

"Strange," Pershing said.

Soon the floating body was out of sight. Gershwin was looming larger in her main display, but the plot passed through a dense cloud of debris.

"Ben, are you sure about your plot?" Kim asked.

"It's the safest way," he replied.

"She's headed straight for a cloud of debris," Pershing said. "Shouldn't we go around?"

"There are some big chunks of metal moving pretty fast around the edges of that cloud," Ben said. "I think the safest way is through it."

"Can the ship handle it?" Nance asked.

"She'll be fine," Ben replied.

"What if there's something inside the cloud?" Kim asked. "We won't see it until it's too late."

"You can risk going around," Ben said. "But that cloud is the last barrier between us and the planet. I'm telling you it's safe. You can fly right through it."

"That's good enough for me," Kim said.

"This is madness," Duke Simeon complained. "You lot take too many risks."

Kim didn't disagree. She felt they had been lucky in the past and couldn't help but worry that their luck might run out. Still, she knew Ben would never do anything to put them in unnecessary danger. And he loved the *Echo* more than just about anything or anyone else. But he could be wrong, and if he was, they would all die.

After saying a silent prayer that all would be well, Kim pressed the throttle forward and flew into the cloud. When she was a child, there were times when rain fell as frozen slivers of ice. She remembered one instance when she took shelter in an ancient work vehicle with a small, enclosed cab. The roof had been metal, covered in rust that had deteriorated the top of the cab until it was dangerously thin. The ice shards had tinkled against it, making a strange sound that was frightening and yet somehow peaceful.

The metal debris in the cloud above Gershwin was the same. There was something peaceful about the sound of debris, much of it barely larger than dust shards, as the ship flew through it. It made a brushing and tinkling sound as it hit the hull and blocked the camera feeds. Kim couldn't see anything. Even the light reflecting off Gershwin wasn't penetrating the cloud.

When something hit hard enough to send a booming echo through the ship, they all ducked instinctively. It was large and Kim hadn't tried to dodge it because she didn't see it coming.

"What was that?" Duke Simeon asked.

"Something hit us," Kim replied.

"Hull's intact," Ben said. "Looks like we lost some of the heat shielding on the port wing."

"Let's hope there's nothing else in this cloud that—"

General Pershing abruptly stopped speaking as the ship broke through the cloud and Gershwin filled the bridge display screen.

"We made it!" Kim said.

They were right on the meridian between day and night. One side of the planet was bright, the other was dark, but everywhere Kim looked were flaming chunks of debris raining downward.

"Just get us on the ground," Pershing said. "Then we can relax."

"Is that heat shielding going to be a problem?" Duke Simeon asked.

"The *Echo* used old-fashioned ceramic plates to shield her from the heat of the atmosphere," Ben said. "I think we'll be okay if Kim makes an inverted entry."

"A what?" the duke asked.

"We're going in upside down," Pershing said. "Do it."

"Yes, ma'am," Kim said, pressing one foot pedal all the way forward, and the other all the way back. The planet spun around in their display, and Kim let the planet's gravity take hold.

The ship shook hard for a few seconds, then smoke began to interfere with the camera feeds. A dull roar sounded from outside the ship.

"What's happening?" Duke Simeon cried.

"Gershwin has a thick upper atmosphere," Ben said. "We'll get through it."

"Without bursting into flames, I hope," Nance said.

Kim almost laughed out loud. Nance never sounded worried or scared, even when she was voicing her actual fears. Glancing at the technical readouts, Kim watched as the altimeter raced lower and lower. An alarm began to sound, and Kim didn't have to look to know it was a heat warning.

"Maybe we should start correcting our descent," Pershing said.

"Already on it," Kim said.

She used the old-fashioned attitude gauge as she slowly turned the ship over.

"Twenty-five thousand feet and falling," Nance said.

"Heat shield is holding steady," Ben added.

Suddenly, the smoke cleared, and Kim could see that they were on the night side of the planet and nearly level with the ground far below. She evened up the wing engines, which played a much bigger part in atmospheric flight than they did in space. Slowly, she fed the engines power, turning their controlled fall into enough thrust to create lift on the old ship.

"I have control," Kim said. "Where should we land?"

"I've got an idea," Pershing said. "Head for these mountains."

An icon came up on Kim's screen, and she turned the ship to bring them in line with the targeted landing zone.

"Heat's rising on the port wing engine," Nance said.

"Must have taken some damage to the cooling system when we took that hit," Ben said. "I can fix it when we're on the ground."

"I need that engine to make a safe landing," Kim said. "I don't want to take any chances in the dark."

"She'll hold," Ben said.

"We're four thousand miles from the landing zone," Nance said. "Altitude is eighteen thousand feet."

"Take us in low and quiet," Pershing said. "Let's make sure our running lights are off."

"Roger that," Nance said. "All exterior lighting is off."

"Can they pick up our radar?" Magnum asked.

"We can't risk flying in the dark without it," Kim replied. "How tall are those mountains?"

"The tallest is fourteen thousand, eight hundred and two feet," Nance said.

"Then I'm holding at fifteen thousand," Kim said. "Once we reach the landing zone, I'll do a Kestrel descent."

"A what?" Pershing asked.

"It's a vertical landing technique," Ben explained. "Kestrel class ships can hover using the three engines, but an emergency descent involves thrusters and repulsor power only. It's quieter."

"And more dangerous," Nance asked.

"As long as the conditions are right, we should be fine," Kim said. "If not, we'll do a traditional landing with the engines."

"Too many chances," Duke Simeon said.

"I live for the pressure," Kim said. "Right on the edge of out of control."

"Is she insane?" the royal asked.

"I'd say we all are," Ben replied.

"Time to our landing zone?" Pershing asked.

"Four hours at this rate," Nance said. "We should be on the ground just before sunrise."

"That's perfect," the general replied. "But let's not take any unnecessary chances. Can we dial back the power on the port engine?"

"Sure," Kim said, making an adjustment on her controls.

"Ben, keep an eye on that heat meter," Pershing warned. "Get us safely on the ground within striking distance of the aliens. That's all I ask."

"Oh, she's asking now," Kim said in a snarky tone.

"For once we're all in agreement," Ben said. "Good job getting us through the debris cloud, by the way."

"Thanks, I never had a doubt in my mind," Kim said.

"For the record," Ben replied, "neither did I."

Chapter 25

The engine heat held steady, and Ben felt relieved when Kim descended into the mountains. They took their time finding a clearing in a deep valley. A river flowed from high up in the mountains and rushed through the valley, but a meadow with no trees made a perfect landing spot.

As soon as the *Echo* touched the ground, the commandos jogged out and disappeared in the darkness. Ben had work to do to repair the damage on the port wing, but he decided to wait until dawn.

"What's our timeline?" Pershing asked as the ramp rose back into place.

"What are you wanting us to do?" Ben replied.

"Ideally, we get airborne until Alpha team had completed their objective," she explained. "We can spy from the stratosphere."

"I can't promise anything," Ben said. "I'll have to see how much damage we sustained coming down."

"Just don't take too long," she warned. "If the Spec Ops team gets lucky, they could be back very soon."

"I'll get to work as soon as there's enough light to see," Ben said.

"In the meantime, I'll be asleep in my cabin," Kim said.

"Magnum, can you give me a hand?" Ben asked.

"Sure," he replied.

"I'll stay on the bridge," Nance said. "I'm running systems diagnostics now. They'll take a couple of hours to complete."

"I guess that leaves kitchen duty to me," Duke Simeon said.

"I'll be monitoring comms in case Alpha team radios in," Pershing said. "Then I want someone up the mountain on overwatch. We need to keep an eye out for any sign of the enemy."

"I'll send Magnum up just as soon as I see what we're dealing with on the ship's port wing section," Ben said.

"If you need him, I'll send the duke," Pershing said. "He wanted to come along, and he'll have to pull his weight."

Ben nodded and started for the stairs. He went down to the engineering bay and gathered his tools, while Magnum got one of the Lancet assault rifles they had stored for personal safety.

"Want to take a look around?" Magnum asked.

"Sure," Ben said, picking up a step ladder that he would need to reach the underside of the *Echo*'s wing. "I'm ready."

The ramp was closed, and Ben led them out of the air lock. It was cool in the minutes just before dawn. They stood outside, breathing the crisp, clean air and letting their eyes adjust to the darkness. When they spoke, both men whispered.

"This seems strange," Ben said. "I don't think I've ever breathed air this fresh."

"The royal family had it good," Magnum agreed.

"What do you think about what we're doing?"

"You mean working with the Imperium?"

"Yeah," Ben said.

"I think we're doing what we have to do," Magnum said. "The food's not bad either."

"Yes, I could get used to real food all the time," Ben said. "But maybe we're risking too much."

"A big risk now or constant risk for the rest of our lives," Magnum said. "At least this path has a spark of hope that we might get free at some point."

"That's the thing," Ben said. "Can we trust the general?"

"No," Magnum said. "We don't trust her and we won't be disappointed when she fails to keep her word."

"Well..." Ben replied. "That's depressing."

"Maybe, but we're putting our trust in people who lie and steal for a living. They just do it in a way that's legal. Would you trust the Scalpers if they promised to let you go once you did a job for them?"

Ben thought for a moment and realized his friend was right. He shook his head, which Magnum could just make out in the semidarkness as dawn turned the sky a pearly-gray color.

"You're right," he said, feeling almost as if someone had punched him hard in the gut.

He leaned forward and put his hands on his knees, breathing as deeply as he could. The cold morning air seared his lungs and made his eyes water. Fatigue set in heavily, and he wondered how many hours he'd been awake. Sometimes it was hard to keep track, with so many changes happening in such rapid succession.

He realized he had to put a plan in place. When the opportunity came, he needed to find a way to get the *Echo* and his friends to safety. Not that there would be much safety if he double-crossed the Royal Imperium. But there was a sliver of hope. The government was fractured, and it might take decades for the diminished Royal Imperium to get all the renegade systems back into the fold. That left a lot of cracks for a ship to hide in and even more opportunity to get work for a crew who knew how to deliver. If they had proven anything in their short tenure, it was that the *Modulus Echo* and her crew could get things done.

"Let's go check on that damaged wing," Ben said.

It wasn't hard to find where the ship had collided with something in the debris cloud. The *Echo* was covered with octagon heat tiles. Several were missing from the underside of the wing, and others around the missing tiles had bucked up. Replacing them would be easy enough. Ben knew he could make that particular repair at any time. Even if they had to go back up into orbit without replacing them, it wouldn't hurt the ship. It was the damage inside the wing that concerned him.

Ben set up the ladder and climbed up. The peaks of the mountain were catching the early-morning sunbeams, but down in the valley, the gloom was thick. He pulled out a small flashlight and began looking around, hoping the artificial light wouldn't attract the attention of the aliens.

The metal that contained the components was torn open and blackened. He used the light to look inside. The ship was contained in layers, almost like a nesting doll. He could see the electric wiring and conduits running to the wing engine. Beyond that, he saw the inner hull, and while he couldn't see it, he knew that beyond the inner hull was the space beneath the crew quarters.

"How's it look?" Magnum asked.

"Fried," Ben replied. "I'll need a day at least."

"You need help?"

"No, not until I'm putting the heat shielding back on. Why don't you go on up the mountain and find a good spot to keep watch? I'll have someone relieve you in a few hours."

Without a word, the big man headed off into the darkness. Ben descended from his ladder and started back for the air lock, tapping the com-link on his collar as he went.

"General?"

"I'm here, Ben. Go ahead."

"We've got lots of electrical damage," Ben said. "Nothing major, but I suspect the engine coolant won't work until I get it fixed."

"How long?" Pershing asked.

"A full day," Ben said as he climbed back into the ship through the air lock. "I'll have to solder new wiring and get it all insulated. But first, I've got to cut away the torn metal. Once I get all that done, I'll weld a new piece of metal over the gash in the airframe, and if there's time, I'll replace the heat shield tiles."

He picked up a small cutting torch and an angle grinder. The torch was more visible, the angle grinder was louder, but both ran the risk of attracting attention.

"Any sign of the aliens?" Ben asked as he headed back toward the air lock.

"No," Pershing said. "Alpha team gave the all-clear through the valley. That doesn't mean we shouldn't be careful, though."

"Okay," Ben replied. "I sent Magnum up to watch for any sign of trouble. With your permission, I'm going to get busy making repairs."

"Granted," Pershing replied. "If you run into trouble, I want to know ASAP."

"Okay, you've got it," Ben said.

He walked back out of the air lock and made his way to the ladder. The thick grass was visible beneath his feet. Nearby, he could hear the gurgle of the river as it gushed over and around the rocks in its wide bed. There was a peacefulness to the pristine world and being out in the wilderness. They weren't safe, yet he felt as if the dangers they had barely escaped from were far away.

With a flick, he powered on the cutting torch, then adjusted the flame until it was a bright-blue cone. He raised the torch and let it burn through the ship's metal hull. It always amazed Ben how thin the metal was and how little actually separated them from the harsh atmosphere of space. One tiny hole could spell disaster for the entire vessel. One simple crack in the fuselage could rip the ship apart under the rigors of outer space and hard vacuum.

He took his time, cutting into the undamaged portion of the hull, trying not to cause more damage to the delicate components inside. Once he had the bent and damaged metal cut away, he traded the torch for the angle grinder. It was a simple tool, just a motor and a small grind wheel that would turn at great speed. The device itself wasn't loud, but once he began grinding, the sound would carry through the valley between the massive mountains.

Ben tapped his com-link again. "Magnum?"

"I'm here," he replied.

"How's it look up there?"

"Beautiful," he replied. "I might just stay."

"Wouldn't that be hilarious?" Ben said. "There's plenty of space out there."

"No kidding. What's up?"

"Any sign of trouble?"

"Nothing," Magnum said. "Some wild game, but no aliens."

"I'm going to use the angle grinder," Ben said. "If it's too loud, let me know."

"Sure," Magnum replied.

Ben switched on the device, spun the wheel up to speed, then touched it to the metal. Sparks flew, and the noise seemed especially loud, but when he stopped his work and asked Magnum, the big man assured him it wasn't too much.

An hour later, the opening was cleaned. The jagged edges were gone, and the metal was straight around the rectangular opening. Ben headed back inside to get more wiring and his soldering iron. As he walked across the cargo bay, he saw Duke Simeon descending with a thick sandwich in each hand.

"Where are you headed?" Ben asked.

"To relieve Magnum," the duke replied. "Here, I made you a sandwich."

Ben took the food gratefully. "I appreciate it."

"Any idea where he is?" Simeon asked.

"Up the mountainside," Ben replied. "That's all I know. If you're going out there, you better take one of these."

Ben opened a storage panel and pulled out his Lancet assault rifle. He handed the weapon to the duke.

"Nice gun," he said. "Is this a Brimex Lancet?"

"It is," Ben replied. "You ever use one?"

"Sure, just for fun."

"Well, hopefully you won't have to today. Use the com-link and Magnum will guide you up to his position."

"Alright, thanks," Duke Simeon said.

Ben watched the duke leave the cargo bay as he unwrapped his sandwich. It seemed strange that a member of the royal family was fixing him meals. The entire galaxy was upside down, and the best he could hope for was a slim chance that he and his friends might find a way to survive.

Chapter 26

Pershing got the transmission from Alpha team without any problems. It was a surprise, since their signals could be picked up by the enemy. Normally, unless the commandos were sure their radio transmissions wouldn't be intercepted, their SOP was to maintain radio silence until they were ready to leave. But the first word the general got from Staff Sergeant Visher and his team of highly skilled operators was a video transmission.

She hit the button to play the video and saw from the point of view of the staff sergeant's helmet camera. It panned across the opening between the mountains. The commandos were on one side of the river, and on the other side, the aliens had built a wall of stone and timber. There were a number of aliens working on the outer portion of the wall.

Dial, Staff Sergeant Visher said on the video, his voice barely more than a whisper. *Climb a tree and get us eyes inside the compound they're constructing.*

Yes, Staff Sergeant. Corporal Dial replied.

Pershing marveled at the aliens. They were humanoid, but taller, with thickly muscled bodies. Most had some sort of prosthetics. She saw arms and legs made of metal that looked almost robotic. It was amazing to see how natural the artificial limbs moved. The aliens were almost graceful and certainly athletic in their movements. She saw them lifting heavy tree trunks and boulders that would take multiple men to lift.

She also noticed their weapons. They carried a variety of axes, knives, and even swords and clubs, but no firearms. It was almost shocking to see the aliens who had crossed space through a wormhole from another galaxy building a timber palisade and carrying what looked to her like primitive weapons.

But what she saw next surprised her even more than the aliens with their waving tendrils that surrounded their heads, or their frightening faces that looked like flattened versions of vicious carnivores'. She had expected to see the aliens and even anticipated their superiority. The shock came when she saw a human working with them.

Holy shit, is that Major Le Croix? Staff Sergeant Visher proclaimed.

General Pershing's first thought was that the staff sergeant was speaking too loudly. She wanted to hush him, but his words had been spoken from far away and in the past. She was just watching a recording that had picked up his voice. And what she saw made her feel hollow inside.

Major Robert Luc Le Croix was indeed helping the aliens. Only, he looked different. His thin, curving prosthetic legs had been replaced by massive robotic legs. And across his head was a band of metal. His eye glowed with a strange light that made him seem alien and almost monstrous. A single tendril hung from the band of metal, and he had an exotic-looking ax hanging from a belt around his waist just above his new artificial legs.

Looks like him, Corporal Amadi said.

I guess, Corporal Miller added. *But he don't look human to me.*

Alright, can that chatter. We still have a job to do, Visher said. *The fact is, the aliens got to him one way or another. And that means he was picked up in space.*

With the last pod, Corporal Amadi said. *They could have the king or the crown prince held hostage.*

Alright, let's pull back, Staff Sergeant Visher said. *I want to touch base with the general before we go any further into this shit show.*

The video suddenly panned and Pershing saw the rest of Alpha team hidden among some bushes. They began creeping back into the trees when the video ended. She leaned back in her seat and glanced at Nance, who was studying her computer display. Pershing couldn't see the monitor that was built into Nance's console, and for all she knew, the computer expert was watching the video Pershing had just finished. Nance was like a robot, with no visible emotions. When she spoke, it was always calm and steady, as if she were merely an extension of the computers she managed. There was no way to know what she had seen simply by looking at the young woman.

"Have we gotten any more transmissions?" Pershing asked.

"Negative," Nance said without looking up. "Just the one you saw."

"What did you see?" Pershing asked.

Nance looked up for the first time. "I'm studying the data compiled by my systems check. Did you need something from me?"

"No," Pershing said.

She didn't know why she felt so secretive. The crew members of the *Echo* weren't military, which made them outsiders in Pershing's mind. Yet they were her people, as much as she hated to admit it. Their lack of discipline and respect for the chain of command aside, she valued their abilities. So why did she want to keep private the transmission from Alpha team? Perhaps it was because of the shocking revelation that Major Le Croix had defected to the enemy.

Pershing backed through the video until she found the image of Le Croix. She zoomed in until the image was grainy, but there was no doubt the human working with the aliens was her former senior officer. But two questions remained. First, was he a prisoner forced to help the aliens build their defenses? She didn't think so. The ax hanging from his belt was a weapon —it was too ornate to be a tool, and either way, you didn't give a prisoner something that he could use to cause you harm. Second, was that really Le Croix, or merely his body? Perhaps the aliens had taken over his mind. The band around his head might suggest that they were using some strange alien technology to control his body. His eyes glowed strangely, as if they were more machine than flesh and blood.

Brigadier General Alicia Pershing had no answers. She was a warrior in what would go down in history as the most significant conflict in over a century, perhaps even more important than the Great War that had unified most of the galaxy under the Royal Imperium. Yet, she found her old subordinate's treachery painful. Pershing considered Le Croix a friend. Never would she have imagined that he might reject his own people in favor of the strange aliens, yet she could deny what she had seen.

The communications system beeped with an incoming transmission. Pershing pressed the transmit button and spoke into the small microphone built into her console.

"This is *Modulus Echo* actual. Over," she said.

Modulus Echo, this is Alpha one. Did you receive our video transmission? Over.

"Affirmative," Pershing said, glancing over at Nance, who seemed oblivious to the conversation.

What are your orders, General? Should we continue as planned? Over.

Pershing thought for a few seconds before responding. The revelation about Le Croix was disturbing, but it didn't change their priorities. She needed an alien captured alive and returned to the ship. It was the only way to truly study her enemy.

"Proceed as planned," Pershing said. "Your first and highest priority is to bring one of them back alive. Over."

Roger that, Staff Sergeant Visher said. *They're staying busy, but we'll catch one unaware and get it to you, General. Over.*

"Just make sure you don't bring the enemy back to this location," Pershing said. "The ship is under repair, and I don't want to have to run for it when we aren't at full strength. Over."

No worries, General. This isn't our first rodeo. Alpha team, out.

The transmission went dead, and Pershing felt herself tense. She didn't mind danger, but she felt too much responsibility. The Fleet was decimated, and what remained was led by incompetent political appointees. Without her, they were lost, and if she wasn't careful, the little ship that could get her off Gershwin and back into space wouldn't survive. The aliens didn't appear to have modern weapons, but that might just be a fluke. Perhaps they weren't expecting trouble. Or maybe they weren't carrying weapons so that they could focus on the work being done. Pershing knew better than to pin her hopes on wishful thinking when it came to assessing her enemies.

Their ships didn't appear to have weapons either. They used grappling arms to capture ships rather than weapons that would disable or potentially destroy the vessels. Not that ripping a ship to pieces was unheard of. Pershing had seen firsthand that the aliens wouldn't hesitate to rip a ship apart as long as they were able to capture all the pieces.

So why didn't they use weapons? Why didn't they fight back with weapons when her forces had used them against the aliens' ships? The only reasonable answer was that they didn't have them. For some strange reason, the aggressive aliens from another galaxy didn't use modern weapons. It seemed ludicrous and yet it was the only explanation for their behavior. They were advanced beings, capable of space flight and sophisticated prosthetics, perhaps even mind control. The only reason Pershing could fathom regarding their choice of weapons was that perhaps they had never considered projectiles before. Perhaps in their evolution of warfare, they had never developed firearms at all.

She could only hope that was true. If so, a few of the Royal Imperium capital ships could destroy their entire fleet. But she had to plan for the possibility that they would adapt. If the aliens never used a missile or cannon against them, that would be the most desirable circumstance. But she would plan for the aliens to adapt, especially since her tiny group of vessels had forced them out of the Celeste system. They were cut off and would be desperate, which meant they would have to adapt or die, and she was betting her life that they would find a way to fight back. The sooner she got what she wanted on Gershwin and returned to space, the better.

She tapped the ship's com-link and contacted Ben.

"What's your status?" she asked.

"Just getting started on rewiring the wing engine, port thrusters, repulsors, and the rotator mounts," Ben replied. "It's slow, tedious work, but I'll get it done."

"How soon?" Pershing asked.

"A few hours at least," Ben said.

"Can we fly?" Pershing asked.

"It's possible that we could fly in atmo, but I wouldn't suggest trying to make orbit, especially with that debris cloud. Without this engine, we cut our maneuverability down almost in half."

"Then get it done," Pershing said. "We're sitting ducks until you do."

"Is there trouble?" Ben asked.

"Always assume the answer to that question is yes," Pershing said. "Finish up as quickly as you can. I want us ready to move on a moment's notice."

"Okay," Ben said. "I'll do my best."

Pershing cut the transmission and wondered if their best would be good enough, when the entire galaxy hung in the balance.

Chapter 27

There were still occasional flaming objects streaking across the sky, but the Krah no longer paid attention. Grubat had them working diligently on the defenses for Alpha Vistol's settlement. They were in a good position, on high ground with the mountains at their back. And building defenses was easy enough, but Grubat worried about an attack from the air. The alpha was having trouble understanding that the humans didn't fight with honor. They might come in and drop bombs from the sky that completely obliterated the Krah settlement without ever setting foot on the ground.

Oddly enough, the Krah chieftain was growing to like the human better and better as each day passed. He worked tirelessly and never complained, even though he knew better than anyone just how futile their rock and timber walls were in the event that the humans attacked.

"The workers are finishing the fighting platforms," Le Croix said as Grubat approached. "The walls are strong."

"They are for show," Grubat said. "The enemy will never try and defeat us this way."

"We can't know that for certain," Le Croix said. "If the Royal Imperium has retaken the system, they might send troops. This is the royal family's world, after all. They might choose to fight in the least destructive way possible."

"Unless the Krah return, we can only hope to die with honor," Grubat said. "We don't have enough warriors to hold out long."

"There are always the mountains," Le Croix said. "We should begin formulating a contingency plan. A safe route through the mountains with caches of supplies for the children."

"The mountains offer excellent ambush opportunities," Grubat said. "But we do not retreat."

"Don't think of it that way," Le Croix replied. "It isn't a retreat but an overall strategy. If the Royal Imperium comes against us here, we will coax them into the mountains by making it look like a retreat."

"Alpha Vistol could be persuaded, but it would require him to leave his chambers and live rough with the rest of us. I do not think he will agree."

"What choice does he have?" Le Croix said.

"The communication equipment is linked to his ship."

"We can carry portable communicators capable of reaching orbit," Le Croix said. "When the fleet returns, we'll be able to reach them, even from the mountains."

Grubat grunted. He couldn't find a flaw in the human's logic. But Alpha Vistol would not be so easy to convince. It took over an hour just to get an audience with Vistol, and the alpha was not in favor of the plan.

"Are you suggesting that we run and hide, Chieftain Grubat?" the alpha said. "Please tell me that I have not put my trust in a coward."

"No, my lord, I will fight to the death, but in order to protect the young ones from the humans' cowardly weapons, which they would fling at us from a distance or drop on us from the skies, we must make them believe that we are running away from battle."

"To draw them into our trap?"

"Exactly, my lord. We will find a path into the mountains that gives us the greatest advantage. Then we will begin moving supplies, perhaps even the young ones to ensure their safety," Grubat explained.

"But we will fight the hue-mans," Alpha Vistol vowed. "We will make them beg for our mercy."

"Yes," Grubat agreed, his head tendrils stiffening in anticipation of a great battle.

"Proceed, Chieftain Grubat."

Grubat bowed low, then left the alpha's spaceship. Back outside, he moved quickly to where his son, Yarl Cherbak, waited. His injuries from the fight with Trooper Le Croix had healed, but there was no way to know if Yarl Quissi had saved the *En'Galla* or if the ship had been lost in the battle above New Krah. Until the fleet returned, they were a Thralldom with neither ships nor army. Only a handful of troopers remained loyal to the disgraced chieftain, and while Yarl Cherbak longed for an opportunity to increase his fortune and fling off the disgrace of his father's failures, he had no other option but to stay with Grubat and hope for the chance to return to space.

"Did he agree with your plan?" Yarl Cherbak asked.

"He did," Grubat explained. "Gather those still loyal to us. We will scout for the best path into the mountains."

"What about the human?"

"Trooper Le Croix was accepted by the warlords and blessed by the high priest. It is time that you accept him as well."

"He is a traitor," Cherbak said. "You cannot trust him."

They walked toward the edge of the settlement. All around them, young Krah played while casteless females watched over them. Workers continued building the settlement's defenses. Fighting platforms were being erected, and a strong gate was being built that would enclose the inner compound in the event of an attack. Food was cooking, and all around him, Grubat could see the joy on the faces of the Krah. Never before had any of them been in a world as beautiful and clean as the planet they were on. It seemed almost unbelievable that an attack was imminent or that violence could shatter the idyllic existence they had discovered on New Krah.

"You are bitter," Grubat said.

"Of course I am. Could he not have at least given me an honorable death?"

"He spared you as a favor to me," Grubat said.

"And now I must live with the shame of defeat. It wasn't enough that you have tainted our Thralldom, but you have let your sentiments for the human corrupt your mind."

"Believe what you will," Grubat said. "It makes no difference to me. If you wish to find another master, I release you."

"None would have me now," Yarl Cherbak grumbled.

"It is you that is corrupt. You have let your shame rob you of the opportunity to learn from your mistakes. We both underestimated our enemy. Even the warlords with a mighty armada were driven away by only a handful of humans. We must not repeat our mistakes over and over."

Cherbak had nothing to say.

"If Trooper Le Croix wishes to accompany us, he is welcome," Grubat said. "But we must leave at once. The humans could attack at any moment."

"I will do as you command," Cherbak said.

Grubat could still hear the pain in his son's voice. But sooner or later, he would come to terms with his mistake. Cherbak had been in a rush to defeat his own father, hoping that it would somehow separate him from the shame of the loss of nine ships, which until the battle in space around New Krah had been the largest defeat in the history of the Krah unification. Nine vessels, all their crews, lost in a single battle. It was unheard of, but the warlords, even with the knowledge of Grubat's loss in the Yelsin system, had lost even more ships, and worse still, been forced to flee the system.

Alpha Vistol didn't want to give the appearance of retreat, but Grubat knew that even the combined might of the warlords with their massed Thralldoms, had been forced to run or die. It was a dark hour for the Krah, but Grubat knew that his people had never encountered an enemy like the humans. It would take time to carve out a portion of the new galaxy for the Krah to take root in. And if he could keep the young ones from Alpha Vistol's colony ship alive long enough, they could reinforce the Krah forces and lead the next wave of conquest over the humans.

"We are ready," Yarl Cherbak informed him after gathering their loyal troopers.

Grubat had stopped for a quick meal and to gather some supplies. Water was abundant, but he didn't want to risk moving into drier country without supplies.

To Grubat's satisfaction, he saw that Trooper Le Croix stood with the other troopers. There were nine in total, more than enough to scout the mountains and carry supplies, but Grubat knew that if the *En'Galla* was lost, then he was no longer truly a chieftain. Most Yarls commanded more respect, and some had far more troopers loyal to them. In some respects, Grubat was ruined, but he didn't care. How could he feel shame or loss of status when he was surrounded by the greatest bounty he had ever seen? The planet he was on was grander than anything he'd ever imagined before. And if it was his fate to die in the pristine world, then he would gladly give his all. Death and defeat were not something he regularly dwelt on, but he had always assumed his death would come at the hands of an ambitious Yarl or a rival chieftain in the cold confines of a spacecraft. To die in the open air of a beautiful planet was truly an honor, one that he did not dread.

"Our goal is to find a way into the mountains," Grubat said. "When the humans attack, we will feign retreat, drawing them into our trap where they cannot escape our fury."

The troopers raised their tor'axes and cheered the plan. Their rough voices echoed around him, but Grubat feared his tiny Thralldom was too weak to resist the humans who would soon rise against them. Still, all he could do was lead his troopers and die beside them. It would be an honorable death, and while Grubat longed to explore the new planet they had found, he would be content to die with what little renown he had left.

"Let us go, then. We move fast," Grubat said. "Try and keep up."

Chapter 28

"Alpha team, we are going silent," Staff Sergeant Visher said into his throat mic.

Their com-link was set to a team-only channel. And the seven commandos were spread out on a hill behind trees and boulders. Below them, the valley narrowed, and there were eleven aliens counting whatever Major Le Croix had become. In Visher's mind, his former commander was no longer human.

Visher was at the narrowest point of the valley, and to his right, he could see Corporal Dial. His subordinate was the only other team member the staff sergeant could see, but beyond Dial was Private First Class Rhoades. They alternated rank, each commando spread so that only one could be seen in either direction.

Through his scope, Visher could easily make out the details of the rearmost alien. He was a hulking brute with two robotic arms. Dial had spotted the group jogging up the valley, and Visher had given the order to take cover. They needed one of the brutes alive, just one. The staff sergeant had pointed out the one he wanted to keep alive at the center of the group of aliens. The rest of them, including Le Croix if he wasn't careful, were collateral damage.

It didn't help that the aliens were moving up the valley where the *Modulus Echo* had landed. If Visher's team didn't stop them, their only ride off the planet would be overrun. Things had been easy since landing on Gershwin because the aliens didn't know they were there, but that was about to change. Visher's shot was the signal for the rest of his squad, whom he knew had already sighted their targets.

Visher centered the crosshairs of his rifle's scope on the alien's upper back. He had to wait until the group was past the narrow point in the valley. Visher took a slow breath, held it for a moment, then gently stroked the trigger.

The Royal Imperium military used a Grissom all-purpose rifle, but the Special Forces commandos preferred a Bailey Shock and Awe rifle or BSA. The weapon had an extendable barrel for sniper shots, which Visher's entire team had employed. They could fire a range of ammunition, but Visher preferred good old-fashioned soft metal projectiles. His BSA was loaded with depleted uranium rounds, and as he pulled the trigger, it bucked hard against his shoulder. Visher's eye never left the scope, and while the bullet was moving too fast to be seen, he saw the damage. The projectile smashed through the alien's back leaving a tiny hole, but after ripping through the vital organs, it exploded out the other side with a much larger exit wound.

Right on cue, the other commandos fired their shots. The reports rolled through the valley like a cascade of thunder, and seven of the aliens dropped to the ground. The remaining four, including Major Le Croix, reacted to the shots in different ways. One drew his weapon, a polished metal ax of some sort, and roared in defiance, only to be the next alien killed.

The other three ran for cover in different directions. The commandos took more shots, but all missed their marks.

"We got eight," Corporal Dial said.

"They never saw it coming," Private Felix said. "Sorry bastards."

"Dial, Amadi, and Rhoades, with me," Visher said as he slipped from the boulder he was hiding behind. "The rest of you, cover us. No more kill shots. If you have to shoot, go for the legs."

There were three acknowledgments to his orders, but Visher barely heard them. His heart was thundering in his chest as he ran down the steep hillside, dodging trees and trying to get to the narrow point in the valley before the aliens could flee.

He burst out of the trees as Le Croix and another of the aliens raced past him. Staff Sergeant Visher's hands worked the controls of his rifle without any conscious thought. His thumb pulled back the switch that transitioned the BSA from a sniper rifle to a close-quarters, nonlethal assault rifle. His free hand reached forward, rotated the long barrel, and slid the telescoping section back toward the stock, shortening the weapon by half. Another shot from high above Visher rang out. He glanced down the valley and saw the target. He was different from most of the others, with two robotic legs and long tendrils that were jerking spasmodically as the alien tried to get back up.

"Good shot, Miller," Visher said.

"Thanks, Staff Sergeant," Corporal Miller replied.

"Looks like you were right," Dial said, his breath coming in hard puffs as he raced down the mountain slightly behind Visher. "The legs are a weak point."

"So are mine," the staff sergeant replied.

He finally reached the valley floor and circled around the choke point. The alien and Le Croix were nowhere to be seen. Visher's first instinct was to chase after them, but something in the back of his mind warned him of danger. He put a hand up to stop Dial, who was hard on his heels. He pointed to the rocky outcropping that narrowed the valley, then waved his hand in that direction before pointing to himself and motioning the other way.

Dial nodded, and both men moved forward slowly.

"Staff Sergeant, we've got the alien," Corporal Amadi said over their com-link.

Visher didn't reply. If he was right, the aliens were waiting just behind the large rocks. He came around the boulders, his gun held at the ready, but there was no one in sight. He quickly turned around, expecting Dial to be under attack, but he wasn't. The corporal just shrugged his shoulders, and Visher felt a sense of disappointment. One alien and a former major in the Royal Imperium Special Forces had escaped.

"Miller, Felix, Wriggles, move down the valley. I want eyes open for those last two survivors."

"Roger that," Corporal Miller replied.

"I can't believe Le Croix ran," Private Wriggles said. "It was the perfect opportunity to escape from the aliens."

"I guess he didn't want to escape," Dial said. "Dirty traitor."

"He hasn't gone far," Visher said. "We'll get him eventually."

The staff sergeant moved back up the valley and looked at the dead aliens. He had seen dead men and women, even children. It chilled his blood every time he saw death up close. But the aliens were different. They were familiar, yet completely foreign. He couldn't say why, but he felt no remorse as he gazed at their bloody corpses.

Toby Neighbors

"Miller, is that prisoner locked down?" Visher asked.

He could see the big corporal kneeling on the alien's back. Miller had the creature's arms pulled back and fastened with plastic cable ties.

"Trussed up like turkey at Thanksgiving, Staff Sergeant," Miller replied.

"Outstanding," Visher said. "Our first priority is to get the prisoner to General Pershing on the *Echo*. Amadi and Rhoades will see to the prisoner. Dial and I are moving at least one of the dead back with us for study by the eggheads. Miller, Wriggles, and Felix, stay put and keep an eye out for the other two that escaped. If you see them, try and take them alive, but don't take unnecessary chances."

"Roger that, Staff Sergeant," Corporal Miller responded.

"Alright, Dial, you think you can carry one of these brutes?"

The aliens were all bigger than the commandos, but Corporal Dial didn't seem to think that was a problem. He picked out the smallest of the aliens, one with only a single prosthetic arm. He kicked the alien, and when it didn't move, he poked his gun barrel into the alien's eye.

"Looks dead to me," Dial said.

"We can carry him together," Visher said.

Dial grabbed the alien's natural arm and heaved the body to an upright position. Then he grabbed the body around the waist and hoisted it up over his shoulder. He grunted a little, but looked steady.

"I can handle this one, Staff Sergeant," Dial said.

"Trying to make me look bad, Corporal?" Visher asked.

"Nah, you do that all on your own, Staff Sergeant."

"Funny, you can clean the gear all by yourself when this op is over," Visher said.

He picked out another of the aliens. Lifting the body so that he could get it over his shoulder was difficult, but once he had the alien and was standing upright, the deadweight was manageable.

"Let's move," Visher said. "The sooner we deliver these prisoners, the sooner we can set up a good position overlooking the alien camp. I don't want to lose the light."

Miller and Rhoades had their prisoner on his feet. One of the robotic legs was mangled by Miller's bullet, but the other worked well enough. Amadi held the alien's right arm, and Rhoades had the left. The alien's thick tendrils waved spasmodically, and even though they were long enough to reach the commandos marching the alien forward, they didn't seem to want to touch the humans. The group moved slowly, but Visher had been a soldier for a long time. He knew that great distances could be covered if a person didn't give up. One step at a time, they moved closer and closer to the small ship that had brought them to Gershwin. The prisoner didn't struggle. It was clear that without the use of his leg, the robotic prosthetic was simply dead weight. And it looked heavy to Visher. The alien he carried had a robotic arm, and part of his chest and back were covered with the same material. The staff sergeant guessed his load was well over two hundred pounds. As long as he didn't stop, he could carry the weight. The danger would be in putting the body down. Visher didn't know if he would ever be able to hoist it back up again, and they didn't have time to rest. He didn't like splitting his team, but they didn't have a choice. It would be better if the aliens just disappeared with no trace. If they escaped, they could warn the others. Not that there would be much doubt about what had happened, but the mystery was better than certain knowledge. Visher was determined to deliver his prisoners, both dead and alive, to the general, then reform his team. So despite the weight and the burden, he kept moving forward.

Chapter 29

Le Croix was lying prone next to Yarl Cherbak. They were under an overhang of rock and covered by dense shrubs. After dashing through the narrow point of the canyon and taking cover behind the rocks, Le Croix meant to ambush the commandos. He knew their tactics, knew they would come looking, and if he stayed close to the big boulders, he could get close to them without coming under fire, at least for a while. But when he saw the small overhang not far away, he took a chance.

Yarl Cherbak was dazed, not from gunfire, but from the almost instant deaths of the Krah. Knowing that the humans fought with firearms was one thing, but coming under fire without warning had been shocking for the Yarl. They hadn't even seen their enemy and death was raining down on them. At first, Le Croix had run toward the river, thinking of dropping down the bank for cover from the snipers, but when he saw Yarl Cherbak running aimlessly, he instantly changed his mind.

"What now?" Cherbak whispered after Staff Sergeant Visher and Corporal Dial had gone back on the other side of the outcropping.

Le Croix hadn't been close enough to hear Visher's orders or to realize they were the same team of commandos that had been under his command during their rescue mission in space above Gershwin. But he knew how the soldiers would think. They knew he couldn't have just disappeared, and they wouldn't give up the hunt. What he needed was a way to get to safety without being seen.

"They are leaving. We should run for it," Cherbak said.

"No, they're watching," Le Croix said. "We need to get to the river bank."

"It's across the valley," Cherbak said. "We can make it if we run."

Le Croix knew better. They couldn't outrun bullets, but Cherbak was near panic. He had to calm the frightened Yarl down and come up with a plan.

"Running won't help us," Le Croix said.

"Then we stand and fight," Cherbak said. "I will not cower here, hoping to slink away."

"That's exactly what we're going to do," Le Croix said. "Those snipers are just waiting for a chance to shoot us down, and getting killed won't help anyone."

"Dying in battle is honorable," Cherbak said.

"It's not battle when you can't get close enough to even use your weapon," Le Croix said. "We'll just be two more dead bodies. We have to report back to Alpha Vistol. The humans are already here."

"He'll know that when we don't return," Cherbak argued.

"No, he won't," Le Croix countered. "Look, right now all they know is that we left the settlement. But what he needs to know is that Special Forces assault teams have infiltrated the wilderness around that encampment. The best we can hope for is to man the battlements and hope that the fleet returns before the camp is overrun."

"You are a coward."

"I'm a realist," Le Croix said. "The humans won't stop and we don't know how many they have."

"So what do you propose we do?"

"Wait for nightfall," Le Croix said.

"Then slink away in the darkness?"

"No," Le Croix said. "But we'll have an advantage. They can't see in the dark like we can. If we start a fire, they'll be distracted. Then we can attack on our terms."

"You're sure?"

"Yes," Le Croix said.

But he wasn't sure. In fact, he didn't even think the plan would work, but there were a few hours of daylight left, and he hoped that before night fell, he could come up with a better plan.

Chapter 30

Grubat had experienced many things in his life, but utter defeat was not one of them. When the shots rang out, he knew immediately they were under attack, yet there was nothing he could do to save his troopers. Those around him fell to the ground, blood spewing from terrible wounds inflicted by human weapons. He had heard of their firearms, Le Croix had even described the damage they could do, but nothing had prepared him for the sudden, thunderous devastation.

His second thought was that if he could get to cover, perhaps he could draw them out. If he was going to die, it would be better to do so fighting. His hand was on his tor'ax as he ran toward a large boulder near the river, but a shot from the humans disabled his leg. He had fallen hard, and no matter what he tried, he couldn't move his right leg. The limb was suddenly heavy and cumbersome. There was no pain, but that didn't save him. He tried to find a way to rise up and face his attackers, but he couldn't even roll over.

The extrasensory tendrils sensed the approach of his enemies. He felt them stiffen, and he heard their boots slapping hard as they ran, occasionally grinding rocks together. Every instinct in his body screamed for him to get up and fight, but before he could, a human landed hard on his back, knocking the wind out of him and pinning his arms behind him.

Grubat's humiliation grew with each insult. They bound his hands with a thin filament that was too strong for him to break. He was unable to rise on his own, but the humans hoisted him up easily. Their bare faces and short hair were unnatural and distasteful to him, especially as they reveled in their victory, showing their short, blunt-looking teeth.

They marched for nearly three hours. It was late in the day when the human ship finally came into view. Grubat recognized it as the same ship that had mysteriously defied the efforts of the Krah vessels to capture it. Part of him wished he'd never seen the little ship. It was much smaller than a Krah vessel, even an explorer ship was bigger, yet it had been present at every defeat his people had faced since coming to the new galaxy.

The soldiers didn't speak often. Two were burdened with the bodies of Grubat's troopers. He was surprised at the strength and stamina of the humans. Grubat would not have thought them capable of carrying full-grown Krah to such a distance. He could see on their pale faces the effort it took. By the time they reached the little human ship, the soldiers were exhausted.

They were met outside the ship by several more humans, two of them females, which Grubat found even more interesting. Only one was a warrior; she was their Yarl. The others were workers, but none had enhancements. When they spoke, Grubat's translator deep inside his ear did its work so that he understood everything they said.

"Good work, Staff Sergeant," the warrior woman said.

The leader of the soldiers was too exhausted to reply. An older human with gray hair on his face and bald pate handed the soldiers containers with drink of some sort, then bent over the dead bodies.

"Fascinating," the older man said.

"They smell," said the younger woman. She was cocky, almost flippant, but her attitude was a disguise to hide her fear. Grubat could sense it with his tendrils, which were sampling the new scents of the band of humans.

"Get him on board," the warrior woman said. "Have you searched him for weapons?"

"We have," the one the others called Staff Sergeant said. "He had an ax, like the others, but no other weapons that we could find. And we disabled his right leg. It's heavy."

"You can say that again," said one of the guards who had helped Grubat hobble through the valley. "I don't see how they can walk with them."

"He can't do much with it the way it is now," the staff sergeant added.

"Good," said the warrior woman. "If he gets loose, we'll have to kill him, and that's not what I want."

Grubat was surprised. The humans had killed the troopers in his Thralldom without hesitation. Despite the shame and humiliation he felt over being captured, his mind began to list the reasons why the female Yarl wanted to keep him alive. The most obvious was to interrogate him, but they might have other plans as well. They could be planning a public execution. Perhaps they wanted to keep him alive in captivity to lord their victory over him for the rest of his days.

Another thought occurred to him as the soldiers led him up into the cargo hold of the ship, which was stacked with supplies. There was enough food to feed a small army. And Grubat saw munitions as well. Some of the pallets and crates were marked for medical supplies. Grubat's eye enhancements were old and in need of updating, but they were able to translate the words printed on the containers. Was it possible that the human workers wanted to experiment on him, the way his people had enhanced Trooper Le Croix? The thought frightened him more than death. To be cut into by the humans, his body explored and prodded as he slowly died, was humiliating. He wished he had the strength to break free and force the humans to kill him outright.

"Put him in the rec room," a voice boomed from the speakers mounted around the large cargo hold.

"Yes, ma'am," one of the soldiers pushing him along replied.

The voice had been female, but Grubat had no idea where it came from. It could be from a human, or perhaps some type of artificial intelligence. Neither Le Croix nor the sniveling coward Godfred had mentioned such devices, but they were not unheard of, even in the Krah galaxy.

The soldiers escorted Grubat, half pushing, half carrying him, through the cargo bay and into what appeared to be the engineering section. Grubat had never bothered to learn about the inner workings of his ships. That was beneath him. As a member of the Warrior caste, his sole concern was conquest. The engineering section was small and led to another portion of the ship. The soldiers bypassed the odd-looking furniture and pushed him down against the wall. They cut the ties that bound his hands behind his back, but they added more, stretching his arms to either side of his body and fastening them to pipes that rose up from the floor and disappeared into the ceiling.

"That should hold him," one of the soldiers named Miller said.

"Even if it can't, he isn't strong enough to get up," the other replied. "Let's go."

They left him alone in the room. Grubat tested his bonds. The thin filament was strong, and the soldiers had doubled them up. He could tell, if he kept trying, the plastic bands would cut into his flesh. He would willingly trade the pain of deep lacerations for freedom, but the bands would not pass the bones in his arms, and the soldiers had been right about his leg. He had never noticed the its weight before, but the metal components were heavy. The disabled leg was like an anchor holding him down.

His only choice was to wait and see what the humans wanted from him. If their intentions were nefarious, he would find a way to strike back or die in the attempt. He may have been beaten, but it was not in Grubat's nature to give up.

His mind replayed the ambush. It was perfectly executed. The troopers were all killed, except for Le Croix, and Grubat couldn't help but wonder if the entire idea of leading the humans into the mountains wasn't really Le Croix's way of leading Grubat and this troopers into the trap. Could he have been so foolish as to trust the enemy in their midst? Cherbak had warned him that Le Croix couldn't be trusted. He tried desperately to understand if he had made a fatal mistake in believing that Trooper Le Croix had forsaken the humans and embraced the way of the Krah.

The only other survivor had been Yarl Cherbak. Grubat had tried to see his son, to see if he lived or died, but he had failed in that effort too. It seemed he was doomed to fail no matter what he tried to do. If Le Croix was an enemy, Grubat would know soon enough. And if he wasn't, it might be possible that he and Cherbak would help each other escape. Grubat couldn't think of any reason why it would matter, but he couldn't extinguish the spark of hope he felt for his son, and even for the human whom he considered a friend.

Chapter 31

"How close are we?" Pershing asked.

"Another hour," Ben said. "All I have left to do is weld the new metal patch onto the fuselage and replace the missing heat shield tiles."

"Is it possible to do that in orbit?" Pershing said. "We have what we came for, but every second we spend on the ground, we are vulnerable."

"I suppose," Ben said.

She could see the worry in his eyes. There really was no safe option. The commandos had attacked the aliens, which meant that odds were high that their presence was known. It had taken the Spec Ops team hours to deliver the prisoner, and if they stayed much longer, their luck was bound to run out.

"Magnum and Duke Simeon are due back any minute," Pershing explained. "If we can fly, I want us moving ASAP."

"I'll gather my tools," Ben said.

Pershing tapped her com-link. It was a sophisticated device that made the little buttons the crew wore seem like relics that belonged in a museum. Hers was voice activated and could scan dozens of frequencies, even encrypt messages. But all she needed was to send the crew on the bridge a message.

"Prepare for takeoff," she said. "We leave as soon as the duke and Magnum return."

"Yes, ma'am," Nance replied.

"We're on it," Kim added.

Pershing had everything she needed. The bodies of the dead aliens were on new emergency gurneys that she had commandeered from the supplies on Yelsin Prime as part of the agreement she had brokered with the crew of the *Modulus Echo*. The gurneys were equipped with tiny repulsors, which would lift them into the air and make moving even the heavy bodies of the aliens simple enough. Once they were underway, she intended to have the professor do a thorough dissection. But in the meantime, she had a prisoner to question.

She was still in the cargo hold when Ben returned with a small toolbox and a crate of supplies. She saw a spool of wire and several pieces of conduit pipe sticking out.

"I need a weapon," she explained.

Ben gave her a look of surprise and distrust, but he nodded and set his tools down.

"Rifle or pistol?" he asked.

"A pistol is sufficient," she said. "In fact, as long as we have prisoners on board, we should all be armed."

"That's not a problem," Ben said.

He went to a plain-looking section of the wall and pressed it. The panel concealed a small compartment, and it opened as he triggered the spring that held the panel shut with a simple latch. Inside were four Lancet assault rifles and a variety of pistols. Ben stepped back, and Pershing frowned.

"I suppose it's necessary to have a hidden cache of weapons," she said.

"We weren't hiding them from you," Ben said. "Magnum and Duke Simeon both have rifles right now. This is a good place to store them."

"I suppose this ship has more hidden compartments," Pershing said as she selected a slim laser pistol and inserted a battery pack.

"She has secrets that I'm still learning," Ben said. "But we're not hiding anything from you."

"Very well," Pershing said. "I'll be with the prisoner, and I don't want to be disturbed. Use the com-link once we're ready for takeoff."

"Alright," Ben said, the same look of distrust crossing his face.

Pershing held back her smile. She was not sadistic. Torturing prisoners was not something she wanted to do, nor did she expect to have to. But she didn't mind having the crew believe she would. They were too close, too undisciplined for her taste, and fearing their commander would be helpful in keeping them in line.

She checked the pistol's settings as she moved through the engineering bay. The weapon was a simple laser weapon, yet it had stun capabilities, which was what she needed. She set the stun setting to its highest capacity. There was no telling how the alien's body would respond to the weapon, and the last thing she wanted was to kill or permanently damage it, yet she couldn't risk it getting free and trying to hurt her either.

Pershing's uniform had no place for a weapon. She was an officer, and while she preferred to lead from the front, she didn't have a holster on her belt. She slipped the gun between her belt and the small of her back. It was snug and secure there, but easy to retrieve if she needed it.

The alien looked up as she walked into the rec area where it was bound to the wall. The small plastic bonds seemed too delicate to hold the alien, but she knew they were almost unbreakable. And she detected no blood or even chaffing on the creature's arms, which told her it wasn't struggling to free itself the way she would have been.

"Can you understand me?" Pershing asked.

The alien looked at her, its headdress tendrils writhing like a nest of snakes. It nodded slowly, as if the gesture was unnatural. Yet if the aliens had taken Le Croix and Prince Godfred prisoners, then she had guessed they had found a way to communicate. It felt like a tiny victory that she had been right.

"Good, we have a lot to talk about," Pershing said.

She turned a chair around and sat down. The alien watched her. Its eyes were unusual. They looked like human eyes, yet there was something mechanical about them. She imagined she could hear the servos whirring as the alien looked at her.

"Do you have a name?"

The alien gave a reply, but the sounds were indecipherable. It sounded to Pershing like he was an animal; the words were more of a pronounced growl. But from somewhere on the alien, perhaps from the ornate headdress the writhing tendrils were attached to, a translation was emitted.

"Chieftain Grubat." The translator sounded small and strange. It was oddly robotic, but foreign to Pershing's ears.

"What is your kind called?" Pershing asked.

"We are the Krah."

"Thank you for speaking so freely," Pershing said. "Now tell me everything about your people and why you are here."

Chapter 32

Ben was frustrated as he carried the last of his gear back into the ship. The dead aliens had begun to smell, and Pershing was doing things he couldn't imagine to the captive in the recreation room. He didn't like leaving a job unfinished, and no matter how hard he tried, he couldn't help but worry that an army of aliens was about to appear and slaughter everyone he cared about.

"You look like a man with a lot on his mind," Kim said.

She was in the pilot's seat on the bridge, but she swiveled around to face the consoles that were normally behind her as she flew. Ben couldn't help but smile as he realized how lucky he was. Kim was beautiful, and caring in her own way. And she was the best pilot he'd ever seen or heard of.

"Well, I'm not happy," Ben said.

"What's wrong?" Nance asked.

"Besides having aliens on the ship?" Ben asked. "I didn't get to finish my repairs."

"I just ran a systems check," Nance said. "The port engine is fully operational."

"Yes, but I didn't get to seal it back up," Ben said. "I only needed another hour."

"Why's the general in such a hurry?" Kim asked. "Our lookouts haven't seen any sign of trouble."

"I don't know," Ben said.

"Can you finish the repairs in orbit?" Nance asked.

"Yes, but we've got to get through the debris cloud before we can even think about extravehicular activity," Ben said.

"And if we get in that same spot, we could lose the wing, maybe even have a hull breach."

"That's not going to happen," Kim said. "I'll get us through, and you'll get the ship repaired, good as new."

Ben dropped into his seat and checked the status of the ship's engines. Everything looked okay, but he had a nagging feeling that something was amiss. Perhaps it was just the fact that General Pershing had an alien on board the ship. He didn't like the idea of fighting on board the *Echo* or that someone he cared about might get hurt.

"Any word on Magnum and the duke?" Ben asked.

"They're almost here," Nance said.

Ben brought up another screen and checked their Zexum supply. They had three-quarters of a tank left, both banks of auxiliary batteries were fully charged, and all the ship's systems were in the green.

There was nothing to worry about, he told himself, but he couldn't relax. It was as if he were going out in public half-dressed.

"I could have had the new section welded on by now," Ben complained.

"What do you think the general wants to do with the bodies of the aliens?" Kim said.

"Are you just ignoring me now?" Ben said.

"Not now," Kim said with a smile. "Just whenever I get bored."

"Magnum and Duke Simeon are at the air lock," Nance said.

"Good. I'm going to get our guns," Ben said. "The general doesn't want us going unarmed now that we've got the enemy down in the rec room."

"Don't forget mine," Kim said. "I'll be here, flying the ship."

Ben heard Nance alerting General Pershing, which only made him wonder what the general was up to. He felt the engines power on. The entire hull thrummed and the air was suddenly filled with power. He loved the sense that anything was possible when he was on the Kestrel class ship. He could anywhere, do anything. He was home, but his home could take him across the galaxy.

Ben stopped just inside his quarters and leaned against the wall. Somewhere below him, there was a hole on his ship. That wasn't the way he liked to do things. It felt wrong to leave the *Echo* less than a hundred percent when all their lives depended on her.

He had his pistol stashed in the drawer of his bedside table. The power pack was fully charged and sitting beside the weapon. Ben picked it up and slipped the battery into the handle of the gun. He liked the feel of the pistol. It had a weight to it that suggested potency, and yet it also had just the right balance. It felt fast and accurate and just a little dangerous. He slid the gun into the loop holster on his belt, then went across the atrium to Kim's quarters. She sometimes locked the door, not to keep him out, but just to give herself the privacy she needed on a small spaceship.

The door opened and he was amazed. Not that it should have been a surprise, but the colors in Kim's small corner of the ship were so bright and inviting that he couldn't help but smile. There was more to her than the cool, confident pilot. She was a woman after all, and her tastes reflected that. Bright tapestries covered the bland metal walls. Ben was sure that at some point, the *Echo* had been polished and sleek, but time had taken its toll. He had scrubbed every inch of the ship, and there wasn't a speck of rust anywhere, but the signs that there had been remained. But Kim had covered all that. There were thick rugs on the deck, and colorful scarves hung in graceful arcs across the ceiling.

The furniture was the same in all the crew cabins. A narrow bunk, with a bedside table built into the bulkhead. A larger table and room for chairs nearer the door. And on the far side of the small berth, a private bathroom.

Kim's room was neat and clean. Ben knew she kept her pistol in a locker beside the door. He got and left the room, running into Magnum as the big man came up the stairs.

"Any trouble?" Ben asked.

Magnum shook his head.

"We've got aliens on board, so we're all wearing our pistols until further notice. Can you get Nance's sidearm?"

Magnum nodded, and Ben headed for the bridge. He could see on the main display screens that they were flying through the mountains. The art grav generator blocked out the gravity from Gershwin so that the only sign that the ship was moving came from the slight vibration produced by the engines.

"I've got your weapon," Ben said to Kim as he sat down at his station.

"Thanks," Kim said without turning around.

"I was forced to leave Royal City without mine," the duke said from where he sat at the communications console. "I don't suppose we have time to swing by there."

Ben looked at Nance, who was studying her console display. She answered without looking up.

"That would take several hours of flight time," Nance said. "The general's orders were to make orbit and find a way through the debris cloud."

"Hopefully the Royal Imperium ships have cleared a path," Kim said.

The *Echo* banked sharply, but the crew didn't even notice.

"I'll get myself something new the first chance I get," the duke said.

"I'm sure Magnum has something you can use until then," Ben said. "He's a talented gunsmith."

"Doesn't talk much, though," Duke Simeon said. "He's a man of action. I respect that."

The ship rocked several times as they passed through the upper atmosphere. Ben brought up the exterior camera feeds. Gershwin looked pristine and peaceful. He could see the curvature of the planet, and when he switched from the stern cameras to the bow, the sky faded away. Above the planet was a thick barrier of wreckage. Ben couldn't help but wonder what would happen to Gershwin if it was left in the decaying orbit that would pull tons of space junk down to the unspoiled world below. Would it, in time, become a junk world like Torrent Four? Ben didn't know, but he was confident that the Royal Imperium would never allow that to happen.

"We're in the lowest possible orbit," Kim said. "Any idea how we get out of this mess?"

"Where are the Royal Imperium capital ships?" Ben asked. "They've had hours to work on clearing a path."

"I'm looking," Nance said.

Ben wasn't surprised to find the barrier of space debris seemingly untouched. They had navigated the gauntlet of deadly, floating remnants of the alien fleet once, and if they were going to leave the planet, it looked like they would have to do so again.

"I've got a new ship on radar," Nance said. "The feed is difficult to piece together through all this garbage."

"Alien?" Ben asked.

"Negative," Nance replied. "It looks like a Royal Imperium ship."

"That's good, right?" Kim said.

"I'm picking up some communications," Duke Simeon said.

...hold your position and prepare to be boarded...

The transmission was filled with static and hard to make out, even as it boomed through the ship's speakers.

...we have... Confederate soldiers... await instructions.

"We better get the general up here," Ben said. "That's got to be the ship she sent to pick up the Confederate army on Gemli."

Ben used his com-link to notify Pershing, but she was already on her way up. Ben feared that she might be covered in blood and gore from torturing the alien. But when she appeared a moment later, she was neat and composed, although Ben thought she looked pale.

"You okay, General?" Ben asked.

Pershing gave a curt nod in reply.

"Status," she said.

"We're in the lowest possible orbit," Kim said. "I'm afraid to get any higher with all that debris out there."

On the display screens that filled one side of the bridge, all that could be seen was the floating debris, almost as if it were a solid mass. Ben couldn't believe they had actually navigated it once before. And as if to illustrate Kim's point, a large chunk of metal so bent and warped that it was unrecognizable suddenly dropped from space. It spun as it fell, leaving a trail of black smoke from the sudden friction of its passage through the planet's atmosphere.

"We're picking up another ship in the system," Nance said. "I believe it's the *Plato*. They have the Confederate soldiers from Gemli, in the Lebbanon system."

"Excellent," Pershing said. "Where is the gap in the debris field?"

"Wouldn't we all like to know," Kim said.

"Unfortunately, I can't see it on radar," Nance said.

"Perhaps it's on the other side of the planet," Duke Simeon suggested.

"None of the capital ships are working on it," Ben said. "It looks like they've surrounded the *Plato* as if it were an enemy ship."

"Admiral Dietz is a fool," Pershing said. "Patch me through."

"That's the other problem," Duke Simeon said. "Communication is sketchy. There's too much interference."

"Then find me a way through the debris," Pershing said. "This farce has gone on long enough."

"I'm trying," Kim said. "But it's hard this close. I see some gaps, but they close as fast as they appear. Everything is moving at different speeds."

"Are you saying it's impossible?"

"No," Kim replied. "But I'm not taking any chances either. Not without the shield."

"We can't use the flux shield without making the debris completely unstable," Ben said.

"Alright," Pershing said with no outward sign of the rage Ben guessed was building inside of her. "Transmit this message on a repeating broadcast. Even if they don't get it all at once, they'll be able to piece it together until we find a way through the debris field."

Ben brought up the radar on his console and tried to help Kim find a way through the swirling mass of destroyed ships. The problem lay in the copious amounts of space dust. There were vast clouds of tiny fragments that might not hurt the ship, but on radar they looked like one solid mass, making it impossible to guess if it was navigable. Not to mention the fact that anything could be floating in the clouds, including weather probes that had yet to detonate. Bumping into one of those would do more than minor damage.

General Pershing cleared her throat and looked down at her console so that the ship's communications system could record her image as well as her words.

"This is Brigadier General Pershing on the *Modulus Echo*," she began. "We are in low orbit around the planet and searching for a way through the debris field in order to deliver an alien prisoner and two alien bodies to the *Everest*. It is my intention to send the Confederate soldiers to Gershwin with orders to eradicate the aliens there. Please do not hinder their progress."

She repeated the message again, then ordered Duke Simeon to send it through.

"I think I see a way," Kim said. "At least part of the way."

"You have to be sure," Ben said. "Once we're in that field of debris, there's no turning back."

"If you can do it, you have my authority," Pershing said.

"Radar still shows no gap in the debris field," Nance said.

"You sure, Kim?" Ben asked.

"I wouldn't go otherwise," she replied. "I can't guarantee anything, but I think we can make it."

"Go ahead, then," he told her. "I've got the flux shield standing by."

"Everyone needs to get their emergency gear on," Pershing said, standing up. "No exceptions. Contact me when you get through the cloud."

"Yes, General," Ben said.

He could feel his hands getting sweaty at the prospects before them. Ben carried Kim's helmet over to her.

"Are you ready for me to put this on you?"

"You bet," Kim replied, flashing him a wink.

He settled the dome-shaped helmet over her head and fastened the seals. Her suit and helmet were connected to her seat so that she had oxygen and power, without the need for air tanks that might hinder her ability to fly.

When he turned, he saw that Magnum had returned. He was wearing the large, old-fashioned revolver he liked so much, and everyone on the bridge had their helmets on. Pershing had gone back down below. All that remained was to fly through the debris field. It was dangerous; only the extreme need of their mission made taking the chance worthwhile. Yet as Ben put his helmet on and settled back at his console, he wondered again why they were risking so much for a cause they had so little to do with. Perhaps it was the guilt over having opened the wormhole, or just his desire for immunity from the crimes they had committed against the Royal Imperium. Yet the deal he had struck with General Pershing was getting more and more dangerous. And it made him wonder if perhaps they wouldn't be better off slipping away from the general and disappearing somewhere in the vast galaxy.

"Here we go, people," Kim said. "Rub your lucky charm and say a prayer. We need all the help we can get on this one."

"You can do it," Ben said. "I have no doubt."

But in truth he was riddled with doubt. Still, there was nothing to be done until they were free of the debris cloud that separated them from the rest of the galaxy. When—or if, he corrected himself—they made it out, he would rethink this deal he'd made. It was time he put his crew first. They had taken enough chances. Whatever debt he felt he owed the galaxy, they had more than repaid.

Chapter 33

The *Echo* moved slowly through the drifting cloud of debris. Fortunately, enough time had passed that gravity had most of the larger pieces moving the same way. It made navigation a little easier for Kim, who was concentrating fully on flying the ship.

She had all six display monitors showing the different views from the ship's external cameras. It wasn't the same as being in a cockpit with actual windows or flying a racing kite as she hung in a harness below, but Kim had a good feel for the Kestrel class ship. She was in the center between the wings and with slightly more of the vessel below than above her. As unbelievable as it appeared, she had been successful in finding a seam in the floating parade of ruined components, burned-out hull segments, and clouds of dust that had once been interstellar spaceships.

It wasn't perfect, and more than once she'd had to perform delicate corkscrews, usually around larger sections of the destroyed ships that were out of proportion or between large chunks of steel that clashed together and threatened to destroy the *Echo* if she hadn't slipped past them. The bridge was quiet behind her. Kim wasn't sure if no one was talking or maybe she was just concentrating so hard that she couldn't hear them.

They had nearly found their way through the debris field and were drifting slowly in the lee of a huge engine that had once powered a ship many times the size of the *Echo* through space. Beyond them was a cloud of debris that was too thick to see through. Kim wanted to go around it, but there were too many fast-moving pieces around the cloud. She preferred flying among the large sections of spaceships that moved slowly, rather than the smaller pieces that would do less damage if she hit one but were moving faster.

"Any chance you can tell me what's in that cloud?" Kim asked.

"Radar doesn't penetrate," Nance said.

"I have an idea," Ben said. "Are we safe here for a minute?"

"I think so," Kim said.

"Magnum, can we fire the last missile without arming it?" Ben asked.

"Yes," Magnum said.

"What good would that do?" Duke Simeon said.

"Maybe nothing," Ben said. "But an object moving at speed through the dust cloud should swirl it enough that we can see what's ahead of us."

"And if something swings into our path, we're dead," Kim said.

"You don't like the idea?" Ben replied.

"I didn't say that," Kim said. "Just reminding myself what's at stake."

"I would prefer not to die," Duke Simeon said, "if I have a vote."

"We all get a vote," Kim said. "Unfortunately, this idea is running opposed. Go ahead, Magnum."

It took the big man less than a minute to configure the missile. When he fired it, the weapon jumped away from the *Echo* and shot into the dust cloud at massive speed. The cloud of dust was blown outward from the missile's exhaust, creating a tiny tunnel through the cloud.

"It's clear," Nance said. "Radar shows the missile ran straight through."

"Our turn," Kim said.

Unfortunately, the tunnel didn't hold its shape for long and was too small for the *Echo* to fly through. The ship's impact on the dust, which went flying into the space left by the missile, soon obscured their view. Kim flew straight, and there was nothing they could do but wait, hoping that nothing larger lurked in the cloud that might compromise the ship.

When they broke out of the cloud on the other side, there were only a few more obstacles to avoid, and then they were free.

"Made it," Ben said. "That was amazing flying, Kim."

"No sweat," Kim said as she slumped in the pilot's seat.

The truth was, she was drenched in sweat. Not from fear, but from intense concentration and the bulky space suit she'd worn just in case the worst happened. She set a course for the cluster of Royal Imperium ships that were nearly two hundred miles from the debris cloud. It was clear that they hadn't bothered trying to move the junk circling the planet. Kim guessed that once they lost contact with the *Echo*, they must have decided that General Pershing was lost and they no longer needed to carry out her orders.

"I'll notify the general," Nance said.

"Who wants to bet they aren't happy to see her?" Kim said.

"No, thanks," Ben said. "That's a lousy bet."

"I can't believe we made it," Duke Simeon said.

"Believe it or not," Kim said as she turned her seat around, "all that matters is that we're still here."

"You have to be the best pilot in the galaxy," the duke said.

"I like him," Kim replied.

"She is," Ben said. "But we shouldn't have had to prove it. If the Royal Imperium is going to survive this war, you need to get behind a single leader and make sure that people follow orders."

"If only things were that simple," the duke said.

"That's why I have no interest in politics," Kim replied. "Just give me a good ship and a solid destination, not endless debates and constant striving for power."

"Is that really how you see it?" Duke Simeon asked.

"Don't you?" Ben asked.

"No," the royal said with sincerity. "I know it may look confusing and perhaps even a little out of control, but with the right leadership, all parties come together in unity. It's like a symphony—everyone has a part, and together it creates a masterpiece."

"Maybe," Kim said. "But right now, it seems like everyone has their own agenda."

"Maybe we can change that," Duke Simeon said. "I intend to try."

"We wish you luck," Ben said.

Kim thought he was going to say more, but General Pershing came up the stairs and the bridge fell silent. She looked exhausted, and Kim wondered just what was happening down in the rec room.

"Make for the *Everest*," the general ordered. "I want the prisoner detained properly."

"Is it giving you trouble?" Ben asked.

"Just the opposite, actually," Pershing said. "Chieftain Grubat seems to be cooperating fully."

"Who saw that coming?" Kim said.

"Makes sense," Duke Simeon said. "It's not like the aliens have a prayer against the Royal Imperium."

Kim thought the duke was talking pretty big for a government that couldn't bring more than a few ships together against the alien fleet. They had gotten lucky, there was no doubt about that. But their victories against the aliens had come at a price.

"Incoming message," Nance announced.

"Put it on the speakers," Pershing said.

Modulus Echo, this is the Everest. You are ordered to come aboard and explain the purpose of the rebels on board the Plato.

The message repeated. The general looked perturbed, but Kim didn't care. All that really mattered to her was that the *Echo* and the people she cared about were safe.

"Follow their instructions," Pershing said. "I'll see that the prisoner is situated, and then I'll straighten out the misunderstanding with Admiral Dietz."

"I'll go with you," Duke Simeon said.

"We'll make sure the *Echo* is ready when you return," Ben said.

Kim detected a strange note in Ben's voice. He was not a deceptive person, but Kim could have sworn he was trying to hide something. The general didn't seem to notice. Kim swiveled her chair around. Flying through the debris field had been taxing, but all she needed was a chance to stretch her aching muscles, and then she would back Ben's play, no matter what he had in mind.

Being pawns in the Royal Imperium's war had gone on long enough to Kim. She had proven herself, and all that was left was to live long enough to enjoy her hard-won reputation. The last thing she wanted was to become a legend best known for dying too young.

Chapter 34

Ben decided to bide his time. There were things happening that he had no influence over, but he was optimistic that an opportunity to break free from the general's need to be in the center of danger. He had made a deal, but he felt confident that he had more than fulfilled his end of the bargain. General Pershing was constantly pushing them into situations that put the ship and her crew in danger, like flying through the debris cloud with no shielding. It had been his idea, but no other pilot would have even considered trying a crazy mission like that. It was those types of things that had, in his mind, provided the general with more than enough return for the food and Zexum she had given to them.

Leaving would, of course, void any kind of amnesty, but Ben was willing to risk it. He had fallen in love with the life of a smuggler. Flying between worlds, staying off the Royal Imperium's radar, helping people who were in desperate need, all while earning a decent living—that was what he hoped to do. And the longer they stayed in the fight with the aliens, the more likely it was that they would die. Ben still felt responsible for having opened the wormhole, but considering all they'd done to at least slow the alien invasion, it seemed reasonable that others could take up the fight.

The journey across space toward the cluster of Royal Imperium ships was uneventful. And when they approached the *Everest*, the big ship locked onto them with her tractor beam to guide them safely into the cavernous hangar.

Ben met the general, who was at the rear hatch. She hit the button to open the big cargo door as soon as the *Echo* settled on the hangar deck. A squad of soldiers was waiting, all armed with rifles and in full battle armor.

"What's going on?" Ben asked, suddenly afraid that the general had picked up on his desire to break their deal. For a second, he imagined them carrying him off the ship in restraints to be taken straight to the Royal Imperium torture chambers.

"They're here for the prisoner," Pershing said. "Show them where he's being kept."

Ben nodded, and General Pershing began giving orders for the bodies of the aliens to be removed from the *Echo* as well. Ben led a squad of armed guards through his precious engineering bay. His back tingled with the fear that one of them might raise their weapon and shoot him before he had a chance to turn around. His skin seemed to crawl, and sweat began to drip down his back.

When he pushed through the door into the rec room, Ben wasn't sure what he expected to find. The prisoner sat slumped against the wall, his arms outstretched and bound with plastic wire ties. But other than his strange appearance, the alien seemed completely unharmed. Whatever methods of persuasion General Pershing had used, they hadn't caused the alien harm.

"Cut him free," the ranking soldier said.

Ben stepped aside, happy that there was someone for the soldiers to focus on other than him. They cut the plastic bands that held the alien and stood him up. Ben was surprised at how tall the alien was. The creature's long, thick tendrils waved like hair that was underwater.

"Secure his arms behind him," the soldier in charge said.

When the alien spoke, everyone in the rec room froze. Ben felt chill bumps spring up all over his body. The deep voice sounded like an animal, grunting and growling, but a strange robotic voice translated the alien's words.

"My leg is damaged," he said. "I will need help walking."

"Stay on either side of him," the soldier in charge said.

The soldiers took hold of the alien's elbows. Their battle helmets covered their faces, and Ben couldn't see their expressions, but he could tell by their body language that they weren't happy. They escorted their prisoner back through Engineering and toward the wide-open rear hatch. Ben watched them leave, then closed the ramp that served as the cargo bay door. He felt more secure in his ship with the doors battened down than completely exposed in the Royal Imperium battle cruiser's hangar.

"They got rid of the bodies," Kim said as Ben slowly climbed the stairs toward the main deck. "Smells better already."

"Did the duke leave with the general?" Ben asked.

"As a matter of fact, he did."

"Good, I want to have a quick word with everyone. Let's gather in my quarters."

Getting Nance away from her computer station wasn't easy. And Ben knew they could talk on the bridge, but he didn't feel comfortable speaking his mind there. And that was part of the problem. The longer the general was in charge, the less the *Echo* felt like his ship.

They crowded into the narrow berth. The room was large by military standards, and bigger than the passenger cabins, but they weren't made for groups. Two people were comfortable, but four were crowded. Magnum leaned against the door, while Nance sat at the table. Ben sat across from her, and Kim was perched on the foot of his bed.

"Should we get the professor?" Nance asked.

"No," Ben said. "Let him work."

"What's on your mind?" Kim asked. "I could see the wheels turning when the general was on the bridge giving orders."

"I'm thinking it's time we found a way to get out of here," Ben said. "I want to leave without the general."

"I knew it," Kim said with a grin.

"You mean break the deal?" Nance asked.

"I know we gave our word, but we've done enough, don't you think?" Ben argued. "We may have started this mess, but we've done more to fix it than anyone else."

"Here, here," Kim said.

"The longer we stay, the greater the odds that we'll get killed," Magnum said.

Ben saw Nance look at him. She was uncertain and that was no surprise. She didn't like taking risks. Even though working with the Royal Imperium was dangerous, it felt secure in some ways. Having a high-ranking officer on board gave the *Echo* legitimacy that none of them had ever experienced before.

"I know it's scary to think of leaving," Ben said. "We'll be outlaws again, but I doubt there would be many people in a hurry to help the Royal Imperium. From what I've heard, most systems are reforming old alliances and declaring themselves independent."

"If that's true, we could survive outside the government's reach," Nance said.

"I'm sure it's true," Kim said. "The Confederate worlds would jump at the chance to break free, and there are plenty of others who are under the control of politicians who are just as crooked and greedy as the royal family."

"How do we do it?" Magnum asked.

"I've got an idea about that," Ben said. "Nance, can you tell the *Everest* flight controllers that we need to go off-ship to make some repairs?"

"I suppose," Nance replied. "But why would we do that? Can't we make the repairs easier here, in their hangar?"

"We'll tell them we need zero gravity to make the repairs," Ben said. "We'll have to play it cool and drift away from the Royal Imperium ships."

"That will raise some eyebrows," Kim said.

"Not if they see us doing the work," Ben said. "I'll go EVA and repair the wing."

"We could mount the missiles too," Magnum said.

"Good idea," Ben said. "They won't question us if they can see that we're doing what we claimed to be doing."

"But what are we really doing?" Nance asked.

"Preparing to leave the system," Ben said. "That's why we can't wait to get started. I have no idea how long the general will be tied up on this ship."

"If we log onto the Nav Net, the Royal Imperium ships will pick up on it," Nance said.

"True," Kim said. "They might even scan us. They'd know if we were calculating a jump point."

"So we won't," Ben said. "We'll do standard systems checks and make the repairs until we drift out of tractor beam range."

"And then what?" Kim said.

"Then we run for it," Ben said. "I'll fire up the shield, we make for deep space, and do a series of quick jumps."

"We'll be free," Kim said.

"But we'll be wanted fugitives," Nance pointed out. "We'll never have another chance for amnesty again."

"And that brings me to my last thought," Ben said. "I don't think the amnesty will stand, even if we stay."

"You think the general will double-cross us?" Kim asked.

"She wouldn't," Nance said. "She's honor bound to uphold the deal she made."

"Honor or no honor, I don't think she'll be in charge," Ben said.

"What about the duke?" Kim asked.

"If he lives," Ben said, "he won't be made king."

"Why the hell not?" Kim asked.

"The queen," Magnum said.

Ben nodded. It was strange how in sync he and Magnum were. They hadn't discussed Ben's concerns beforehand, but it was almost as if they had.

"I don't think the queen will give up control," Ben said. "Not while there's a chance that the king or her son could still be alive."

"How would she know that?" Kim asked, narrowing her eyes.

"The prisoner," Ben said. "She admitted that he was cooperating. He had a translation device. I heard him use it."

"So?" Kim said.

"I saw the transmission the commandos sent," Nance said, "before they ambushed the aliens and brought back prisoners."

Ben looked at her with surprise, and she shrugged her shoulders. "What? I get bored sometimes," Nance explained.

"What'd they see?" Ben asked.

"The aliens, building a wall to protect their settlement," Nance said.

"That's no big deal," Kim said.

"And Major Le Croix," Nance said. "He was working with the aliens."

"What?" Kim asked.

"The officer who led the rescue operation in orbit?" Ben asked.

"Yes," Nance replied.

"And if he's alive..." Magnum said.

"Then it stands to reason that whoever was in the emergency pod with him could still be alive," Kim said shaking her head. "Ben, did you know that?"

"No," he admitted. "But I got a feeling that something was bothering the general. She looked pale and preoccupied."

"So if the prisoner was spilling his guts to the general, he might have mentioned the other prisoner," Kim said.

"And if he told her, he'll tell whoever else questions him," Ben said. "It'll be the first thing the queen wants to know."

"She won't uphold the deals General Pershing made with us or the Confederates," Magnum said.

Ben shook his head again. "No, I don't think she will. And in my mind, that's too big a risk. We have to get free."

"I agree," Magnum said.

"Me too," Kim added. "I mean, maybe that's why the prisoner was cooperating. Maybe they're planning some kind of prisoner exchange."

"It's just too risky to stay," Ben said. "If we can get away, we have to try, I think. Nance?"

She was thinking it all through, like a chess master going over potential moves in her head and calculating her opponent's responses. Finally, after a long, tense minute when Ben began to doubt that she would agree with them, she nodded.

"Okay," Ben said, relaxing a little. "We're all agreed, then."

"Should we tell the professor?" Nance said.

"No, let him work," Ben said. "He's our ace in the hole. If anyone can solve the wormhole issue, it's Professor Jones. And they probably won't fire on us and risk killing him."

"Good point," Kim said.

"Alright, we don't have a lot of time. Once Pershing is through on this ship, I have a feeling she'll want to leave as soon as possible."

"To go on some other crazy mission," Kim said. "And put us all in danger."

"Let's make our request to do the repairs off-ship," Ben said. "What's the worst that can happen?"

"They can arrest us all and torture us to death," Kim said.

"I was thinking more along the lines that they might say no," Ben said.

"Oh yeah, that too," Kim said with a wink.

Chapter 35

General Pershing was conflicted. The information she had learned about the Krah was frightening. The human race was standing on a razor's edge. If the aliens learned how to fight back in space, they could retake the Celeste system, bring in hundreds, maybe even thousands more ships, and conquer the galaxy. There was no doubt in her mind that they would try to do exactly that. But they needed time, and so did she. Hopefully, she needed less than they did.

But what was really troubling her was the prisoner's information about the crown prince. Godfred was still alive, and giving the aliens whatever they wanted. He had shown them how to access the Nav Net, which put the entire galaxy at risk. Without that information, the aliens were stuck in the Celeste system. Their only way out was by following the human ships with their sophisticated tracking method. She had pushed to know more about it, but the prisoner wasn't knowledgeable about technical matters. Perhaps he was lying, but she couldn't know for certain.

If Godfred was alive, then he was the heir, and rescuing him was the highest priority. But her staunchest supporter was Duke Simeon. If the crown prince still lived, he was just a useless member of the royal family—a cousin to the king, with no power and no influence. Yet she felt duty bound to reveal her knowledge. The aliens might even trade Chieftain Grubat for Prince Godfred. They didn't understand his value to the human race, but Grubat was a member of their warrior class, who had the most experience fighting the humans.

She walked into the admiral's salon. Most politically appointed officers utilized the areas of the ships they commanded in what Pershing thought of as an entirely unnecessary fashion. Admiral Dietz had converted his command center into a social lounge. All tactical decisions were made on the bridge, where the admiral only made the occasional visit. He was more comfortable in his stateroom, the officer's wardroom, or his well-appointed salon with furnishings from his home world of Reaught.

Pershing saw the queen standing by a large observation window. She was standing ramrod straight, but she looked thinner than when she'd been rescued and taken aboard the *Modulus Echo*. Admiral Dietz had a drink in one hand and was stroking the ears of a long-haired cat of some kind with the other. There were rugs on the deck and artwork on the walls, even a large aquarium filled with colorful fish.

"General Pershing," Admiral Dietz said. "Welcome back."

"It's good to be back, Admiral," Pershing said.

"It's Admiral General now," Dietz said. "The queen thought it only fitting that her commander in chief be of proper rank. I thought it was a splendid idea, don't you?"

"I couldn't agree more," Pershing said.

"You have a prisoner," Queen Ultane said without turning. "What have you learned?"

Pershing cast a quick glance at Duke Simeon, who was standing beside her. It felt disloyal to tell the queen the truth and dishonorable to lie.

"That the danger posed by the Krah, that's what they call themselves," Pershing explained, "is even greater than I feared.

They're militaristic and have come here to conquer and pillage."

"I think we could have guessed that much," Dietz said.

"They have a warrior culture," Pershing said. "They have conquered their own galaxy, but it's smaller and less hospitable than ours. The climate and atmosphere of Gershwin are ideal for their kind, and they are without a home world."

"Well, they can't have mine," the queen replied.

"But it is of great value to them, as you can probably guess," Pershing said. "Nothing will stop them short of total annihilation."

"Then we will oblige them," Dietz said.

Duke Simeon finally spoke up. "If we don't close the wormhole, we'll be vulnerable. They could bring in ten thousand ships, for all we know."

"Is that what the prisoner told you?" Queen Ultane asked.

"Not in those exact words," Pershing said. "And we would be wise to believe him if he had. The point is we can't know how many ships they have. But if they've conquered one galaxy, we shouldn't underestimate them."

"They are not the only ones to have accomplished that feat," Queen Ultane replied.

"Don't be absurd," Duke Simeon said. "Even at our strongest, we took control through diplomacy and economic pressure. These Krah know nothing but war."

"Well, they don't appear to be suited for it," Dietz said. "We ran their armada out of the system with just three warships."

General Pershing wanted to point out that Dietz and his trio of ships had arrived late. It was actually her strategy and the work of her people that had won the system back, but he was too arrogant to accept reality. She decided to try another tactic.

"You haven't used your gravity tractor beams to clear a path to the planet," Pershing said. "And you've stopped the *Plato* from delivering the soldiers I sent for. May I ask why?"

"Well, until we found out if you even survived the descent to the surface, we didn't really see the point," Dietz said smugly. "To be honest, at this juncture, I still don't."

"The point," Pershing said, forcing herself to speak in a calm, reasonable tone, "is to eradicate the alien presence on Gershwin. They're already calling the planet New Krah. As long as they have hope of making it their new home world, they will keep trying to retake the system."

"Don't we want the fight to be here?" Queen Ultane said, turning around for the first time. "It makes more sense than chasing them around the galaxy."

"Of course," Pershing said. "But the planet is a rallying point for them. Crushing their hopes will go a long way to taking the fight out of them."

"Maybe they'll even leave peacefully if they see that we won't let them take our planets," Duke Simeon said.

"Either way, the wormhole makes this system too valuable strategically to let the aliens have it," Pershing said. "They will be back and we have to be ready, which is why we need to get the *Plato* onto Gershwin as soon as possible."

"How's that?" Admiral Dietz asked.

Pershing wasn't sure if she wanted to laugh or cry about the admiral general's lack of tactical acumen. It was no surprise that the queen had gone back on her word and made a more pliable political officer her choice for commander in chief. To be honest, Pershing didn't care who held the top spot in the Royal Imperium military, but she had hoped that it would at least be a competent officer during their conflict with the Krah. Dietz was a fool and would only cost the Imperium lives with his impulsive decision making that was based more on whim than on sound military theory.

"Because," Pershing said, almost losing her calm demeanor, "when the aliens return, which they inevitably will, the ground forces on Gershwin will force the Krah to divide their focus. We have taken the upper hand by cutting off their chain of supply when we drove them out of the system."

"You mean the wormhole," Dietz said.

"Exactly," Pershing replied.

"Can't they get whatever they need here?" Queen Ultane asked. "Food, water, air, fuel, whatever they need is here. Not back in their old galaxy. They've shown their hand, General. They take our ships to increase their fleet. They're pirates, nothing more."

Pershing couldn't believe that the queen of the Royal Imperium was actually treating the biggest threat to the galaxy like a minor annoyance.

"I don't see any need to involve the rebels," Queen Ultane continued. "And I don't like the offer you made to them."

"Yes, that was rather foolish," Admiral General Dietz said. "You've only made their petty calls for independence more desperate."

"Please understand," Pershing said, "that we need help. If we don't stop the Krah as quickly as possible, they will take root and we may never get them out."

"You have proof of this?" the queen asked.

"I have spent time questioning the prisoner," Pershing said.

"And I think it's time we do the same," Dietz said. "I'll order a proper interrogation, and we'll revisit this conversation once we've been properly briefed."

"Can we at least send the *Plato* to begin moving the debris from around the planet?" Pershing urged.

"Actually, I think it's best if we keep the rebels right where they are," Dietz said. "I'll decide what to do with the rebels. It might be best to ship them straight to a penal colony where they belong. You are dismissed, General Pershing."

She forced herself to salute the pompous officer before leaving his salon. Duke Simeon followed her. She could feel the uncertainty radiating from him. He had good intentions, but he was easily swayed. Even a foolish argument, made with conviction, caused him to think twice.

"Should we return to the *Echo*?" Duke Simeon asked.

"No," Pershing said. "We need to find out as much as we can from the dissections being done on the aliens."

"But the admiral general doesn't seem interested in carrying on the fight," the duke pointed out.

"It's not up to him," Pershing said. "The Krah will bring the fight to us. All we can do in the meantime is gather as much information on our new enemy as possible."

Chapter 36

"We're cleared to leave the hangar," Nance said.

"Good," Ben said. "Kim, take us out."

"My pleasure," she replied. "This place gives me the creeps."

The little ship rose up and moved swiftly toward the open hangar bay doors. Ben watched on the big bridge displays as they passed through the magnetic shielding that protected the open hangar from the hard vacuum of space.

"Where should we go?" Kim asked.

"Out past the Royal Imperium ships," Ben said. "But go slow."

"Look casual, I got it," Kim replied.

"Move toward the planet," Nance said. "There are more obstacles that way."

They had all agreed not to talk about the plan on the bridge, just in case someone was listening. They had their communications system muted, but they didn't trust the Royal Imperium. Anyone could have put a listening device on the bridge, from the general herself to one of the commandos on her Spec Ops teams.

It didn't take long to fly clear of the other ships. Kim let the *Echo* drift, making it look like she tried to stop their momentum, but did a slipshod job of it.

"We're ready," Kim said. "There's zero friction and we're drifting away. I'd say in half an hour we'll be out of range of their tractor beams."

"Good," Ben said, slipping his helmet onto his head and testing his com-link. "I'll get started on the repairs."

Ben made his way down to the air lock. He already had a piece of metal cut to fit the hole in the underside of the *Echo*'s port wing. He picked up a portable welder and stepped into the air lock.

"Ben, wait," Nance said.

His hand hovered over the switch to cycle the air lock.

"What is it?"

"Ships," Kim said. "Get up here. We're in trouble."

Ben dropped the torch and ran out of the air lock. The space suit was bulky and made running up the stairs difficult.

"Looks like multiple ships," Nance said. "They're all around the system."

"It's the alien ships," Kim said.

Ben got to the main deck where Nance had a plot of the system pulled up on the bridge displays. At the center was a little green plus sign that was labeled *Modulus Echo*. Beside it were several blue V's, each labeled with the name of the Royal Imperium ships.

Ben saw Gershwin and the wormhole, but it was the dozen or so clusters of red V icons that struck fear in his heart. The aliens had come back. Pershing was right. Only, they didn't come in a single formation. They had sent groups of ships to strategic locations throughout the system. Several were around the wormhole, and more hovered just above the debris cloud around Gershwin. Four of the groups had appeared around the cluster of Royal Imperium ships.

"Get us moving!" Ben said as he dashed toward his console.

"I'm already on it," Kim said.

Two of the clusters of alien ships were moving in on either side of the *Echo*'s position. The other two were waiting to see what the humans would do.

"Nance, we need a jump point," Ben said.

"I'm looking for a clear lane," Nance replied.

Ben immediately started the flux shield spinning up, but he knew it would take several minutes to reach full power and actually cast the gravity bubble around the ship. The aliens were spreading out. Ben imagined them like a net, almost inescapable.

"We can't jump while we're this close to those ships," Kim said.

Ben wasn't sure if she meant the Royal Imperium vessels or the alien ships. But he was certain of one thing—they were in trouble. And if he couldn't get the shield up in time, they might all die. There were over a hundred alien ships on the plot, with more appearing like magic as they made the jump into the system.

"This is insane," Kim said.

The only stroke of good luck seemed to be that they were already moving away from the cluster of Royal Imperium ships when the aliens arrived. Kim had the main drive at full throttle, but the alien ships were faster. They would have to depend on the *Echo*'s maneuvering to keep them from being captured or destroyed.

"Oh no," Nance said.

"What?" Ben asked.

"The aliens have weapons," Nance said. "They just launched projectiles at the Royal Imperium capital ships."

"That's not good," Kim said.

Ben brought up the external camera feed on his console screens. The alien ships weren't shooting weapons, but throwing them with their articulated arms. Ben couldn't tell what the projectiles were for sure. They looked like torpedoes made of scrap metal. The projectiles didn't have independent propulsion, like a missile or torpedo. Ben watched as the *Everest* moved behind one of the drone operator ships.

"Ten seconds to impact," Nance said.

"Are they firing at us?" Kim demanded.

"Negative," Magnum replied.

"Ben?"

"It's almost ready," he said, checking on the flux shield.

"They're aiming for the capital ships," Nance said.

The alien projectiles hit the slow-moving drone operator vessel with incredible force. There was no explosion, and Ben guessed that the alien torpedoes had no warheads on their projectiles. Instead of blowing up, they punched through the drone ship. Ben saw the big engine on the drone ship go suddenly cold.

Just as suddenly, the space around the Royal Imperium ships lit up with laser fire. Ben was happy that they were far enough to be out of the way, but he still checked on the flux shield. The progress bar showed that they were more than halfway to having the shield ready.

Several of the alien ships were hit with lasers that blasted away their grappling arms and scorched holes in the ships themselves. But there were so many of the strange, bulbous ships that were closing in from every side. More projectiles were fired. Ben thought the entire mass of Royal Imperium ships looked out of control. Only the *Everest* seemed to be making headway. After ducking between two of the bulky drone operator ships, she fired a hail of missiles straight ahead.

"What are they doing?" Kim asked.

"I don't know," Ben said. "But the shields are up. Let's get out of this mess."

Chapter 37

Pershing was making her way to the lifts, intending to go down to the medical wing of the massive ship, when the alarms sounded. Beside her, Duke Simeon looked shocked, but Pershing sprang immediately into action and sprinted back down the wide hallway, straight to the ship's bridge. She even arrived before Admiral General Dietz, who came stumbling in and looked just as shocked as the duke.

"What's happening?" Dietz demanded.

Pershing could see from the holographic plot exactly what had occurred. The Krah had returned. The *Everest* was a state-of-the-art battleship. At the center of the bridge, which was located in a reinforced section in the middle of the massive ship, was a holo-projector. Unlike the plot on the *Echo*, which only showed tiny icons to indicate the different vessels in a given area around the ship, the holo-plot, as it was often referred to, showed actual images of the ships themselves. Pershing noted right away that they were surrounded by clusters of Krah ships. The aliens were already moving to attack and wasting no time.

"We're under attack," Pershing said in an authoritative tone. "Have all hands report to battle stations. Come around on heading two-one-niner."

The helmsman didn't hesitate to repeat the order. Pershing glanced at Dietz, who looked petrified.

"I'll take command here," Pershing told him. "You're too important to risk losing, Admiral General."

The title came out of her mouth stilted with condescension, but Dietz didn't seem to notice. He nodded.

"Go with him, Your Highness," Pershing ordered Duke Simeon. "Both of you stay with the queen. I'm locking down the ship."

Duke Simeon nodded, and when he moved toward the exit, Admiral General Dietz followed. As soon as they were out of the bridge, Pershing began barking orders to the crew again.

"Order our ships to spread out," she said. "Evasive maneuvers. Prepare to jump out of the system. Have everyone reconvene at the..."

Her eyes spotted a familiar-shaped blip on the plot as she approached the holo-projector in the center of the bridge.

"Why is the *Modulus Echo* not in the hangar bay?" Pershing demanded.

"They requested permission to leave the ship to make repairs, General," the flight control officer said.

Pershing was caught off guard. She knew that they didn't need to leave the *Everest* to make their repairs, which meant they were running. The urgency of the attack was suddenly diminished by her fury at the betrayal by the crew of the little ship.

"Where should I order the other ships to meet?" asked the communications officer.

"The Yelsin system," Pershing said. "Multiple jumps. I don't want anyone leading the Krah straight to our rendezvous point."

"Roger that, General," the communications officer said.

"We have incoming fire from the alien ships," the weapons officer shouted.

"Stay calm and lock down the ship," Pershing said. "Bring up the visual feed."

Just like the *Echo*, the *Everest* had large displays built into the walls of the oval-shaped bridge. Thick steel doors were slowly closing behind her, and emergency lights were flashing out in the hallway. On the display, Pershing saw the projectiles racing through space toward them.

"Helm, get us behind the drone ship," Pershing ordered.

She saw the helmsman bringing the ship's main drive engines to full throttle.

"Navigation, I want a jump point straight ahead," Pershing continued giving instruction to the officers of the big ship. "Fire control, prepare for a heavy barrage, straight ahead."

"General, we have enemy ships moving to block our path," the ship's navigator said.

"Order all ships to open fire," Pershing barked. "What's the status on the *Tempest*?"

"They've lost power," someone said. "And they're venting atmosphere."

"Stay in their lee, helmsman," Pershing said. "Are we ready to make the jump?"

"Almost, General," the navigation officer replied.

"Fire everything we've got, straight ahead," Pershing said. "Don't bother assigning targets."

"Roger that. Firing all forward cannons and missiles."

The barrage blazed out into space. Pershing glanced at the other ships. The drone operators were lost. They simply couldn't get up to speed in time to avoid the projectiles being fired at them. The other two capital ships were holding their own, but both seemed focused on fighting rather than fleeing.

Pershing could see that there were over a hundred Krah ships in the system. At least thirty were moving to attack positions and even more were waiting in reserve. The three Royal Imperium battle cruisers had more firepower, but they couldn't stop thirty ships.

Her eyes darted to where the tiny Kestrel class ship was running from the battle. Pershing silently vowed revenge on the *Modulus Echo* but then turned back to the space in front of the *Everest*. The barrage of missiles and laser fire had cleared a path. Two Krah ships exploded in dazzling balls of fire, and several others that were moving to intercept the big Royal Imperium ship altered course.

"Now, helm. Make the jump," Pershing ordered.

"Aye, General. Transitioning to hyperspace."

The ship seemed to stretch and time slowed for a heartbeat. Pershing feared that the ship would be hit by one of the several projectiles that had been fired at them by the Krah, but fortunately for General Alicia Pershing and over four hundred crew members on board the *Everest*, they disappeared into hyperspace before the ship was hit by the kinetic projectiles.

The blue glow of hyperspace lit the bridge display, and the holo-plot was erased, almost as if someone had tripped on the device's power cord.

"Should we stand down?" asked the ship's first officer, a stout woman in a uniform that was too tight around her bulky middle.

"Negative," Pershing said. "How much time do we have before we drop back into normal space?"

"Two minutes, General," the helmsman said.

"The Krah are capable of following us through hyperspace," Pershing explained. "When we drop back into normal space, I want full speed ahead. Fire control, prepare all stern weapons and fire on anything that follows us."

"Aye, General, preparing stern cannons," the weapons officer said.

"Navigation, I want the next jump plotted, but don't set the jump point until I order you to."

"Roger that, Cap—I mean, General."

Pershing should have relished being back on a proper ship and in the thick of the fighting, but she couldn't. Underlying the tension on the bridge, and her own personal fears, was the hurt that the crew she had trusted and given a second chance to had betrayed her. If it were simply a matter of an official pardon, she might have understood. But Pershing had covered up the *Echo*'s role in opening the wormhole, which had destroyed more than half of the Royal Imperium Fleet. She didn't know what the future held, or how long the war with the Krah would last, but she knew that when it was over, she would focus all her attention on finding the crew of the little ship and making them pay for their disloyalty.

"Fifteen seconds till transition to normal space," the helmsman said.

It took a strong act of will, but Pershing filed her personal vendetta away and focused on the task at hand. *First, the Krah,* she told herself. *Then you can hunt down the Modulus Echo, no matter what it takes.*

Chapter 38

It wasn't hard for the *Modulus Echo* to slip through the lines of the attacking alien ships. They didn't even get fired on as they fled from the battle. But other ships were maneuvering behind the front lines.

"We've four ships moving to intercept," Nance said calmly.

"We need to jump to hyperspace," Ben said.

"Just give me a jump point," Kim snapped.

"Working on it," Nance said. "The aliens have blocked the initial trajectory."

"The *Everest* is gone," Magnum said.

"Gone as in..." Ben said.

"No," Nance replied. "It jumped out of the system. Six of the alien vessels followed it."

"That's bad news," Kim said.

"They're a big prize," Ben said. "We're just a little fish."

He looked at the plot. The drone operator ships were blinking to indicated they were damaged. The *Romulus* and the *Andromeda* were holding their own, but more alien ships were moving toward the battle cruisers. Small arrows indicated projectiles that were picked up on radar as the large torpedo-shaped devices hurtled toward the Royal Imperium ships.

"They've had to stop firing on the aliens and focus on destroying the missiles being fired at them," Ben said.

"How about you worry a little more about us right now?" Kim said.

"The *Plato* is making a run for it," Nance said.

"Kim, let the closest ship get just within range," Ben said. "Let's remind them what happens when they do."

"You're sure the shield can handle it?" Kim asked.

"Positive," Ben said.

Although everything on his console showed that the gravity shield was up and working, they couldn't see it. Unlike the deflector screens, the flux shield covered the entire ship in a swirl of gravity current that was completely invisible and didn't drain their power like traditional shielding. The prototype shield had saved them in the past, but the sheer number of alien ships around them made their current situation feel hopeless.

"The aliens are moving to intercept the *Plato*," Nance said. "Their hyperdrive just went offline."

"They're stuck here," Magnum said.

"Focus, people," Kim said. "I need a jump point."

"It's hard to calculate where to jump from," Nance said. "There are too many alien ships in the system."

"So we jump blind," Kim said. "What choice do we have?"

The nearest alien ship had just come in range. Ben was glued to his console, watching the gangly arms from the alien vessel reach out for them.

"Incoming," Nance said.

The grappling arms were grasping for the *Echo*, determined to take hold of the Kestrel class ship and take her captive. Ben knew that if that happened, they would almost certainly rupture the hull. The atmosphere would be sucked out of even a tiny crack in their fuselage, and the crew would be sucked out into space. There was no hope of help coming, even if they could survive in hard vacuum long enough.

"The *Romulus* is gone," Nance said.

Her tone was even, completely unemotional, yet Ben didn't have to ask if she'd made the jump to light speed. The flash of light as the *Romulus* exploded was more than enough evidence of her demise.

At almost the same time, the alien ship chasing them reached the *Echo*'s gravity shield. The first grappling arm to touch it was knocked away; the second was crushed, ripped from the alien ship, and sent whirling through space.

"The shield is working," Ben said.

"Good, now can we go?" Kim asked.

She slammed the joystick over, pushed the throttle to the stops, and sent the ship spiraling down. They had lulled the alien ships into a false sense of superiority, but while they couldn't outrun their pursuers, they were vastly more maneuverable.

"If we jump, there's no guarantee that we survive," Ben said. "But I'm sure the *Plato* and all those Confederates we talked into joining the fight will die."

"What? Is that what you're worried about?" Kim asked incredulously."

"The *Andromeda* just made the jump, but she was followed," Nance said. "And she was showing damage before going to light speed."

"The *Plato* doesn't have the weapons that the other ships had," Ben said. "They can't blaze a trail out of the system."

"Neither can we," Kim said.

"True, but we can run interference," Ben said. "Until the *Plato* gets to Gershwin."

"No way," Kim said.

"You think the *Plato* can make it through the debris field?" Nance asked.

"They've got a shot," Ben said. "The aliens probably won't follow them. I know they'll take damage, maybe a lot, but at least they'll have a chance of surviving."

"Fine, let them try," Kim said.

"But they won't make it if we don't help," Ben said.

"Haven't we helped enough?" Kim argued.

"You're talking about blocking the aliens," Magnum said. "There are four ships pursuing the *Plato*."

"We got them into this mess," Ben said. "I know it's crazy, but we can't safely make the jump either. Gershwin is our safest option right now."

"I don't think I can fly through that garbage field again," Kim said. "I'd rather jump from the system blind."

"We'll go through the debris field with our shield up," Ben said.

"Didn't you say that was dangerous?" Kim said.

"It is," Ben replied. "It will destabilize the debris field. But that will work in our favor. And we can use the *Plato* to block most of the smaller elements."

"Fine," Kim agreed. "Where are they?"

Nance pointed Kim in the right direction, and the *Echo* went charging past the trio of alien ships that were chasing her. Kim trusted the flux shield, but she didn't rely on it. Instead, she stayed just out of reach of the alien ships, zigging and zagging as they raced toward the *Plato*.

"Can you raise them on comms?" Ben asked.

"The channel is open," Nance said. "Can't promise they're listening."

"R.I.F. *Plato*, this is the *Modulus Echo*," Ben said into the mic that was built into his console. "We are coming to assist you."

The reply was instantaneous.

Negative, Modulus Echo. We have lost our hyperdrive and have no way to leave the system. I repeat, we're stuck here with no hyperdrive. Save yourselves. Over.

"We read you, *Plato*," Ben said. "But we have a plan. Head for Gershwin, and we'll run interference for you."

Ben wasn't sure that the Royal Imperium ship had heard him, or would listen. They had four alien ships chasing them. The aliens were gaining on the *Plato*, their grappling arms extended like the tentacles of giant space monsters.

"They're turning," Nance said.

"Good," Ben replied. "Kim, get behind them."

"Thank you, Captain Obvious," Kim replied. "We should have jumped from the system as soon as we were out of the *Everest*."

"We'll make it," Ben said.

But as they slipped behind the *Plato*, they were almost immediately hit by the alien grappling arms. Nearly thirty of the articulated, extendable arms with pincers at the end to grab their prey with, ran straight into the *Echo*'s gravity shield. The result was instant chaos. Several arms were jerked free and sent flying away from the Kestrel class ship, and others were smashed flat by the powerful gravitational waves. But several were actually caught. They were crushed too, reduced down to atoms that swirled on the gravity currents. There was a sudden surge of energy that made the warning alarm on Ben's console beep.

"What was that?" Kim asked, as she flew up and over the top of the *Plato*.

"Just an energy surge," Ben said.

"They won't try that again," Magnum said. "They're spreading out."

"Trying to take hold of the *Plato* from the sides," Kim said.

She argued and fussed, but Ben knew she wouldn't turn her back on the helpless. The crew members of the *Plato* were professionals in the Royal Imperium Space Navy. Fighting the alien threat to humanity was their duty. If they died in the attempt, it was tragic, but understandable. The Confederate volunteers, however, were completely helpless. They might die fighting on Gershwin, but at least their fate would be in their own hands. If the alien ships managed to rip holes in the *Plato*, the Confederates would die from exposure to hard vacuum, and Kim didn't want that any more than Ben did.

Whatever you did worked once, the voice from the *Plato* said, booming over the bridge speakers on the *Echo. I hope you have a few more tricks up your sleeve. Over.*

"Roger that, *Plato*," Ben said. "Keep heading for the planet. We'll hold off the aliens. Do you have weapons?"

Just two laser batteries. We've used everything else. Over.

"Concentrate your fire on the debris field. We have to clear a seam for you."

Roger that, the voice said.

Ben didn't even know the name of the ship's commander, or what the status was of the two hundred Confederate volunteers. Kim was rolling over the side of the Royal Imperium ship, careful not to get too close to the *Plato* and risk damaging them with the *Echo*'s gravity shield. The aliens, on the other hand, were trying to get close enough to reach the ship, but they had learned to fear the *Echo*'s shield.

Keeping pace with the *Plato*, which Ben guessed was a converted Corvette class battleship, didn't seem to be a problem for the alien vessels. But maneuvering was. They edged closer and closer until Kim flew between them and the *Plato*. At first, they tried just retracting their grappling arms, but Kim flew toward the alien ships and drove them back. It was a constant battle to keep the ships away, and more were moving toward them from all around the system.

"Looks like we're a hit," Kim said.

"All the alien ships are moving toward us," Nance said.

The *Plato* began to fire toward the planet, and after a few minutes, the alien ships pulled back. Ben could see the heavy lasers punching through the debris cloud, but they didn't have much success in opening a corridor. The power level on the flux shield had surged to over sixty percent. And odds were good that it would get too high to keep online once they entered the debris field.

"How are we looking?" Kim asked.

"The aliens realize what we're doing," Nance replied. "They aren't trying to stop us."

"Why should they?" Kim said. "If we make it through the debris field, we'll be stuck on the planet. They can capture us at their leisure."

"We'll make it," Ben said. "And Gershwin is a big place. Getting to the surface will buy us time to find a way out of the system."

"I just love his optimism," Kim said with just a touch of sarcasm. "Even in the face of overwhelming odds, he can find a way to think positively."

"I'm glad you think so," Ben said. "I need to drop the shield."

"You said we could use it in the debris field," Kim snapped. The playfulness that had been in her voice a moment ago was completely gone.

Ben hit a few buttons on his console and cut the power to the gravity shield.

"I'll get it going again," Ben told her. "But it was getting hot."

"What do you think I'm doing?" Kim said, her voice loud enough to be a shout. "I'm on fire. Do something to cool me off, why don't you?"

"The plan is working," Ben said as he ordered the artificial gravity generator to power the flux shield on again. It took the system several minutes to spin the wave generator at a speed great enough to keep the gravity flowing around the ship rather than collapsing back onto it.

"The plan is suicide," Kim snarled. "That Corvette won't make it through the debris field."

"It will with our help," Ben said.

"We can't help without the shield," Kim shot back angrily.

"The *Plato* is slowing down," Nance alerted them.

"What about the alien ships?" Kim asked.

"They're holding back," Nance informed her.

"Told you," Ben said.

"Oh, shut up," Kim said. "When this is over, I'm going to give you a piece of my mind."

"I'm looking forward to it," Ben said.

"Fifteen seconds and the *Plato* will be in the debris cloud," Nance said.

"Slowing us down," Kim said.

"The flux shield is at thirty percent," Ben said.

"We're being followed," Nance said. Her calm voice seemed in contrast with the foul news she was relaying.

"Wonderful," Kim retorted.

"Two ships," Nance continued. "They're moving slowly but coming right in our wake."

"Good for them," Ben said. "We can't worry about the aliens or what they might do. Just concentrate on getting through the debris, Kim. That's all that matters."

"Unless we die," Kim said. "That matters, to me anyway."

Chapter 39

The captain or helmsman of the *Plato* knew their business. The laser fire had reduced the size of most of the debris directly ahead of the Royal Imperium craft. Unfortunately, the real danger was from the chunks of metal and starship components that were drifting in orbit. Kim could maneuver the *Echo* around and through the debris field, but the *Plato* was a long, narrow ship. Her hangar had been emptied to make room for the Confederates, and unlike the battle cruisers, she only carried weapons on the bow module.

Kim moved the *Echo* in the lee created by the larger starship. The flux shield was at seventy-five percent as some desk-sized chunks of space debris crashed into the *Plato*.

"They're taking damage," Nance said.

"Can you get a read on their hull?" Ben asked.

"No, only their active systems, but their radar just went down," Nance said.

"There's nothing we can do without the shield," Kim said.

"We have lasers," Magnum said.

"That's right!" Ben replied. "I completely forgot. Come up over their hull, Kim. You'll have a clean shot at anything that might damage their ship."

"That would put us in too much danger," Kim said. "This isn't a game, Ben. I can't just change directions on a dime."

"We have to do something," Ben said. "They'll get chewed to pieces in this debris."

"Fine, get the shield up, and we'll help. Until then, we're staying safe right here," Kim replied.

"We're being hailed by the *Plato*," Nance said.

"Put them through," Ben said.

What the hell are you doing, Modulus Echo? Tell me you didn't just trick us into the debris field to be your cover to make it through.

"Negative, *Plato*" Ben replied. "We had to reset our shield. It's coming back online in just a minute. When it does, we'll help you out."

You better hurry, the commander of the *Plato* said. *We can't take much more without something breaching the hull.*

"*Plato*," Kim said. "Rotate on your center access. We can't keep you from taking a few shots, but at least you shouldn't take two in the same place."

There was a pause, and Ben knew the commander and crew were considering Kim's advice. When the commander's voice came back over the bridge speaker, it sounded shaky.

Okay, Echo, we're beginning rotation. But our hull integrity is down to seventy percent. We've got almost three hundred souls on board. Don't let us down.

"The alien ships are entering the debris field," Nance said.

Ben glanced at the flux shield progress bar. It was at ninety percent. Then he looked at the aft camera display. The alien ships were following right behind them. And just like the *Echo* was smaller than the *Plato*, one of the alien ships was smaller than the other. Ben knew instantly that they were using the bigger ship like a shield. But he was about to change everything, and when he did, neither of the alien ships would be safe.

"Shield is up," Ben said.

"It's about time," Kim said, as she pulled back on the joystick that controlled the ship's main drive. "You should work on getting the shields up faster."

"Thanks for the advice," Ben said sarcastically.

"Anytime," Kim replied.

They rose up over the slowly spinning Corvette. A large ground transport–sized chunk of twisted metal was drifting straight toward the *Plato*. Kim raced straight toward the object.

"This feels all wrong," she said.

Ben jumped from his seat and carried Kim's helmet to her.

"We should suit up just in case," Ben said.

He slipped the helmet over Kim's head and connected the hose that fed oxygen and power to her helmet.

"I hate this thing," Kim said.

"Me too," Ben said. "Something about putting it on makes my nose itch."

"Thanks for putting that idea in my head," Kim snapped.

"You're welcome," Ben said as he returned to his console.

"I'm bringing the exterior camera feeds up on the main display," Nance said.

Ben glanced up just as the image on the screen changed. He saw the gnarly chunk of metal. It had sharp-looking edges that protruded on two sides.

"Looks like a piece of the engine manifold," Ben said.

A second later, the metal contacted the swirl of gravity waves around the *Echo*. A large section of the metal was instantly compressed and the rest shot off like a bullet from a barrel of a gun. The metal hit another piece of debris, sending it spinning off course, before ramming into a second that shattered like glass.

As things began to move in different directions, there were more impacts. The steady flow of debris slowly became a maelstrom. The *Echo* blocked the larger objects when they could, but a few got through.

It wasn't long before the alien ships were taking impacts as well. They used their grappling arms to swat the objects away when they could. But some were moving too fast, and others had too much mass.

"The alien ships are taking damage," Magnum said.

"Yeah, let's just hope they don't explode and kill us all," Kim said as she blocked a large piece of slightly curved fuselage that looked almost as big as the *Echo*. Fortunately, it was only a few layers of thin metal, some part of a ship's hull that was never intended for impact. It flew away like a disk, spinning straight back toward the alien ships.

"Take that," Kim said without looking away from the monitors that showed her every side of the *Echo*.

"We're almost through," Nance said. "We're only a mile from Gershwin's atmosphere."

"Feels like a million miles," Kim said.

All around them, debris was flying in different directions. Every impact sent the dangerous remnants shooting away in a different direction. There was zero friction, and while Gershwin's gravity had an effect on the debris, the *Echo*'s flux shield was wreaking havoc on whatever it came in contact with.

Ben hit the transmit button on his console and spoke into the mic.

"We're almost through, *Plato*," he said. "How are you looking?"

We'll make it into atmo barring any unexpected collisions, the commander of the Corvette class ship said. *Landing may be a bit messy. This ship was built in orbit. We have atmospheric engines and all, but our helmsman's never flown her anywhere but in space. And I doubt there's a decent landing strip down there.*

"Is it possible?" Ben asked Kim.

"Anything is possible," she replied. "It may not be pretty, and that ship won't ever fly again in all likelihood, but any landing you can walk away from is a good one."

Ben hit the transmit button again. "Roger that, *Plato.* We'll help you find a suitable landing spot. Our pilot has a lot of experience in atmo. We'll walk you through it."

We are in your debt, Echo.

The alien ships blew apart with no warning. First, the smaller ship blasted apart as if a bomb had gone off inside her. There was no fire or signs of explosion, just a shockwave that broke her to pieces and sent them flying in every direction. The shockwave caused a similar reaction in the larger alien vessel an instant later.

"Incoming," Nance said.

"Damn, I knew it was too good to be true," Kim said.

Ben glanced at the power reading on the flux shield. It was holding at forty percent, but Kim was already dropping back to shield the *Plato* from the rain of metal shooting toward them.

For nearly twenty seconds, metal pieces from the size of a door to larger sections of a hull that were nearly as big as the *Echo* rushed toward them. Kim moved the Kestrel class ship in a circle around the rear section of the *Plato.* Most of the debris was sent flying back the way it had come or in a completely

318

new direction. Very few impacted the *Plato*, but some did. One wedged in the engine output like a piece of food stuck between oversized metal teeth.

Some of the debris was sucked into the gravitational flow and compressed, which released energy in the form of heat. The flow of the gravity waves swirled closer and closer to the *Echo* as they picked up more matter. The ship's heat shields were at maximum, and the energy reading was at eighty-five percent. Ben knew that if the rain of metal from the exploding alien ships continued, they would die. Their shield could only do so much before it collapsed on itself like a black hole creating a star.

Fortunately, they dropped out of the debris field and into Gershwin's upper gravity. Ben immediately hit the button to shut down the shield.

"Flux shield is down," Ben said loudly.

"Our hull is too hot," Nance said.

"But we're alive," Kim said. "You're welcome."

Unlike the *Echo*, the *Plato* wasn't built for atmospheric flight. Like most ships, she had emergency components, but she didn't fly, exactly. By the time the *Echo* had joined her in the planet's atmosphere, the larger Corvette class ship had fallen nearly five thousand feet.

"Is the *Plato* okay?" Magnum asked.

On the video feed, Ben could see the long, skinny ship engulfed in flames. He hit the transmit button on his console.

"*Plato*, this is the *Echo*. Do you read me?"

Roger that, Echo. We read you.

Despite their rapid descent, the commander of the *Plato* sounded relieved.

"How is your ship holding up?" Ben asked.

We're taking some heat damage, the commander replied. *But we'll hold together.*

"We're likely to take some heat damage too," Nance said, but only to the crew of the *Echo*. "We absorbed too much heat from the flux shield, and there's no time to cool it down if we're going to help the *Plato*."

"That's a chance we'll have to take," Ben said.

"Fine, fine, I'm going," Kim said in her usual bravado.

They followed the larger ship down through Gershwin's thick atmosphere. Unlike space, moving through air particles created massive amounts of friction. Flames appeared on the ship's external camera feeds, many of which winked out from the heat. Smoke boiled off the Kestrel class ship and they lost all communications for a time. All they could do was wait to see what damage would happen.

"I've got heat warnings all over the ship," Nance said.

"I see that," Ben replied. Every warning and each system that showed damage were like a physical wound to the young engineer.

"Port wing engine is offline," Nance said.

"Wonderful, we survive the gauntlet only to plunge to our deaths on Gershwin," Kim said.

"She'll hold together alright," Ben said. "We've been through too much to give up on her now."

Like magic, the flames winked out and the smoke cleared. They were twenty thousand feet above the surface of the planet.

"*Plato*, open all flaps and extend your landing devices," Kim said. "You need to slow down as much as possible."

Roger that, Echo, the commander on the Royal Imperium vessel replied.

"I have a suitable landing spot," Nance said. "It's clear of trees and relatively flat."

"I see it," Kim said. "Can you send it to the *Plato*?"

"Already done," Nance said.

"*Plato*," Kim continued to give the crew of the Corvette class ship instructions. "Begin a long, slow spiral toward the landing zone. You should be able to slow your descent by gliding, then line up for an emergency landing."

Roger that, Echo, and thanks for the help.

"They sound relieved," Ben said.

"They should be. We saved them from being killed or captured by the aliens," Kim replied.

"For now," Magnum said.

"He's right. The aliens could track us easily," Nance added.

"True," Ben said. "But I don't think anything is getting through the debris field for a while. We have some time to prepare. Does anyone know where we are?"

"About two hundred miles from Royal City," Nance said.

"And the alien settlement?" Kim asked.

"It's on another continent," Nance continued. "Unless they have an aircraft, we should be safe."

"Should be," Kim said. "Famous last words."

Even with one engine down, Kim had no trouble keeping the *Echo* aloft as the *Plato* made her landing. It was rough and ugly. Ben guessed they would have injuries on board, but the ship held together. Kim brought the *Echo* in for a much more graceful and less destructive landing. They still had warnings on four systems. Ben knew the wiring and maybe even part of

321

the hull that he hadn't been given time to fix would be scorched. He would have to run tests to make sure the metal was strong enough to hold up to the rigors of atmospheric flight and the hard vacuum of outer space. Still, he felt good that they were alive and that their actions had saved the two hundred volunteers on board the *Plato*.

"Should we drink or see to the damage first?" Kim said as soon as she pulled off her helmet.

Ben, Kim, and Magnum, who had one of the Lancet assault rifles slung across his back, exited the ship via her rear cargo ramp. It was late in the afternoon on Gershwin. The sunlight slanted in with golden sunbeams that made the distant trees and green grass look almost magical. The air was tainted with the smell of exhaust, melted rubber, and scorched metal, but Ben was glad to smell it. They were alive, and he knew it wouldn't take them long to get the *Echo* shipshape again.

Across the field, the *Plato* lay like a fallen log, half-buried in the rich soil she had landed in. There were pieces of metal littering the ugly scar the ship had gouged in the field as she set down. And smoke rose from various spots on the ship, but a large side hatch opened, allowing the passengers and crew to come flooding out.

"What now?" Kim asked.

"Get the *Echo* flying again," Ben said.

"We're trapped here, you know," she replied.

"That's not so bad," Ben said. "I can think of worse places."

"But if the Royal Imperium comes to the rescue, we'll be arrested for treason," Kim said. "It's sort of a lose-lose situation from my perspective."

"We'll help the Confederates get settled and see to the ship," Ben said. "Then we'll find a way out of the mess with General Pershing."

"I don't think she's the forgiving type," Magnum said.

"I didn't expect to run at the first sign of trouble either," Ben said. "But that's what they did."

"Maybe she wasn't in charge of the *Everest*," Kim said. "She's a force of nature, but that doesn't mean she always gets her way."

"I agree," Ben said. "Which is why I plan to make sure she doesn't get her hands on the *Echo*."

"Or her crew?" Kim asked.

"Exactly," Ben said. "The war isn't over, and we aren't out of it yet. It won't take long and we'll be back in the thick of things."

"That's what I'm afraid of," Kim said.

And they all laughed.